LEE FITTS

a novel

Rich Garon

richgaron.com
Edited by Kiele Raymond

Print ISBN: 978-1-54394-287-3
eBook ISBN: 978-1-54394-288-0

Library of Congress Control Number 2018910270

To Russell J. Campbell

You won't have to sleep in the cold again in the woods

CHAPTER 1

"Once more and you're through. You either work here at the firehouse or you drive the damn school bus; your choice," said the man with the clipboard.

Speakes had never been yelled at like that. He knew he would have to kiss his part-time driving job good-bye. But by evening's end, he recognized how dependent he was on those extra dollars. Maybe he could shave some time from his bus route and get to the firehouse on time.

The next morning, Speakes watched as the Fitts boy walked down the long winding driveway toward the school bus. Once, Speakes had told the boy to walk faster and his mother called the junior high principal. The principal warned Speakes never to harass the kid again. As the boy finally boarded the bus, Speakes closed the door and shifted into gear.

The light at Hillman Road turned green. If he picked up some momentum for the incline ahead and then accelerated just a bit more than usual, he thought he could make up time. He'd only been late to work by two minutes last time.

Speakes always got a rush as he felt the huge vehicle hug the bend before the fast descent. At the bottom of the hill was a short straight-away happening fast on to a double set of railroad tracks. The school was a half-mile beyond those tracks giving Speakes more than enough time to slow his bus down to the speed limit before he turned into the parking lot.

He rose from his seat a little higher than usual that morning as the bus broke the crest of the hill. The students paid little notice to the extra blip of momentum capturing the bus. Speakes looked at his watch and calculated his arrival time at work. He looked in the rear-view mirror and down at his watch again. I'm going to be okay, he concluded. That was until he saw a multi-engine freight train barreling across from his left. It was far away enough that it hadn't tripped the crossing gate and lights. He calibrated distances, speeds, and times much as if he were in an algebra class at the school beyond the tracks. More than a good grade hung on his answer. Other mornings he would have downshifted by now to get a little bit better traction going down the hill. He could still do it, he told himself, would buck some, but he could still do it. But if he did, that was it. No doubt, looking at the length of that train, he'd be late again by the time the train passed.

It wouldn't be long before all the warning signals would announce the train's approach. In that second, he pressed down on the accelerator. The gate began to lower and the lights flashed. His hands froze to the steering wheel as his shaking foot dusted the brake before the bus hit the lip of the first track.

"Stop that screaming," Nelson Speakes yelled. "We're okay, we're okay." He floored it as the gate came down on the bus's hood.

Lee Fitts was thrown against the window as the bus began its quarter-mile trip sideways down the track. He was still all right; his head throbbed a little, but he thought he was okay. But maybe he wasn't. How could he tell anything? He could never have imagined the sights and sounds that were exploding in bursts around him: bodies punctured and twisted, bones splintered, a severed arm identifiable only by the blood-drenched sleeve of a pink sweater, screeches of students up front in horrific harmony with the bending and shearing metal, and shattering glass raining on fountains of piercing sparks. Struggling to pull his friend from a crumbled seat, Lee lost his balance and fell to the floor. His eyes closed on impact. The feverish trainmen, not far from him now, cried as panels of yellow steel sheathing at the point of impact began to separate.

"Am I going to have that report by nine?" Martin Wendell asked.

Jim Fitts collected some papers from his desk and stared at the printer. "Yes sir, I'm almost done. Made sure it would be ready for your meeting. Got in at six this morning to take care of all your edits. We'll be in great shape, great shape."

"Notify the others that we're going to meet at four-thirty to review the next steps in the project," Wendell said gravely, as if the company's contract to modify a water-treatment plant carried the same import as America's efforts to develop the atomic bomb.

"But Mr. Wendell," Jim said to the painfully-thin man. His boss paused and turned around. "I mentioned yesterday that I hoped to leave a little early today. If you remember, I said my son had a football game and I haven't been able to see him play much, and well, I thought you said it would be okay."

Wendell started to purse his lips and touched his forefinger to the rim of his metal-framed glasses. "Look Fitts, that was yesterday. Things change. I'll have to think about this and let you know later."

Jim Fitts shook his head and watched as Wendell hurried down the hall. He looked at the wall of his cubicle where he had hung a photo of Lee in his football uniform and a letter from Lee's coach. Few fathers had such a letter. He and Wendell had such different opinions about what was important.

The phone rang. "This is Jim."

"Jim, you've got to take this call right away; something about your son and a school bus."

CHAPTER 2

Ellie Wilson looked at the newspaper her husband D.H. had tossed on the table. She knew there would be painful headlines; words etched in ink that would frame the event for her as other people saw it: "TEN YEARS AFTER: THE FATAL CRASH of SCHOOL BUS #19." She stared at the twisted, smoking wreckage of the bus. She could only imagine the horror unleashed when two-city long blocks of metal punched into the school bus's vulnerable middle. "Twenty-Nine Students Killed as Moonlighting-Fireman Races to Beat Train. Three Student Survivors Hospitalized." Ellie cleared a place for the paper as she surveyed other photos and sidebar stories. "The Survivors Today, page five." She flipped through the paper and stopped when she saw her brother Lee's picture to the right of two other photos. A photo of the surviving bus driver appeared below. That year, 1981, seemed so far away.

D.H. placed his arm on her shoulder and kissed the top of her head.

"Time was really helping," she said.

"You going to be okay? I can stay longer if you want."

"No, you've got to go to work, and so do I. It's not a holiday or anything. I wish I could reach my father, but still no answer. I'll have to stop by this morning. I just hope Lee's not there. He won't know what today is, but if he sees me crying, he'll pester me until I tell him."

Ellie and her father had declined all recent requests to interview Lee. Over the past ten years, he and his family had been hit over and over again by that train. The story in the paper had just scratched the surface.

"Call me today, I mean it, don't keep everything inside," D.H. said. "Besides, I'll be on the road most of the day, won't be no bother."

As she watched her husband pull away from the house, the phone rang. She lifted the receiver slowly.

"Do you know what today is?" Jim Fitts asked his daughter.

"I do Dad. I've been looking at the paper. You all right?"

"Yeah, I'm all right. I've seen that damn paper too. Got up early this morning to make sure I got it before the boy saw it, though I know he's never up this early."

"Daddy, do you want me to come over?"

"No, no, I'm going to be late for work. I got to get going right now."

"You going to be okay today?"

"I've got to go. Look, after all is said and done this day is no different than any other except to those guys that want to sell newspapers. Make sure you call your brother this afternoon, he's got weeds to pull and a lawn to cut."

Jim Fitts placed the receiver down and picked up his hat and jacket. If he didn't get that frayed cuff fixed, someone was going to complain about him not showing up in a neat uniform. He opened the kitchen drawer and tore off a piece of tape that he placed inside the cuff to hold back the frayed material. Should hold till tonight, he thought. He grabbed a piece of paper towel and wiped it quickly across the shield on his hat and the one on his shirt. He opened the door and walked down the creaking wooden steps in front of the three-room bungalow.

"That day," he muttered to himself. "Piece-of-shit house and piece of-shit job and a twenty-one-year- old son that doesn't know what planet he's on."

He'd thought about taking his son back to the doctor. It had been five years. Maybe there was some new treatment that could help Lee. That was when he still was able to scrape together enough to take him to the doctor. That wasn't possible anymore. Lee was never going to be like he was; no getting around it.

CHAPTER 3

Reid Fletcher's finger stabbed at the doorbell. "C'mon Lee. What the heck's going on here, man? You're supposed to be ready." Reid kept the button depressed as if that would make the bell ring faster. He did the same thing with the pump at the gas station, thinking that if he held the lever tightly the gas would pump faster than its programmed maximum rate. Chime, chime, chime echoed through the small alcove.

Reid stopped and looked hurriedly down the sidewalk. He should have checked sooner. Okay, Mr. Fitts must have left for work. Reid sighed. He still couldn't figure out why Mr. Fitts didn't like him. He renewed his attack on the doorbell and started tapping against the glass. A shadow appeared heading toward the door. The doorbell still chimed and the finger didn't release until the door opened.

"How long does it take you to answer the damn door?"

"I was in the bathroom and I cannot rush when I am in the bathroom," Lee said. Lee cut a lithe figure. He looked out at what could have been his body-double. Beyond that similarity were much different characteristics. Reid's thin, olive-skin face faded into disheveled black hair. Below his lower lip was a two-inch by three-inch brush. Lee's face spoke of a complexion that sunburned but never tanned and his light brown hair fell naturally neat. While Reid swayed impatiently in black sneakers, jeans, dark blue

Insane Clown Posse T- shirt, and black-rimmed sunglasses with oil swirl wrap-around lenses, Lee tucked his golf-style shirt into chino pants that rested on sneaker-type hiking shoes.

"You were in the bathroom and can't be rushed? Are you kidding me or what? If we don't get down to Kaptor's by nine, you ain't gonna have to worry about being rushed. You can stay in the bathroom the whole damn day. Last week we had to hang around in the street for an hour with that mutt who I told you wasn't going to make it after getting whacked by that truck. That whole episode cost us a good job movin' those old appliances at the landfill. Might have only been temporary, but you know what they say: one good job leads to another, Lee Boy," Reid said, using the name he sometimes called his friend since grade school. "You know why we're going to Kaptor's this morning?"

"Yes, I know why we are going to Kaptor's this morning. We are going to Kaptor's this morning because you got us a job. And the pay is good. You said the pay is going to be good at our job at Kaptor's."

"More important, Lee Boy, this is a job I think you're going to be real good at. You got your key? C'mon, we gotta move; I need to stop and get some gas."

The Kaptor's sign was pure-1950s: three-lines of script in a tangle of blackened-out neon tubes made visible by the morning sun. Reid and Lee walked down the alley beside the old brick building and up the crumbling cement steps to a locked steel door. Reid pounded on the door.

"You guys here for the circulars?" asked a man with yellowish-white hair and the name Billy written on a Kaptor's employee badge pinned to a faded blue sweatshirt.

"Yeah, we're here for the advertising circulars," said Reid. "Let me do the talking," he whispered to Lee.

"Well, get in here and sign the forms with the rest of them. You guys need to get here earlier tomorrow."

"Yeah, sorry, we got stuck in a little traffic." He then mumbled to Lee, "You got to be out of the bathroom and waiting for me in front of your house tomorrow. You hear me?"

"Yes, I hear you. I will be outside in front of my house waiting for you tomorrow morning," Lee mumbled back.

There were about twenty of them there to assemble circulars near the loading dock. Reid strained to hear Billy's instructions against the noise of the forklift unloading trailers nearby.

"You guys got ten circulars to work with today. Those crates over there got bundles of each circular. I want you to assemble piles that have all ten circulars in them and then we're going to band them together and stack them back in the crates. These are the inserts for the Sunday paper. How many of you guys read the paper?" Billy asked.

"Sometimes," Reid shrugged as another man raised his hand.

"Well that's real nice. We got a couple of intellectuals with us this morning. Look, these circulars got to be done by five or we start deducting from your pay. You know we got plenty of people who want these good jobs," Billy said as the sputtering hydraulic lines of the nearby forklift smothered the rest of his instructions. "Put a move on it."

"All right, so maybe that wasn't the best job after all," Reid said as he put the key into the ignition and rubbed his hands together. "That Billy turned out to be a real jerk."

"Reid, I tried. I just could not put those circulars together any faster. I did not want to have duplicates in the pile. I did not want to make any mistakes. I do not think I made any mistakes; I just was not able to work as fast as everyone else."

"Can't always worry about being perfect."

"But I did not want to have those people think I could not do the job," Lee said as his eyes glared through the windshield.

"Ah, no sweat man. We'll find another job. We don't need no Billy and his damn piles."

"My mom still sends me forty dollars each month. But she says I cannot tell my dad. But I know he will suspect something if I buy things if I am not working. He still yells at me for not working; but not as much as before. He pretty much says 'Ah, what's the use?' to everything."

"You don't think your dad doesn't know you're getting money from somewhere?"

"I save just about all my mom gives me. And my Dad, cause I guess he sees that I have trouble getting a job, gives me five dollars a week. Says I don't need any more than that because he pays the rent and buys the food and my socks and underwear. And my sister bought me two pair of khakis and three nice golf shirts and my hiking sneakers for Christmas, and sometimes she also gives me a five-dollar bill."

"You are set for life Lee Boy, no question about it, you got everything covered. And now you got that twenty-dollar bill Billy the Circulars King gave you. I need something to eat. Want a cheeseburger?"

"I want a regular hamburger and a large Sprite. But one time I lost about three years' worth of the money my mom sent. I had it under my mattress. I had my money in two big mailing envelopes. But I looked one day and one of the envelopes was gone. I do not know how I lost it. You are the only one I am telling about that Reid. I could not tell anyone."

"Lost it? You don't think someone might have taken it?" Reid asked.

"Who could have taken it? Nothing else in the house was stolen."

"I don't know," Reid said. "But I hope you keep it in a better place now."

Reid stopped in front of Lee's house and looked into the bungalow. "Guess your dad's not home yet."

"It is Tuesday. He gets home late on Tuesdays."

"Where's he go?"

"I asked him once and he told me it is none of my business; that just because I lived in his house did not mean he had to answer all of my stupid questions."

Reid shuffled his palm across his two-day stubble and slurped the last of his Diet Coke. "You know Lee Boy, maybe when we get some good steady work, we can get a place together. You won't have to worry about your father saying it's his house."

"But I love my father."

"Yeah. Well, I got a couple of job leads. They sound pretty good. I think one of them is going to be the one that's just right for us. You remember that fort we built in fifth grade? We really didn't know each other; I mean my mother dumped me at that vacation Bible school at your church. But we got along good. That fort, just a bunch of branches and old 2x4s up against that old tool shed by that steep hill. But we had a lot of fun there. You were always good to me Lee; especially on the team when I got picked-on. I sure wasn't very good, but you were a star and you always stood up for your old fort buddy. We can get a place and you'll see it'll be just like having the fun we had in that old fort."

"We did have fun in that fort. Good night Reid."

The old truck pulled away. Reid's room over the Tammery Inn wasn't too far away; close in fact to where he lived when he and Lee were in junior high. Lee's house then was way across town. The only time they rode the same school bus was after football practice. Damn, Lee was good, Reid thought to himself. Even the coaches said they had never seen anyone in the sixth grade kick a football like that.

CHAPTER 4

It took Lee about a half hour to walk from his house to church. I don't know how I forgot to tell Reid that I have a nice blazer, tie, dress pants and well, I've had these loafers for a long time, but I can get them shined up good, Lee thought to himself as he approached the church parking lot.

"Good morning, Lee," said Mr. Cantoli, one of the greeters handing out church bulletins at the door. John Cantoli had a crisp Windsor knot in his tie, trousers with a razor-edge crease, and sturdy tie shoes with a buffed polish. "Beautiful morning, isn't it?" Mr. Cantoli said, his perfectly shaved jowls drooping a bit over the collar of his white starched shirt as he looked down and placed a bulletin into Lee's hands.

"Yes, it is a beautiful morning, Mr. Cantoli." Mr. Cantoli was the first thing about church that morning that made Lee happy. The second was sitting down in the pew. For while he loved to walk and had the stamina and carriage of a natural athlete, that hard wooden bench was always welcome after what was a two-mile walk.

By this time, Mr. Cantoli was at work on other parishioners, much like the man who first gets your car ready to go through the car wash. One Sunday, Lee thought how being in church: getting met by the greeter, going to your seat, reading scripture, walking up and back to get communion, and then walking out of the church and shaking hands with the priest was like going through God's car wash. He always felt cleaner when he came out of church, but there were always some things, just like at the regular car wash, that the process missed; things that never really got cleaned.

Rev. Warren Taylor read the Gospel and then asked everyone to be seated. He wasn't a big man, but his combed-back red hair made him seem taller and when he got excited and started to raise both arms, the draping sleeves of his vestment gave him the look of a large bird heading through the roof. Sometimes Rev. Taylor had a way of explaining complicated things so that Lee understood them; just like on those nights at home five years ago. Lee didn't understand why his mother and father didn't love each other anymore, why his mother said she would be leaving, and why he and his father would be moving to a small house his father kept calling a bungalow on the other side of town. "Son," Rev. Taylor had told him again. "God works in mysterious ways." Sometimes moms and dads can't make things work no matter how much they try. The accident, and well, the bad affect it had on you and what you can and can't do has been tough for them. It doesn't mean they don't love you anymore. It's just something they can't work out together. They might be able to after a while, but not right now. God will be with you, Lee. When we look back at all this, you'll see it was for the better."

Lee understood that a mystery was something he couldn't understand. And if the accident had changed him from the boy in the photos and videos his parents had shown him every night until they would stop and yell at each other, then that was okay with him. God, the God that Rev. Taylor described, had his reasons. There was nothing Lee could do to become the boy his mother and father had cried for each night; the boy he could hardly remember. Lee lived in God's mystery and felt safe there. He didn't know why his parents couldn't join him.

Lee doubted that his parents would ever get back together; but he had to admit that home had become much better without his mom and dad's constant fighting. He thought he would turn out all right, and once Reid found him a good job, well, everything would be fine. Maybe his father would be nicer to him.

Rev. Taylor shifted from one foot to the other as he stood in the center of the altar. One never knew if he were going to start his sermon by speaking softly or by raising his voice and asking the congregation a question that he would begin to answer.

"I'm going to let you in on a little secret," Rev. Taylor said as he let his forefinger dance from one side of the congregation to the other. And then the rocket blasted off. "Our Gospel asks us whom we honor more; our mother and father or God? Whom do you honor more, your parents or God?" The preacher's searching gaze, like the final slot on a spinning wheel of fortune at a carnival, landed on Lee's pew. "Whom do you think you should honor more?"

That was one bad thing about Rev. Taylor, sometimes he asked too many questions all in a row about things that Lee thought otherwise had easy answers. But there was no mistaking the important tone carrying these interrogatories.

Lee learned about the Pharisees in Sunday school back when he and his mother and father and his sister, Ellie, went to church together. It was his mother that got everyone out of the house on Sunday morning. His father didn't see why they had to go every Sunday and sometimes complained to his mother that he needed to "unwind a little;" that he knew God would understand. Lee's father went to church every day for several months after the accident, Ellie said. Then he stopped going altogether when the doctors became unanimous in their prognosis for Lee. "They said we're going to have to be very patient with you," Ellie told her brother, "that you would be slower to pick things up now, that your emotions and your ability to concentrate and to communicate were affected by what you went through during the crash." Lee wasn't sure if his mother still went to church after she moved out. Ellie and her husband went only on holidays, and Rev. Taylor hadn't seen Lee's father in a long time.

Lee didn't like the Pharisees and he knew that Jesus always could twist them up in riddles just when the Pharisees thought they had finally stumped Jesus. Rev. Taylor had left Lee that morning in the dust of confusing thoughts and revelations about what Jesus was saying. Maybe someday, I'll understand what Rev. Taylor is talking about. All I know, Lee told himself, is that I think Jesus loves me and has been good to me. I think Jesus would let me love God and my mother and father. I can't choose.

Lee returned the small smiles and "good mornings" to the congregants he had known since his mother held his hand while he stood in the coffee line. Back then, amidst the buzzing echoes in the fellowship hall, he thought of it only as the juice and donut line. Now, he liked standing by the old upright piano near the window as he ate his donut and drank his juice. Sometimes other people would use the piano to hold their donuts as they drank their coffee or juice, then they would set down their cups and eat their donuts. Lee and Mrs. Plennington were regulars.

Audrey Plennington's blond hair was cut sharply in a 1970s style she must have thought would make a comeback. She had been one of his mother's closest friends and spent a lot of time at his home before his mother finally left. She would alternately embrace his mother, his sister and him during a time when there was a lot of crying in the house. He never forgot the smell of her perfume and her hair spray or how smooth her dress felt as she held him. Sometimes he thought one of the reasons he came to church was because Mrs. Plennington always hugged him. She spoke from experience about the questions Lee's mother would ask her about divorce. It hit Audrey Plennington hard that day her husband said he was leaving. It was a year before she wore any make-up, she said, and she had been a model since she was ten. She recovered, at least that's what she told Lee, and couldn't be any happier now that she owned the Fitness Fling Spa in the mall near where Lee used to live.

As Mrs. Plennington put her arms around him the perfume sprung from her clothes. She was as tall as Lee, and looking at her from the back, it was hard to tell she was as old as his mother. She drew back and patted his stomach. "Lee, are you sure you're eating? Look at you, you're getting too thin."

"Yes, Mrs. Plennington. I have a Hungry Man dinner every night, milk, and sometimes, if my dad has left any, a Little Debbie's apple bar. Sometimes, when he is home for dinner, we will share two different Hungry Man dinners, kind of like getting Chinese food and I will have some of yours and you will have some of mine."

She looked at him with a physician's eye that sought more information about a patient. "Are you eating breakfast, and lunch?"

"Yes, every day, I keep track of those things every day. Breakfast is jelly and butter on a piece of toast, and coffee. And lunch is peanut butter and crackers and milk and I know I need my fruit, so twice a week I have an apple after I have my peanut butter and crackers and milk."

She looked at him as she started taking off her coat. "I don't like the sound of that; you might have to start eating with me. That's not a proper diet. Maybe you should come over to the spa and have lunch with me, we'll have to see what we can work out. Are you still walking like you used to?"

Lee smiled proudly. "It is even better than I used to. I always walk four miles every day, even if it is raining. And some days, before I even realize it, I walk eight miles. I measured these distances when I am in Reid's truck. He reads his odometer and calls off the miles to me from the places where I walk. But I have special rules if it is snowing. If the ruler measures more than four inches of snow on the front steps, I do not walk that day. I wish I could, but I do not. I fell too many times when I did."

"That sounds like a good system, Lee, exercise is very important. Look at me, I exercise and diet very scientifically. Don't you think I look twenty years younger than I am?" as she motioned her hands to accent those parts of her body she had sworn in as witnesses.

His "yes" came involuntarily.

She smiled, but her lips knew how far they could go so as not to disrupt the ecology of a face whose lines were practiced at not revealing the identity their years had given them. "Yes, scientific diet and exercise can do that" as she smiled approvingly to her student. She changed gears quickly. "Lee, I have the best news for you. You're still looking for a job, aren't you?"

"Well, I had one, Reid got it for us. But I think we got fired because I could not sort the circulars fast enough. So, you are right, I am looking for a job."

"Another string bean; hasn't your father and sister, and haven't I told you about Reid. He's worthless, a bum; those sloppy clothes and that cat's tail hanging off his chin. You think you'll ever amount to much hanging around him?"

"I am not sure what I am going to amount to. But, you see, no one knows Reid like I do. He has always tried to help me."

"Oh Lee, you can do very well without his help. Forget him for now. Look, what I'm trying to tell you is I found you a job, not permanent, but four, five months something like that. Mrs. Calvert is a regular at my fitness club. She's a very nice lady and her husband, Dan Calvert, is running for town council. That's a big position Lee, representing a whole part of the town. Anyway, they're looking for someone to hand out their campaign material, you know, go door-to-door and hand out things and tell people why Mr. Calvert is the best candidate. I told her I knew just the person for the job. I know you love to walk and you're very polite and you'll have a card with you to tell you what to say. The pay is only five dollars an hour; but it will be like getting paid for doing your walking."

Lee sucked in part of the skin on the side of his face as he often did when he was making an important decision. "I like that idea, Mrs. Plennington. I like that idea a lot. Can Reid have a job like that too?"

"Lee, I told you to forget about Reid. I'm going to call Mrs. Calvert and tell her you would love to work for her husband." She handed him her coat and then slid her arms into the sleeves.

"Good morning Audrey, Lee," Rev. Taylor said softly as he walked by. He didn't have a back-slapping "Good Morning, how you doing buddy?" No, more as if he were out for a stroll and on the lookout for troubled sheep. He had a sermon voice that spoke to the whole congregation and another, softer one, when he spoke one-on-one to a member of his flock.

"Good morning Warren," Mrs. Plennington called out. "Good sermon this morning, short and to the point."

"Do you think my other sermons have been too long?" he asked concerned that he had found a sheep not understanding his sermons' full import.

She blushed. "I love all your sermons, but today's was just extra special."

Lee said nothing, hoping the now seemingly-reassured Rev. Taylor wouldn't look his way.

Mrs. Plennington's smile followed the reverend who by now had stopped to take the measure of some other sheep. She snapped her head back and looked at Lee. "So, Hon, I will call you as soon as I talk to Mrs. Calvert. I'm sure Mr. Calvert will want to speak with you also. This is going to work; you're a good worker and very polite and I think you'll meet people and maybe someone will be so impressed they'll give you a regular job when this is all over."

"Thank you Mrs. Plennington, I think I can do a good job too. You have always been very nice to me." He wondered if he should tell her about the forty dollars his mother sent him every month. A shiver went through him just at the thought. No, if Mrs. Plennington knew, she might think he didn't need the job with Mr. Calvert's campaign.

She hugged him and kissed him on the cheek. He would pat at his jacket on the walk home. Sometimes, he could pat the scent of Mrs. Plennington's perfume off his jacket for several days.

CHAPTER 5

He went to bed early that night. He knew it was important to get a good night's sleep. He wanted to be up and dressed in the morning earlier than usual just in case Mrs. Plennington called. His father had fallen asleep in the over-stuffed LA-Z-Boy that took up half the living room. Lee heard the spring creek and the footrest hit the bottom of the chair. His father was awake, would be shuffling off to the bathroom, and then to bed.

The angry man at the door was gone; the man who yelled out that he knew Mr. Calvert and was going to call him right away. As soon as he realized it had been a dream, Lee sat up and leaned against the headboard. He looked at the clock. If he fell asleep right now, at most he would only get three hours of sleep before it was time to get up. He hoped Mrs. Plennington didn't call today. He would be too nervous to meet Mr. Calvert. The man at the door returned. Why, he asked, was Lee bothering them with all this talk about Dan Calvert? The man said he would call Mr. Calvert if Lee didn't stop. The man's wife started yelling at Lee. They were going to ask Mr. Calvert how he could ever hire someone like this boy. This boy was making people start to dislike Mr. Calvert. Everyone was starting to dislike Mr. Calvert so much that they were not going to vote for him on election day. Lee's eyes snapped open and a silent "no, please no" leapt from his throat. He got up and sat at the kitchen table for the rest of the night.

"What are you doing up so early?" Lee's father asked. He looked at the Mr. Coffee. "You think you could have at least made the damn coffee."

"I am sorry, Dad. I did not sleep good last night."

"You know if you actually did some work and didn't get up so damn late every morning, you'd be able to sleep at night. Did you ever think about that?"

Lee wondered why his father always asked him if he had ever thought about something. He thought about a lot of things, in fact, he thought about too many things and never had enough answers about all the things he would think about. His father never gave him answers that helped. He only doled out questions one after the other as if they were bills from the big wad of money the man in the ice cream truck had. But Lee found he could not buy anything with questions.

"Dad, it might make you happy to know that I could have a job real soon."

"What, another one of those winners Reid Fletcher comes up with?

"No, this time I think it is going to be a good job. Mrs. Plennington is helping me."

"Damn, that's just what we need, more help from Audrey Plennington. Hasn't she helped enough? Just about single-handedly drove your mother out of the house. What does Mrs. Plennington have in mind for you this time, another job like the one at the county old folks' hospital working the swill truck?"

"Dad, Mrs. Plennington did not drive Mom away. Mom was just, you know very upset. I think I made Mom upset. You know she said she would be back when she could understand what was happening to us."

"Audrey Plennington gave your mother all those ideas. Don't you ever forget who hung around to take care of you. And do I get any gratitude? Any thanks?"

"Dad, I know it was you. When I get this new job, I will have some money to help you with things around here."

"What type of job is your good friend Mrs. Plennington getting for you?"

"I am going to go around and knock on people's doors and ask them to vote for Mr. Calvert."

"Who the hell is Mr. Calvert?" Jim Fitts asked as he lowered his head to look into the back of the refrigerator.

"He is running for town council and Mrs. Calvert goes to Mrs. Plennington's fitness spa and she is going to ask Mrs. Calvert if I can have the job and Mrs. Plennington might call this morning, and that is why I was trying to get a good night's sleep in case I had to see Mr. Calvert today about the job I might get with his campaign."

"What a bunch of nonsense. You don't even have the job yet with some politician who is probably some asshole phony. And you think you, of all people, are going to be able to go around and knock on people's doors and talk a bunch of crap about some damn politician?"

"Dad, you do not know Mr. Calvert, why do you say he is like that?" Lee asked, knowing that when his father picked up his jacket and lunch bag it was time for the older Fitts to leave for work.

"How do I know? They're all the same. Even if he's stupid enough to give you the job, you won't last very long." His father laughed. "Those people will be calling Calvert and asking him why he hired a character like you."

"Dad, I am not a character. Nobody calls me a character except you."

"No one knows you like I do. I just face facts. I'm going to have to support you for the rest of your life." He threw open the door. "And your mother, don't get me started; I never hear from her. She doesn't help with a damn thing."

Jim Fitts was about to be swallowed up by a ten-hour shift as a security guard at Locust Shade Mall. That shift usually spit him out to Pete's Pub. There wasn't much left of him these days when he came home. Lee watched the last trace of his father walking down the street and then turned to the narrow bookcase they had brought from their old house. He remembered how his father used to clean one of the picture frames. Inside was the photo of Lee in that blue and white uniform with his Dad holding that blue helmet and smiling that huge smile. The picture was gone now and so was any way to capture that smile in a new photo.

CHAPTER 6

"Lee, remember, be there on time! That's an important first impression; jacket and tie too. And remember, a nice firm handshake when you meet Mr. Herman; he sounded very nice on the phone. Don't forget to remind him you're being referred by Mrs. Plennington who is a friend of Mrs. Calvert's. Do you have all that, honey?"

"Yes, Mrs. Plennington, I have written that all down on my pad. And I have been waiting for this call, so I am all dressed and ready to go. And I will be very polite to Mr. Andy Herman, Mr. Calvert's campaign manager," Lee said.

"I want you to come over when you're done and tell me everything."

"I will Mrs. Plennington."

Lee had fifteen minutes to get to the second floor. He hit the elevator button again. The light was on, but the indicator arrow above the door remained on the B. He looked at his watch. A rush went through his arms as he realized he'd lost a minute, maybe two waiting for the elevator. I am a walker, why am I waiting for the elevator? he thought. Maybe I am a character. Maybe Andy Herman would recognize that right away and tell me I don't care how good a friend Mrs. Plennington is of Mrs. Calvert, you're just not right for the job. Sorry.

Lee pressed against the banged-up gray steel door that led to the stairs and hustled up two steps at a time. There was the room, just where, Mrs. Plennington said it would be. A piece of paper with the hand-written words Friends of Calvert was taped to a half-open door. Lee grimaced as he tapped on the door hoping he was not making too much noise.

"May I help you?" the heavy-set woman asked. She hadn't looked up yet or maybe that was as far up as she could lift her head upon which a pyramid of red ringlets rested. Her voice was soft and high; he never would have pictured the woman before him if he were talking to her on the phone.

"Yes, ma'am, my name is Lee Fitts and I am here to see Mr. Herman."

"Mr. Herman didn't tell me he was expecting anyone. I'm Terri Herman, his sister, and he usually tells me if he's expecting someone. But as you can see, we're still getting organized; just moved into this rat trap last week." Lee looked around at the stacks of unopened boxes and pieces of computer equipment to be set up. She pointed to a chair that had been treated only to a perfunctory dusting. "Have a seat, Mr. Herman's on the phone. I'll let him know you're here."

Lee wished there were some way he could let Mr. Herman know he had arrived at the office early. "I am a friend of Mrs. Plennington."

"Don't know her," Terri said as she continued writing.

"She's a friend of Mrs. Calvert's. My friend Mrs. Plennington owns a fitness spa; it is called the Fitness Fling and Mrs. Calvert goes there."

Terri Herman frowned. "Why don't you hold all that until you talk with Mr. Herman." The talking in the other room stopped. "Andy, there's a Lee Fitts out here, says he has an appointment with you."

"Fitts? Send him back."

Lee wiped his sweaty palms on his shirt and rose slowly.

"You can go in now," Terri said.

Andy Herman was a little man whose narrow shoulders gave him the look of a pre-teen. He had a comb-over of unnaturally dark hair betrayed by grayish eyebrows and sideburns. From under his open collar, the two ends of his unknotted tie swayed as he shook Lee's hand.

"You Fitts? I'm Andy Herman. This won't take long, sit down. I spoke to your friend, Mrs. Plennington. She said some pretty nice things about you. You tell me a little about yourself."

"My name is Lee Fitts, Mr. Herman." Lee stuck out his hand. He would make sure that he gave Mr. Herman a firm handshake. He remembered how important Mrs. Plennington said that was.

"Yeah, yeah, have a seat, tell me about yourself and what you think you have to offer to help Mr. Calvert," Andy said.

"Well," Lee took a deep breath. "I am very polite and like to walk."

"That's good Lee 'cause you would be meeting a lot of people and you'd have to be very polite and you'd have to walk a lot, visit many houses. Do you know anything about politics?"

"Yes, I do. I know there is an election and people try to get the most votes, and the one with the most votes wins."

"You got it pretty much on the money Lee, and I can tell you're very polite also."

"Thank you, Mr. Herman, I think it is very important to be polite."

"Well there's other things you'd have to do in this job; you have to read a short message when you talk to the people at their houses. You a good reader, Lee?"

"Yes, I am a good reader; I like to read."

"Why don't you take a look at this and pretend you're at the door." Andy handed Lee a small card."

Lee looked at the card and began reading. "Hello, my name is . . . . , wait, I have to fill in that blank. Let me start over. Hello, my name is Lee Fitts and I am representing Dan Calvert who is running for town council. May I ask you some short questions that won't take much of your time?"

"Okay, that's good Lee. You are a good reader and after a while you probably won't have to look at the card. But you see that sheet with all the names and addresses, and you'll have a lot of those sheets, make sure you fill in the answers in the right spaces." If you can do that, I think I'd like to welcome you to the Calvert for Council team."

"I know I can do that Mr. Herman. Does that mean I have the job?"

"Yup, you have the job, start tomorrow, five bucks an hour. But you have to understand, it's important you get all this information right, we can't have any foul-ups."

"Oh, I understand, Mr. Herman, you can count on me." Lee extended his hand.

"That's good, you like to shake hands, that's important for a politician." Andy said. "Maybe you'll run for office one day and I'll be working for you." Lee smiled and strained to keep smiling as Andy Herman gave him one of the deadest-fish handshakes of all time.

"Now, when I'm not here, Terri's the boss and you report to her. Terri works with Sanford Black who's in charge of all our canvassers. You'll meet Sanford when you start. Now, you go out and see Terri; she'll give you all the particulars."

"Thank you again Mr. Herman."

Andy waited until he heard Lee leaving the front office. "What did you think?" he asked his sister.

"What do I think? I think he's not the type of guy you usually hire. He's pleasant, but he's . . ."

"Yeah, I know he's just a shade off. But here's the deal, the kid's a good friend of a good friend of the candidate's wife. We've both been in this game long enough to know what that's like. We've had worse over the years. His friend said something about his being shy; I think there's more to it than that. He can read, he's very polite and I'll have Sanford go out with him the first day. He'll be all right. We've got to get this operation underway; this election is going to be tougher than we thought."

CHAPTER 7

As soon as he walked in, Lee realized he should have called. Mrs. Plennington was on the far side of her studio leading a group of twisting, bending women in assorted pastel workout outfits to the thumping beat of disco. He had hoped to find her between classes in her small office where all the exercisers in the spa wouldn't be looking at him. But it was too late to turn around and leave; Mrs. Plennington had spotted him. She raised her finger and pointed to her office. Her small group turned in unison and looked at Lee. One was old enough to be his grandmother, maybe a few were younger than Mrs. Plennington. It was clear they all would need many more sessions at the spa if they were to look the way Mrs. Plennington did.

Lee asked himself why he didn't just call. He could have told her all about his meeting with Andy Herman and how now he was a member of the Calvert for Council team. But no, he had to come to the spa. He liked Mrs. Plennington a lot. She was always very helpful. But he was always nervous when he was with her. Lee was never sure how he was supposed to respond, especially when she ran her hands along his neck and shoulder and sometimes his waist and then said, "Okay Sweetie?" But he liked being with her. And he knew also he liked to come to the spa to see Christie Veit. He had gone to junior high with Christie. She never paid any attention to him until one day when he was getting on the late bus that took home football players and cheerleaders and any other students who had after-school activities. She smiled and said hello to him and he fell in love. He remembered that afternoon. She was so pretty. He didn't know how he would make it through the night without seeing her. He spent so much time combing his hair and fixing his shirt the next morning that he almost missed the bus. They never to this day spoke about what happened that morning. Lee remembered only that Christie's brother lay in the middle of the bus with blood rushing from his head and a bone in his neck sticking out through his skin.

Lee still carried those feelings toward Christie, but she didn't say much to him. He usually got the same smile she gave out freely to anyone who came into the spa; it was not the smile that had told a school boy one afternoon that Christie wanted to kiss him, and hold him, and marry him. He had overheard Mrs. Plennington tell Christie that he was different now, he'd never be the same. Others too said that about Lee; none though ever as despairingly as his father.

"So, how did it go?" Mrs. Plennington asked him as she pulled a towel from a hook next to her desk and patted down her arms and face. She held the towel over her mouth making her stare seem even more penetrating. She bent over slightly and patted the back of her neck. She pulled out the elastic in her hair and placed the towel over her shoulders. "So, how did it go?"

"It went very well Mrs. Pennington. I spoke with Mr. Andy Herman and he told me I am now a member of the Calvert for Council team. That is why I came over here, to tell you in person and to thank you for getting me a job that I think I will really like. But, maybe I should have called because I know you are always very busy."

"Lee, don't you ever think you just can't come over here anytime you want. I'm never too busy for you and I want you to remember that. Your mother and I were very good friends, even though I wish she'd stay in touch a little more. And you know I've tried with your dad; I mean, well I don't know, for some reason I don't think he's very fond of me."

"My dad sometimes does not mean some of things he says; he works very hard and he just gets tired."

"Maybe you're right. Anyhow, Lee, there is no doubt in my mind that you will do a great job for Mr. Calvert. He's a very nice man and will make an excellent councilman. Did you see his campaign sign I put in the front window?"

"Yes, it is a very colorful sign."

Audrey leaned over and gave him a lightning-quick smooch on his forehead. "You're going to do very well, Lee. You're a very bright boy, don't ever forget that." Her voice cracked slightly as if she were overcome at the thought of all the comments spoken behind Lee's back.

Christie was up by the front door helping a stooped, frail woman whose blueish white hair clashed with her lime sweat suit. "You look mighty dapper today, Lee. I don't believe I've ever seen you in a jacket and tie before," Christie said.

"Oh, that is because I just got a job with Mr. Calvert. Mrs. Plennington has his poster in the front window. I am a member of the Calvert for Council team." He looked at her face. *That* smile wasn't there.

"Good luck," Christie said.

"Thank you. I am sure Andy Herman knows how to get enough people to vote for Mr. Calvert."

Lee had fallen asleep in his father's reclining chair. Lee was always very careful to make sure the pillows and arm covers were the way his father had left them. Very careful, ever since that night his father came home and caught him. "I told you to stay out of my chair. Damn it, can't I have one thing of mine that you don't screw up?"

The phone rang and Lee's head shot up. His heavy sleep was still pulling on him as the phone continued to ring. He reached over to get the receiver, but as he pulled it toward him, it knocked into a half-finished glass of Coke. A brown spot expanded as it absorbed into the side of the chair.

"Oh no! Oh no! Please God no," he screamed as the receiver bounced on the seat.

"Lee, Lee, what's going on? You all right?" Reid called out from the receiver. "Lee, answer me, it's Reid."

"Reid, I need help big time."

"What the hell happened, are you all right?"

"I just spilled soda on my father's reclining chair."

"What?"

"This chair may be my father's favorite thing in the whole world, and he does not want me sitting in it and I was sitting in it and when the phone rang, I reached for it and knocked over the soda and now there is a big stain on the side of the chair. I do not know how I am going to get this stain out."

Reid had never heard Lee so upset. "All right look, I'm on my way over. I've got some stuff I've used on my car upholstery. I'll get the stain out, just get yourself together. Man, get yourself together, it's only a damn chair."

"You do not understand. Can you come over right away?"

"I'm leaving right now."

Lee stared out the window the whole time. Finally, he saw Reid's truck pull in front of the house.

"See, I got that cleaner on there and most of that stain's out already. Just fire up this old trusty hair dryer and no one will know anything ever happened here at the scene of the crime," Reid said as he began waving the dryer over the stain.

"I thought getting my job would make this one of my best days, and now this."

"What do you mean job and best days?"

"I wanted to know if they had a job for you too."

What the hell are you talking about? As a matter of fact, that's why I was calling you, I got something for us tomorrow; it's a landscaping job. No counting any dopey circulars or anything. All we have to do is haul dirt with a wheelbarrow. And you know what? I think this job could last most of the summer."

"But I cannot do a landscaping job because I am working for Mr. Calvert. I'm part of the Calvert for Council team."

"Calvert for Council team?"

"Yes, Mrs. Plennington got me this job. I asked if you could get a job there too, but she said it would probably only be me. I met Andy Herman, Mr. Calvert's campaign manager, and he hired me right then and there. He said that they were looking for someone to go from door to door and talk to people about Mr. Calvert and they said since I was polite and liked to walk, I had the job."

"So, let me see if I understand this. You got a job and don't need this landscape job I got for both of us?"

"Are you angry, Reid?"

"Damn, I don't know, Lee. I thought we was a team. Ah, I guess if you got that opportunity, I mean you probably would have taken the landscape job if you didn't know about the job with this Calvert guy."

"You are right Reid, I just did not know about your job. I know you have always looked after me. You are my best friend."

"Yeah, all right, no big deal. Ya know, who knows how long the land-scape job will last." Reid looked down at the open magazine on the small table next to Jim Fitts' chair. He reached for the issue. "Dan Tamara: The Best Pressure Kicker Ever?" read the big letters on top of the article which was book-marked with tape. "Your dad still pushing this crap?" Reid asked.

"Well he told me not to move that magazine. I had to read it aloud to him two nights in a row when it first came out."

Reid looked at the glossy color photo of Dan Tamara depicting the kicker as he made contact with a football that just cleared the outstretched, mud-caked arms of a huge, rushing lineman.

"Tamara is the man," Reid said. "Your old man still think you could be the man?"

"Sometimes he tells me so much and I tell him I cannot do that."

"Lee, you must admit you were pretty good in school. Damn for a sixth-grader you could kick the shit out of the ball. Remember when the coaches were standing on the sidelines and you kicked the ball twenty yards past them? I still remember the look on their faces. They had to stretch their necks back to see that ball flying way over their heads. Maybe you should try kicking again. Maybe you'd be in a magazine too."

"I do not think so, Reid. I tried some with my dad. I just get very nervous out there and I cannot kick too good. Then my dad would raise his voice at me and tell me to try harder, don't be a quitter. Then he would yell out 'Speakes, I hope you rot in hell.'"

"Well, let's forget about it then," Reid said as he put the magazine down. "Not your fault Lee. You're doing pretty good, same thing could have happened to anyone, that's what your mom said. She was just happy to have you alive." Reid remembered the day Lee's mom took him aside and told him what the doctors said about how traumatized Lee was after being trapped in that bus, and how understanding Lee's friends were going to have to be. "Reid," she said. "He's never going to be the same."

"I just get nervous out there. You know how sometimes your arms and legs feel all wiggly," Lee said with a grimace.

"Not worth thinking about. Look at that spot, I can't even see it any more. Your father won't even know what happened. Maybe I should become an upholstery cleaner. I bet I could make some good money."

Lee stared at the chair. "I am okay now. I am glad you know how to clean a chair. You are real good at it, Reid."

CHAPTER 8

Ellie and D.H. Wilson lived about a half-mile from the home that Lee and his father shared. It was a demarcation that Ellie never thought would separate her from her father. She and her husband backed out of their driveway on to newly-paved streets lined with little trees held by wire to wooden stakes. Heather Hills was a nice starter community. And the way D.H. hustled at work, well, Ellie knew it wouldn't be long before she'd be able to quit her job, be a mom, and move to one of those houses in a nearby subdivision with the expansive rock gardens that you could light up at night.

Her dad didn't visit often even though the bus he took to and from work stopped at the community park a block away from her house. The first time was bad, but the second time was worse. She saw him as she looked out her window early one evening just as the street lamps came on. He was carrying his security guard jacket and hat, with his black tie open on his royal blue shirt. A flicker of the light bounced off the badge on his breast pocket. Ellie stood silent as he staggered closer. He was only fifty yards from the house. He was starting to stagger more. If she went out to steady him, someone might see her and realize that she knew this man who it was clear didn't live in Heather Hills. If she remained at the window, she would be no help to him if he started to fall. He started to cross the street and she began to head for the door. She looked left and right as she opened the door. She saw no one other than her father who was now beginning up the driveway.

"Ellie," he yelled. "How the hell is my only daughter?"

"Dad!" she called in a whisper tone.

"What's wrong?" he asked as he stopped in the middle of the driveway. "Aren't you glad to see your dear old father? I mean you keep telling me I should come over to visit. So right there on the bus, I said to myself I'm going to stop and see my daughter out at that fancy new house of hers and maybe have a couple of beers with D.H. So here I am. Hey, where's D.H.? D.H., want to have a few beers?"

"I'll get him," D.H. said, just as he had told her the first time. Her husband was able to shsssh and guide Jim into the house and help him onto one of the two large chairs in front of the TV. Ellie moved an array of ornamental pillows and lowered herself on to the couch. She looked down at the untied black half-boots Jim wore. She remembered buying them for him several years ago after he complained that his feet hurt from standing all day at the mall. "I don't need anyone buying anything for me," he had scolded. "Think I can't provide for myself? Just who the hell do you think you are young lady?" But he kept the boots, even though they stayed in his closet until several weeks later when it must have become just unbearable for him to wear the black loafers so worn-out that little of the stitching remained to hold the tops to the bottoms.

On both occasions, it didn't take her father long to start in on "the woman" who abandoned him and their son during their time of need. Ellie tried to talk to him through the alcoholic fog between them. She couldn't reach him. D.H. couldn't reach him either. She knew that her mother had tried for many years after the accident to keep the family together. Her mother knew nothing could be done to help Lee, but she had, through many conversations with God, accepted that. She loved her son and she loved Jim Fitts, but it was clear that the accident had cut into her husband far deeper than into her. She recognized that after he kept losing jobs, and continued to scream out at Speakes and at God for ruining their son's life. She recognized too that her husband's life had been so tied to their son's that Jim Fitts couldn't help himself from falling into a rapid spiral. Lee was okay with where he was, if only his Dad could see that. I might have made it too, Marian Fitts had told her daughter, but I couldn't hold your father from falling, worse, he was pulling me down with him. Ellie didn't know what or whom to be mad at, yet it was her mother who had left them. Either way she knew her family now centered around her husband. Her mother would never come back, her father angrily walked in circles, and her brother – her brother – was she responsible for rescuing him? Did he think he needed to be rescued?

"Hello," she said after picking up the receiver.

"Ellie, I do not know if Dad told you about my new job. Did he?"

"No Lee, he didn't," Ellie smiled. It was her little brother's voice from when they were small, before so many people were talking about his gift and how all the colleges would be after him. So many memories rushed into her head as she listened to her brother describe his new job with the "this is the most important thing in the world" tone he used to describe his Lego creations or his acorn collection. She wished she could go back in time. But her eyes now open, she knew it was all behind them.

"So, you start tomorrow?"

"Yes," he said. "I have got my clothes all ready, shoes, everything. Nine o'clock tomorrow Andy Herman and his sister are going to tell me everything I need to know. I am going to bring my own pencils, though, and a pen also. I am sure they have those things, but I do not want to take a chance. I found a canvas bag to carry things in because I think I am giving people things when I visit them. I heard the weather report; tomorrow is supposed to be a beautiful day, sunny and in the low 80s. I know just the right pace for walking on a beautiful sunny day in the low 80s. I am bringing a sandwich, an apple, Vienna Fingers, and water, but I am not going to spend a lot of time on lunch. Maybe I will just work through lunch and eat when I am done with my new job."

"Lee, I know you want to do a good job, but you have to stop and have lunch. Promise me you'll do that."

"Ellie, you do not understand, I might not have time to stop for lunch. You want me to do a good job, right?"

"Yes, I do and you will, but you have to stop and have a break."

"Well, okay, but it might just be a short break."

"Please call me when you're done tomorrow."

"Okay. I have to heat up Dad's Hungry Man now. He should be home soon. I am making him the all-white meat turkey dinner."

"That's his favorite, isn't it?"

"I do not know; he will not tell me anymore. He just tells me to mix it up when I go to the store, so I get different types, but not the ham, he told me never buy him ham."

Lee's father dug into his Hungry Man, responding in a lifeless tone to his son's talk about the next day. Jim Fitts took his guard's shirt and tie off and headed for the recliner. Lee took in a deep breath, all thoughts about the next day chased away by panic as his father sat down and reached for the lever on the side of the chair. His father's hand missed the spot where the cleaned-up stain was probably still drying. Jim Fitts put his hands in his lap. Ten minutes later he was asleep. The beers on his father's way home were doing their work.

CHAPTER 9

Two wrinkled twenty-dollar bills lay on the table; the signal that Jim Fitts had decided it was time for his son to buy groceries. Lee would always leave the receipt on the table after he shopped. He wasn't sure his father checked the receipts anymore. He grabbed the money and stuffed it into his pocket. He left the house at 6:59; one minute before the clock radio his father had set would go off at an ungodly volume and blast out the morning's news. His father hated hearing the news so much that he was up quickly to press the off button. He had never overslept.

Lee walked at a pace just short of a trot and arrived at the Calvert for Council office at 7:20. The hallway was dark and he waited outside the door. His green-collared shirt had several spots of sweat and he walked up and down the hallway hoping they would dry. He had taken such good care of that shirt. He didn't know if Terri and Andy Herman would think he looked sloppy. And if that were the case, he might be unacceptable as a representative of Mr. Calvert. He looked at his khakis; they too had spots of sweat below the knees. He wondered why he had walked so fast. He had had plenty of time to get to work. He stood fanning his clothes as the outside door two flights below opened.

"Son-of-a bitch, that damn elevator hasn't worked right since we got here," said Terri, the twang in her high voice ricocheting in the hall like marbles as she opened the door to the stairway. "These damn stairs are going to kill me. You should have known better than to put us in this rat hole of a building. I mean I don't know what you were thinking."

"I'm sorry, it's just this rent was hard to beat and that damn Calvert is such a cheapskate. I guess I just didn't think it would be that bad for a little while," Andy Herman told his sister. He grabbed the large woman's arm and helped her up the stairs.

"Didn't think it would be so bad? Look at me. I'm sweating like a pig on a spit and I'm not even up to the first floor yet." Lee looked down through the banisters and saw Terri, her pistachio shift stained in sweat below her arms as she struggled with a canvas bag much like the one he had carried to work. Her reddish ringlets struggled to stay upright much like a maharajah atop an elephant ascending a hill. A man with horn-rimmed glasses, a blue blazer, and black hair combed like Superman's followed behind Lee and Terri. Lee wondered if he should run up the stairs to the next floor so that Terri wouldn't know he was there and had heard her use bad language when she yelled at Andy. He started to but realized they were about to turn the corner. He moved quickly to stand by the door, but forgot to pick up his canvas bag.

"Son-of-a bitch, what kind of idiot would leave a bag there?" Terri shouted at the top of the stairs, regaining her balance as the two men reached to steady her. Lee's jaw dropped and he stared at the trio who were staring back at him.

"That is my bag, Mrs. Herman. It was very wrong of me to leave it there. I will never leave my bag there again where someone can trip on it as you just did," Lee said still unable to move.

"Listen here," the man with the Superman hair said. "Mrs. Herman could have been seriously injured, tripping on that stupid bag. She could have fallen down the stairs."

"Oh, I know, and that is why I feel so badly. She could have fallen backwards and taken the two of you with her."

"Little shit," Terri mumbled.

"That's the guy you'll be breaking in today Sanford," Andy said. "Good luck. I'm sure you've had many interesting challenges in your, long distinguished career as a political operative."

Andy flipped on the light switch and tossed his jacket on to a small chair that like the other furniture in his office looked as if it were picked up at either a garage sale or a thrift shop. Andy's office décor was typical campaign make-shift. His desk was a mess of papers and on his wall hung charts and news clips with yellow highlighting.

Two elderly men walked in and said good morning to Terri as Andy gave them a quick military salute. "Morning boys, got a lot of ground to cover. Get your supplies then go spread the gospel. Lee, you'll be doing the same thing: getting the word out about Dan Calvert. Remember, 'Dan Calvert –Let's Start Today.' Damn, Sanford, I like that slogan. Every candidate I've given that slogan to likes it a lot too. Not all of them won; as a matter of fact, my track record's been slipping a little bit of late, but hell, I still like that slogan."

"It's a good slogan, Andy, it's a good slogan," Sanford nodded as if he were pondering the origins of the universe. "With the 'Let's' contraction you subliminally inject an inclusiveness that makes a potential voter feel as if he has an investment in the candidate. 'Start,' well it's a word with feeling that gives a primitive image of a horse beginning to pull a wagon as well as the awakening starter of a present-day race car. And of course, 'today,' well it means get going now, a candidate who won't waste time getting things accomplished."

"I never quite thought of it that way," Andy interrupted. "Lee, let me introduce you to Sanford Black. Sanford used to be a college professor.

Guess he still thinks he's in the classroom sometimes. Anyway, he's helping me get this campaign into gear and after he goes over a few things with you this morning, he's going to go out with you as you start knocking on doors. Sanford, why don't you take Lee into the war room and get him oriented."

"My pleasure, let's get this pup up to speed on the art of campaigning," Sanford said as he picked up his brief case, which matched his spit-polished tie shoes draped by the double-break length cuff of perfectly-pressed gray trousers.

The other men had already left when Sanford and Lee walked into the war room. Three long folding tables contained boxes of envelopes, campaign brochures, empty coffee cups, and scraps of office debris. The wall had photos of Dan Calvert, and newspaper articles. Charts listing people and the streets where they lived and maps of different neighborhoods were either thumbtacked or stapled to the wall. An ink smell wafted from "Vote Calvert for Council" signs stacked in a corner with boxes of campaign literature. Two computers were propped on phone directories.

"Okay Lee, let's get down to business. Shouldn't take us more than an hour or so. I've got this down to a science by now," Sanford said as he sat down and motioned toward a chair across the table. Lee sat down.

"Lee, I like to have my people have a sense of what they're doing. I don't like just sending them out into the field without having a sense of what they're doing. Now, what does politics and more specifically the political campaign mean to you?"

"Well, Mr. Black, I think it means one person trying to get the most votes so he wins," Lee said into the serious eyes behind the sloping glasses.

"Ho, Ho, wait one second; hold it right there, pal. Now I see why I have these talks with my people before I send them into the field. Politics is a lot more complicated than that. Lee, I'm going to tell you one thing and I want you to promise you won't forget it. Promise?"

"I promise."

"Don't ever forget to look at the big picture. Do you know what the big picture is?"

"I know what a picture is, but I don't know if I know what the big picture is."

"That's okay pal. I didn't know what the big picture was right away, but I'll tell you one thing, I found out quickly and that's how I survived all the political wars I've been in. Look around this room, the brochures, envelopes, stamps, bumper stickers, maps, computers. Smell the ink from those signs. Think about Andy in the next room doing what he does, and Terri outside doing what she does. And then think about Dan Calvert and his wife and their children doing what they do. And then the voters and the media doing what they do. And that's where I like to say I come in when I meet a neophyte such as yourself. Because everything I just described, you put it all together and that's what I call the big picture. And that's my gift to you, letting you know what the big picture is. And do you know why we need to know about the big picture?" he asked as he took off his glasses.

Lee smiled but was too nervous to answer.

"I'll tell you why," Sanford said eyes looking upward as if some sign from above would acknowledge this moment of truth. "Because one person tries to get the most votes to win."

"I think that was what I said," Lee offered in a low voice.

"Lee, you have to forget about what you said and remember what I said. Didn't you hear what Andy said about my distinguished career?"

"Yes, now I remember what Mr. Herman said. And I will make sure I remember what you said."

"Good, now we're getting somewhere. Just work with me. I have a premonition that you'll be rounding that learning curve with a velocity you never anticipated. I'm good at what I do Lee and I'm willing to bring you along."

"And while we're at it little brother, you still never stop amazing me. I mean I thought we said we had had enough of Sanford Black; that we weren't going to work with him anymore. I don't care how smart he tries to act and to fool people into thinking he's some kind of mastermind, he is, and you know he is, one dumb son-of-a-bitch. The only reason he works for us so dirt-cheap is because no one else will hire him. Yesterday he made a big deal of handing me a magazine with a 'good article he knew I'd be interested in.' Dr. Sanford Black was on the mailing label. You said yourself he doesn't have no damn Ph.D." Terri said, winded after getting her whole statement out under one breath. She scratched at the subdued volcano of ringlets atop her head with a letter opener and looked down at her paperwork.

Her brother sighed. "C'mon Terri, he's not that bad. I told you the budget's tight right now and I don't have time to break these new people in. Besides, I don't think a lot of people know him around here, and having a doctor on our staff, well, lends our operation a little class."

"That's bullshit and you know it. Your good Dr. Black has had that new kid in there now for almost an hour, who the hell knows what Sanford's telling him about a simple job where you only have to ring the damn door bell and give somebody a piece of damn campaign literature. And you know it's not really fair, that kid's not right and he's just the type who'll get sucked into all Sanford's phony baloney."

The door opened and a pleased Sanford presented his newest acolyte with the distinct privilege of graduating from the Sanford Black Campaign College; at least the abbreviated course. "Put it there, pal," Sanford said as he thrust his palm towards an unsuspecting but smiling Lee. "Andy, you've done it again; you've supplied me with a lad who my instincts tell me will be an integral cog in the cadre of canvassers that will carry our Calvert team to victory."

Maybe Terri was right about Sanford, Andy thought. His sister stuck her forefinger into her mouth and wretched forward "All right, Sanford, you're going to take Lee out, show him the ropes."

"Got it, Boss."

"Lee, any questions?" Andy asked.

"No thank you, Mr. Herman. Dr. Black taught me an awful lot already, I just hope I can remember it all."

Terri's forefinger went back into her mouth. Andy thought for a minute he might do the same thing.

"I'll be back in a couple of hours, just as soon as I feel comfortable the kid can be on his own," Sanford said. "You've got another one coming in for me this afternoon, right?"

"Yeah, there's another one for you this afternoon," Andy replied.

CHAPTER 10

Lee had never been down Hanover Street.

"Okay, Hanover Street, the troops have landed; we've established a beachhead, let's get rolling Lee," Sanford Black said as he got out of his car. "And don't forget to put a Calvert for Council sticker on your shirt. These voters want to know who they're talking to. Don't ever forget your sticker."

During the next two hours Lee and Sanford would walk up one side of Hanover and after reaching the cul-de-sac, head back on the other side until they reached the car. It was an old subdivision where small, one-story houses were often suffocated by rangy trees and bushes. Some houses were carefully painted boxes with brush-cut grass and garden hoses neatly rolled. Others were sun-bleached and covered with paint blisters, with yards crowded with weeds reaching out in all directions to ensnare prey of old toys and other debris. It was a working-class neighborhood, but better than where Lee lived. As long as he was dressed nicely and was polite he didn't think the people in these houses or any houses, might suspect he lived in a bungalow. By the time he walked to the end of the street, he found himself determining if the people who answered the door were a match with the house in which they lived.

Lee watched very closely as Sanford stared at the walk sheets listing the names of the people, their addresses, dates of birth, party registration, and date they last voted. "We're just concentrating on the Repubs," Sanford told him when they began. "The people with an R in the column next to their name. No use wasting our time with the Democrats, so skip a house if you see a D next to a name. There is a strategy here and you're going to see that it is a winning strategy. Just do what I do."

Lee didn't know if the people would take him as seriously as they did Sanford. Sanford looked very official. "I'll do the first five houses and you just watch," he told Lee. "Then it's your turn, so watch carefully everything I do. Everything I do is part of the larger package which forms the strategy, so watch carefully."

Lee did exactly as he was told.

Sanford took choppy steps up the first driveway, shuffling and studying papers and preparing his lines for when that first door opened much as a theater curtain being raised as the play began. He rang the bell and waited. He rang again; still no answer.

"Come up here pal," he called down to Lee who hurried to the front step, his canvas bag flapping against his leg. "Did you see what just happened here?" Sanford asked.

"No one was home?" Lee responded.

"Yes, no one was home; that's a situation you'll be facing and timing is essential. I usually give them twenty seconds to answer the door. I'm not going to stand there all day. And you know what's next?"

"You leave them some campaign literature."

"That's very good pal. I see you were paying attention during my talk at the office; but here's the trick, here's where years of experience come into play. You don't leave the campaign literature any old place. What are you going to do, leave it on the doormat and have it blow away? No. You roll the handout slightly and stick it between the doorknob and the door jam. If there's a screen door never open it; someone might think you're trying to break in. Roll it slightly and slip it behind the handle on the screen door and there will be enough tension to keep it wedged in place. Think you'll be able to remember that?"

"I, I think so."

"Good. Now on to the next house and *be prepared for anything.*"

No one was home at the second house or the third house. Sanford had Lee place the literature on the door and then the older man flicked the piece of paper with his finger to make sure the tension was right.

No one was home at the fourth house either. Lee began to think they wouldn't find anyone at home. But just as Sanford was about to leave the fifth house and fight his way back through the hedges commandeering the sidewalk, the door swung open and an elderly man in an oversized sweater stared out at the two men wearing Calvert for Council stickers.

Sanford put on his game face. This was a potential Calvert voter and Sanford strapped himself into the captain's chair and prepared to show his young acolyte how a big fish was landed.

"Good morning, sir. My assistant and I are part of the Calvert for Council team. Dan Calvert's a good man and we need only a few minutes of your time to tell you why we believe you should vote for him," Sanford told the old man as he tamped down on his half-combed hair.

Lee noticed a musty odor coming from the house and a whiff too of burnt toast. The old man breathed through his mouth, eyes flinched as if trying to find the right focus.

"I don't vote anymore. My wife died two years ago and I don't vote anymore, so we can stop wasting each other's time and besides that I've got to go to the bathroom," the old man said in a raspy voice.

"I've very sorry to hear about your wife, sir, but really you know you still have a civic duty to vote. We'd like to have a bit of your time to tell you why Dan Calvert is the best man in this race."

"You got a problem with your hearing, Mister?" the old man spat. "I told you my wife died two years ago and I don't vote anymore, damn it." The door slammed shut.

The two canvassers walked silently to the road. "All right Lee, you see how it's done. Sometimes there are people home and sometimes not. It's about time for me to get back to the office and help Andy with some big-picture strategic thinking. You finish up here on Hanover, do Waverly, and Oten Streets, then come back to the office and let us know how things went," Sanford said as he climbed into his car. Lee watched as his mentor drove to the end of the street and turned on to the main road in the opposite direction of the office.

CHAPTER 11

Lee planned to skip lunch; he wanted to cover as much ground as possible so Andy Herman would be impressed. Now, he stood standing on the sidewalk holding his canvas bag and wearing his Calvert for Council sticker and wondering why he had ever taken the job. He had been frightened by the old man and he thought that Sanford, even though he was an expert, had been shaken as well. This job was going to be much harder than he thought; it would take more than being polite and liking to walk to do this job the right way. He didn't know if he would be able to remember everything Sanford had taught him. Suppose people he spoke to, like the mean man in his dream, got angry and called Andy and complained and then he called Mrs. Plennington and told her that "He's very sorry, but Lee might be a better fit doing something else." What would Mrs. Plennington say? Would she be embarrassed? Oh boy, what would his father say, or would he just shake his head and throw up his hands? Lee should probably get in touch with Reid to see if that landscaping job were still available. Reid would watch out for him; tell him how to do things the right way. A car passed by and the driver looked at Lee. The woman had two children in the back seat and she stared at Lee. He realized he had remained frozen on the sidewalk and began walking toward the main road. He could walk back to the office in twenty minutes and thank Andy Herman for giving him a chance to be part of the Calvert for Council team and that would have to be that. Andy would have to understand that Lee had tried his best. He was sorry if he disappointed them, especially since Sanford had taken all that time to share his political expertise.

As Lee stood at the end of the road, a car came to a full stop at the sign. An elderly woman, who looked like she had just stepped out of a beauty parlor, looked out her open window. "Hello," she said to Lee, in a tone so pleasant he knew she had to be a loving grandmother.

"Hello," Lee said in response. How many more kindly grandmothers and grandfathers and mothers and other nice people lived in those houses? Maybe there wouldn't be another person like the old man whose wife died two years ago. Lee thought he could remember all the things Sanford had taught him, especially the part about getting the right tension on the campaign literature when he placed it between the door knob and door jamb. The women's smile told him not to give up. He smoothed out his Calvert for Council sticker and started to walk towards the house just past the old man's.

C.T. Agarrwal lived at that house and was born in 1958. The sheet said C.T. and K.S. Agarrwal, Lee assumed K.S. was C.T.'s wife, had voted in the last election. A light blue Taurus with a faded American flag decal in the window was parked in the carport. Landscaping in the front of the house did not seem to be a priority for the Agarrwals. Lee just barely made out the word welcome on a mat heavy with dirt when his nostrils felt the slight burn of sweet spices. He was so mesmerized by the pile of assorted worn sandals near the door that he rang the doorbell with none of the trepidation he had anticipated on this his first solo. The doorbell, like a detonator, had set off inside the house shuffling sounds and the patter of words he didn't understand. The door started to open. There stood an old man with white hair and dark skin who appeared no friendlier than his neighbor. Lee froze, his mouth agape, and thought he might soon be calling Reid about the landscaping job. A slight woman in a blue wrap-dress moved past the man and approached Lee. The dining table stood behind her in front of a large painting of an elephant whose head had a covering of jewels and some kind of fancy material.

"Ma'am, I am terribly sorry if I have disturbed your lunch. It smells like a good lunch and I promise I will not take much of your time." He paused. "Ma'am my name is Lee Fitts and I am here on behalf of Dan Calvert who is running for town council. I'm here to give you information about why you should vote for Dan Calvert. He is a good Republican, just, and I am looking at my sheet for a second, like you and Mr. Aggarwal. I have a packet of interesting campaign material for you, and Mr. Aggarwal. I only have one question left for you, can Dan Calvert count on the votes of Mr. and Mrs. Aggarwal on Election day? Are you Mr. Aggarwal sir?"

The old man said nothing. He just stared at Lee who wondered if the old man was about to yell at him. The woman looked at the materials Lee had handed her and her mouth broke into a smile.

"Thank you very much for these things about the election" she said as her mouth plucked out words through a smile that was polite but not welcoming. "My father does not vote, but I will show these things to my husband and we will read them before the election." She seemed satisfied.

"Thank you very much for your time ma'am and sir."

"You are very welcome," she said nodding her head several times.

Lee walked down the driveway and made a check next to the Aggarwals' name. He circled the box, just as Sanford had told him in a case like this, containing the words: did not commit. Mrs. Aggarwal and her father had been very pleasant, Lee thought. Maybe he could do a good job at this after all. Maybe he didn't need Reid's landscaping job. It had been a long time since Lee felt this good about himself. Surely there must be other people out there as nice as Mrs. Agarrwal and her father. And, Lee told himself, if these other people just gave him a chance he would give them a very polite presentation on behalf of Dan Calvert. Maybe they might even call Andy Herman and say he had a very nice, polite man out there working for Dan Calvert.

Lee walked up the next driveway. No cars, Christmas icicle lights on the gutters, black mold stains on the roof, two weather-worn lawn chairs, and tattered shades hanging in the window. He rang the bell, counted. No answer. He rolled the handout, placed it by the door knob and checked the tension; perfect. He checked the box on the sheet on his clipboard: left lit, which meant left campaign literature. Okay, that's good, Lee imagined Sanford saying.

The next house had an addition that didn't fit the original structure very well. Whiskey barrel halves with flower remnants choked by weeds lined the driveway. The window on the rusted screen door had a faded sticker to inform firemen that pets were inside. Lee rang the bell and the shrill bark suggested it was a very small dog. Lee stood still waiting, but there was no answer. His fingers flew to the rolling motion that he had mastered and the handout slid behind the door handle. Lee tapped the sheet of paper. Perfect tension. He tallied his results on his clipboard.

He visited three more houses before the first drop of rain landed on his clipboard. The water hit one of the words he had circled and the ink began to seep into a raised, wet wrinkle. Lee looked in horror at what had happened. He had been so careful to have his sheet look perfectly neat. Now his sheet had a glaring ink smudge. He felt a drop hit his head and then his sheet took another hit. Lee quickly pulled the clipboard toward his chest and walked down the driveway. He hadn't seen anyone since the Aggarwals and with each empty house he became less confident that he could do a good presentation. If only he had encountered someone else, he was sure he could have started to get his presentation down pat -- practice made perfect. He remembered his father telling him that when Lee had been good at kicking the football.

But now Lee was getting anxious. He almost hoped no one answered the door. He was getting very good at getting the paper to stay where it was supposed to stay, he knew how to get the perfect tension. But he started having doubts again; maybe the Aggarwals had been a fluke.

More drops started to fall and soon they were landing all over Lee. Lee didn't think he would be presentable much longer. He didn't want to look like some wet rat if he found someone home to whom he could make his presentation on behalf of Dan Calvert. At least his sheet seemed to be safe. As horrible as the smudges were, they hadn't gotten any worse. He pulled the clipboard toward his chest. He thought if he let the sheet dry, maybe he could doctor those smudges with some white out. Then he saw the identical smudges on his gold shirt. Forgetting he was holding the clipboard away from his body, he watched in horror as the sheet took at least a half-dozen more hits. He put the clipboard in his canvas bag and held it tightly against his chest. He would have to stop right now. He needed to get to the bus stop shelter at the end of the street as soon as possible so he could think about what he should do next.

Lee stood inside the shelter and listened to the rain pound the roof. He was trapped; the bus passed about six blocks away from the Calvert for Council office. The rain was coming down harder and the sky was smoky gray. He reached into his canvas bag to retrieve his peanut butter and jelly sandwich. He was through that and on to an apple when the truck with one windshield wiper drove by. Lee began to smile as the brake lights came on and the car did a wiggly U-turn on the slippery road.

"Is this some type of new diner or something?" Reid called over as he rolled down his window.

"I am stuck." Lee said. "I do not have an umbrella or a raincoat and I am already very wet." Lee pushed the remains of his lunch into his canvas bag.

"Well, you better hurry up and get in," Reid said as he reached over to unlock the passenger door.

"This is very lucky to have you go by when you did."

"Yeah, well they pulled the plug on our landscape job. We were putting in sod and the ground we had spent most of the morning raking started to turn to mud and the sod was tearing and what a mess. We're going to have start all over again tomorrow; that is if the rain lets up. So, tell me how's your job coming? Cover a lot of houses? Meet any interesting people?"

"I think I like my job. I was not sure if I was doing a good job, but then I met the Aggarwals and I thought I was doing a good job, but then the rain came and I really did not see anyone else, but I did hand out a lot of Calvert for Council campaign literature."

"You need an umbrella if you're going to be walking around in the rain. Don't they have a Calvert for Council umbrella or poncho at that office of yours?"

"They did not tell me about any umbrellas or ponchos. Boy, maybe I should have asked. Maybe they thought I would be bringing my own umbrella, but Sanford never said anything about bringing one. But that is where I have to go, back to that office of mine."

"Yeah, yeah, that's no problem. Who the hell is Sanford? Ah, who cares. Why don't I pick you up later, I got some cash – off the books with these characters—we'll get some burgers, then I've got something you won't believe in my apartment, you gotta see this. Seven o'clock, okay?"

"Yes, that is a good time for me. It is this next building where I have to get out."

Reid pulled over to the curb. "Lee what happened to your shirt? Those are nasty-looking smudges? You usually don't go around looking like that."

Lee had forgotten about the smudges. "I did not have those when I left home this morning, I got them from my check sheet when it was raining."

"Yeah, well whatever, you better get that washed or something. Later," Reid called out.

Lee ran towards the door holding his canvas bag against his chest. He didn't know what Andy Herman was going to say.

CHAPTER 12

"Speak of the devil, there's Lee now," Andy said, his narrow body seeming even more so as he stood between two athletically-fit women both noticeably taller than the campaign manager. "Sanford said you were doing just fine out there, but looks like the rain got you. Did you bring an umbrella?"

Before Lee could respond, Audrey Plennington was by his side with a small cloth to dry off Lee's hair. "Lee," she said. "Did you bring an umbrella, and how did you get those smudges on your shirt? You don't have an umbrella, do you? I want you to take mine and when it dries, keep it in your bag. You can't be doing all that walking without an umbrella, these storms come out of nowhere this time of year. Lee, this is Mrs. Calvert."

"Hello Mrs. Calvert," Lee said as he fumbled with the yellow umbrella and looked away. If he felt this nervous meeting Mrs. Calvert he didn't know how he'd feel when he actually got to meet Dan Calvert. He wished Mrs. Plennington hadn't started drying his hair with her cloth and making such a fuss about his not having an umbrella. He already felt as if he hadn't done a good job and now he was back early because of the rain that wasn't his fault, but the smudges probably were. And now standing there were three important people smiling at him: Mrs. Plennington, because she had never, ever been cross with Lee; Andy Herman, because even if he might think Lee couldn't do the job, Dan Calvert's wife was smiling because her friend was smiling.

"Let's call it a day out there, Lee. Leave your check sheets with Terri and we'll get going at this again in the morning. I'd say you did pretty well today," Andy said in a "what do I have to lose by saying that if I please the boss' wife and her friend tone."

"Hear that Lee? I told you that you'd do a good job," Mrs. Plennington said.

Lee walked over to Terri's desk and handed her his check sheets. Her eyes told him she wished to say nothing; she would contribute only a smile to the foolishness playing in front of her. His eyes could talk to hers and he was told that the world always needed people like her, people who kept things going in the face of foolishness. Her eyes told him further that she didn't blame him.

"Lee, we've got to get you out of those wet clothes. Valerie do you think you'll be ready soon? I can drop Lee off at his house and then drive you home." Audrey said.

"Don't worry about me, Audrey," Mrs. Calvert said. "I'll get a cab from here, I have a few calls to make. I'll be fine."

"Are you sure?"

"I am sure. See you at the spa in the morning. It was very nice to meet you Lee, I'm glad you're on our team."

"Thank you, Mrs. Calvert. I am glad I am on the Dan Calvert for Council team. I'm going to work very hard and do everything Andy, and Terri, and Sanford tell me to do."

"Well you can be sure that I'll pass that along to Mr. Calvert."

"You see, I told you you'd do a fine job." Audrey whispered into Lee's ear as she guided him out of the office. "The candidate's very own wife is going to tell her husband about the good job you're doing." Lee imagined kneeling on one knee before King Dan Calvert as Queen Valerie told the king about the good job his servant was doing. "You've done well," King Dan said. "Keep up the good work, I'm counting on you." "I will," Lee promised. Queen Valerie smiled.

The rain had left little beads of water on the metallic finish of Audrey Plennington's Lincoln Town Car.

"I don't want to get your seat all wet," Lee said as he opened the door.

"Don't worry, it'll be fine; but just look at my hair. This humidity shows no mercy on my poor hair," she said. She leaned over and guided the rear-view mirror in her direction, then touched her fingers to the hair just above Lee's ear. "Your hair is so cute when it's wet."

Audrey Plennington's house was a sprawling rambler of white brick. A beautiful flat stone retaining wall lined the driveway and crisp dark green plants lay in beautifully manicured beds of bronze mulch. Lee had never been to Mrs. Plennington's house before and thought how different her yard was from the one of bare grass spots and shrubs of half-bare branches in front of the tiny house he shared with his father.

"You have a very beautiful yard, Mrs. Plennington."

"Well, I pay that landscaping company enough. Problem is, I'm never home to enjoy it. That fitness center just takes so much out of me."

"But you do a very good job. Every time I come in you have a lot of customers, so you must have a very good business."

"I do have a good business," she said as the tip of her forefinger touched Lee's nose. "Come on, let's get in so you can take care of those wet clothes." As she opened the door, her mid-cut skirt rose to her thigh. Lee self-consciously realized he was staring and quickly opened the door and got out of the car. Mrs. Plennington's leg didn't have any fat on it at all. It was beautiful muscle that she must have gotten from all her workouts in the spa. He thought about his legs and how his father once told him about how perfectly muscled they were. You have legs that look like you've been working out forever, his father said. His father used to keep a notebook containing the measurements he took of Lee's calves starting at the end of fifth grade. The leg strengthening exercises began at the beginning of the sixth grade. One day during the following spring, Mr. Richards, the football coach, came to Lee after school and told him that they would be meeting Lee's dad on the football field. "Mr. Fitts, I never seen anything like it. I'm telling you I never seen anything like it, and I've been coaching twenty years. Never seen a leg snap forward with so much follow through. He'll be kicking them from fifty yards out when he gets to high school." Lee didn't remember as well as his father.

"Lee, are you coming or are you going to stare at that plant all day?" Audrey Plennington said from her front door.

"I am sorry, Mrs. Plennington, I guess I was having a daydream."

"Was it about me?

"Excuse me ma'am?" Lee said confused.

"I'm just kidding, silly, now come on, inside."

Audrey Plennington's front door opened on to a natural slate-floored foyer beyond which the sunlight from the clearing sky ramped in through the high windows just below the cathedral ceiling. Lee had forgotten how wealthy Mrs. Plennington's family was. Multi-directional lights shone on huge paintings, and ornate draperies, over-sized chairs and sofas dressed in burnt oranges, yellows, and blues stood before the perfectly-cropped shrubbery visible in the yard beyond. Audrey placed her large purse and keys on a narrow table holding a vase of fresh-cut flowers.

"Well, what do you think?" she asked.

"I have never been in a house like this," Lee said. "There are so many things in that big room that are very beautiful. Your house looks like it belongs in a magazine."

"Well, I'm glad you like it. I've been meaning to show it to you and this afternoon just seemed to be the perfect time. You can leave your wet sneakers and socks right by the door then let's get those wet clothes taken care of. Want something to drink; soda, juice?"

"A soda, and it can be any kind at all. I like all sodas." He did what he was told, a little uncomfortably, and took off his sneakers and socks.

"That's fine, I won't be a minute."

Mrs. Plennington walked through the dining area and through a swinging door that led into the kitchen. Several minutes later he heard her call from a hallway that led off the big room.

"Lee, come on down here, I want to show you something."

He followed her voice and found her standing in front of a huge window at the end of the hall on either side of which were French doors leading to separate rooms. His bare feet sank into the thick pile of an Oriental rug leading to the window.

"Isn't this a spectacular view?" she asked as she handed him his soda and pointed to a waterfall that splashed into a pool lined with rocks and brightly colored flowers. "I had that pool designed from a photo I saw in just the kind of magazine you were talking about. Actually, it's much nicer than the photo. It was finished last month and swimming in that pool in the early morning, when it's very still, is the most peaceful thing in the world. You have to come over one morning, we can go for a swim, then I'll fix you a nice breakfast."

Lee watched the falling water hit the pool. Trees swayed in the distance.

"It is very, very beautiful, Mrs. Plennington. You are very lucky to have that view out this special window."

"I know, in some ways I'm very fortunate. But it's nice to be able to share things with someone." She placed her hand on his shoulder. She pointed into the room whose French doors were held open by identical slender wooden containers of artificial flowers. "The robe on the chair is for you. Give me your wet clothes and I'll throw them into the wash. There are some magazines next to the chair you can look at and I'll let you know as soon as your clothes are ready."

Lee moved away from the open door and standing between twin beds, removed his shirt and pants and put on the fluffy terrycloth robe. He went back to the hallway and handed his clothes to Mrs. Plennington who smiled and walked up the hall.

Two women's fitness magazines, a healthy-cooking magazine, and an oversized photo book on home landscaping sat on a glass table next to the chair. Lee plopped the book on to his lap. He was very comfortable in that soft chair, and the landscaping photos of artfully-placed bushes, stone, flowers, and pools brought a restfulness to his mind. Lee caught sight of Mrs. Plennington walking down the hall. She turned and walked barefoot into the bedroom across from him. She said nothing and Lee thought it best to continue reading his book. He heard a clicking sound from Mrs. Plennington's room like the magnetic clip on a door pulling away from the metal catch. He turned his head and saw Audrey Plennington standing in front of a large open closet. But she wasn't just standing any more, she was starting to unzip her dress which was soon off and on a hanger she had gotten out of the closet. Lee quickly turned his eyes back to the landscaping book. His mind tried to get him out of the chair and under the bridge so Mrs. Plennington wouldn't think he was looking at her. When he looked up, Mrs. Plennington was standing there wearing only her underwear and staring out the window. She walked toward the window and then turned back and stopped. She looked at Lee and smiled. She began changing into a one-piece workout outfit and then stepped into a pair of red warm-up pants.

"There," she said. "I'm ready for work. I'll let you know when your clothes are ready and then I'll drop you home before I go to my spa."

CHAPTER 13

Lee looked down at his clean khakis; he could wear them tomorrow for work. That was one good thing, he thought, as he looked at the stuffed bag on the back of his door, I won't have to go to the laundromat tonight. It seemed every other thought he had was about Mrs. Plennington. She had been very quiet in the car and when they got to Lee's house she just told him to do a good job the next day and handed him the bag of fruit and health food drinks she had prepared for him. Lee tried to remember when he saw Mrs. Plennington as his mother's best friend. And yet she had known he was sitting there and she had turned and smiled at him. He didn't know if he should see her again.

Reid rapped at the door and when Lee turned, his friend was already in the house. "Wouldn't that be funny if one Tuesday night your father was home and I just walked in like that?"

"I do not know if it would be funny," Lee said. "But I think you are still pretty safe. Dad has not been home till late on Tuesdays for at least the past three years."

"You're not hiding back there are you, Mr. Fitts? I know you really like me, even if you don't show it."

"Why do you think my dad is back there hiding? I just told you he has not been home on Tuesday nights for the past three years. And Reid,

I think you are wrong, Dad really does not like you. I have asked him to change his mind, but he has not."

"Lee, chill man, I'm only kidding. You always take everything so seriously. I know your Dad isn't hiding back there and I definitely know he doesn't like me. But, hey, we're still best buds, always have been and always will, right?"

"Right, Reid, best buds."

"All right, let's go, I told you I've got something great to show you at my apartment."

Lee made sure all the lights in the house were off and turned on the porch light. If he left any lights on in the house when no one was there, his father would yell that he was trying to make the electric company rich. Lee thought leaving a small light on would make burglars think someone was home. Lee's father told him there was no burglar stupid enough to want to break into their rat trap of a house.

"So, all ready for another big day on your job? You going to stay at that job?"

"Yes, I am going to do my best tomorrow. I like being part of the Dan Calvert for Council team and I will just have to see if my boss, Andy Herman, thinks I'm doing a good job." The image of Mrs. Plennington bolted through his mind. He shivered as he looked at Reid. Reid could never know; no one could ever know. It was hard enough for Lee to think about things and now Mrs. Plennington had found hiding places in his brain from which to pop out when he would not expect it.

"You okay, boy, you daydreaming or something?"

"I am okay. What is the big surprise at your apartment?"

"Won't be long now," Reid said as he pulled the key out of the ignition. Something continued to gurgle under the hood and the worn hinges let out a grinding sound as the two occupants opened the doors. If Reid's truck had been a horse, he would have had to shoot it. "Damn, the lot's pretty full; the Tammery's got some new Tuesday night special, must be working whatever it is."

"Yeah, it seems to be working alright, whatever it is," Lee agreed.

The Tammery Inn was a simple two-story building, asphalt shingles on the walls and a wooden awning that supported a neon sign new probably during Eisenhower's first term. The faded black paint on the neon tubing would make first-time customers believe they were going into the Tamery Inn. The light stood right outside of two windows that Reid had never been able to open and the old table cloth hanging in the windows did little to keep the light from flooding into Reid's apartment.

"I always told myself this apartment was a real find," Reid said as the friends walked up the narrow staircase.

"Remember, you got to jump over those two steps, and watch out for the second from the top, it's just about to go." Lee braced his hand on the wall that vibrated from the bass line of the jukebox in the bar on the other side.

The apartment was the size of two small U-Haul trucks if they were side-by-side and didn't have any walls between. Each piece of furniture: a single bed, coffee table, a couch with one of the arms missing, fought for any available inch in the small room. A shower curtain hung in place of a bathroom door.

"Wait till you see this," Reid said as he walked over to a TV framed by a box of corn flakes on one side and a bag of Doritos on the other. He clicked on the remote. "Ta Da. What do you think man, I got cable?"

Sure enough, as Lee looked at the screen, there was a perfect picture. "Wow Reid, it is cable."

"Damn right it's cable. Now here's the deal, and mum's the word. I got this cable connector and found where the wire runs into the bar and voila, I got cable. This guy at work; he's from Bolivia or someplace close to Mexico, and he told me exactly what I had to do. And those guys in the bar don't know anything; it doesn't affect their picture at all. I got your HBO and ESPN and some movie channel, is this hitting the jackpot or what?"

"Are you sure the guys that own the bar do not know? You do not want them to find out and kick you out of this apartment that you love."

"Stop worrying. This is a gift from above. Do you know how much cable costs?"

"My dad says we cannot afford it and called me a jerk because I did not understand that."

"Maybe I should ask him if he wants to come over here and watch a few shows. But you know he'd turn my ass in if he knew I was getting free cable. Look at this, Atlanta Braves playing the Dodgers; is this something or what? I got some beer, a little wine, or I think there is some ginger ale, may be flat though."

"I would like the ginger ale."

Reid handed Lee a Wendy's plastic drink cup. "It's a little flat but it's wet. Matter of fact, I like my ginger ale flat. Don't you think it tastes good flat?"

"I like ginger ale flat or not flat," Lee said. "But when you buy soda in those big bottles, I know it is cheaper that way, but the soda is usually flat by the time you get to the middle of the bottle. Are you at the middle of the bottle?" Reid held up the bottle. "You are near the bottom of the bottle; it will always be flat when you get that far down the bottle. Thank you for the ginger ale."

"What's important is the cable. Look at that picture! Ever see a baseball game like that? They're probably watching the same thing downstairs, but here we are, got the same thing, but all the comforts of home. I got to bring Lope from work over to show him how well it worked."

"Does Lope like the landscaping job?"

"He doesn't mind it. I don't think anyone minds it. But I don't think he likes it. It gets hot out there and dusty and sometimes when you run into all those little roots, raking can be a bitch. But I guess it's good exercise and lots of fresh air. You drink a lot of water, man and even so, sometimes it's so hot you don't have to piss, you just sweat it all out. Yeah, Lope probably doesn't like it, but he's not even supposed to be here. He and his brother came up here from Mexico or Bolivia or somewhere near there. Good thing our boss don't ask many questions. He just wants someone out there steady, doing a good job and not stealing any tools. I guess me and Lope and his brother all got the right stuff for landscape work. And what I really like is not having to do a lot of thinking about how to do the job; it's pretty automatic after the first couple of days. Damn, I knew that ball was out of there. Look at that picture, see how good you can see that dirt on the bat."

"Yeah, I have not seen pictures of dirt so close up and realistic."

"So, what about your new job with what's his name, Dan Cramer?"

"No, his name is Dan Calvert. I work for the Dan Calvert for Council Campaign."

"So, this Dan Calvert, is he a nice guy, like what's his deal?

"I have heard he is a very nice man, but I have not met Dan Calvert yet. I met Mrs. Calvert today when she was at our office with Mrs. Plennington. Mrs. Calvert is a very nice woman."

"Yeah, so do you like your job, what do you actually do?"

"Yes, I think I like it. I go to each house and give people campaign handouts about Dan Calvert and ask them to please vote for him. You have to be very polite and not answer questions that you do not know anything about. But most times, there was no one home, so after you ring the door bell and no one answers, you have to very carefully roll the handout and fit it into the door handle. There was one man home who was not very nice to Sanford Black, but then later when I was by myself I found the Aggarwals and they were nice to me. I definitely know how to leave the campaign handouts in the door if no one is home and I just have to see if I meet more people like the Aggarwals and not like the mean man that did not want anyone bothering him."

Reid looked at his friend in the folding chair with the paint stains on its legs. The job didn't seem that hard, a little walking; a little talking. But the more he thought about the name Dan Calvert; it just seemed so familiar. He tried to think where he had heard the name before, but then was caught by the find of the roving camera as it panned the seats. "Damn, look at that chick; pretty hot. Those cameramen know who to look for. Hi baby! Go on Lee, wave back to her." Lee's face had no intention of even the slightest smile. "Hey you know who that chick reminds me of? Christie, Christie Veit. I saw her the other day at the gas station. Pretty hot man. Didn't she used to like you in junior high? I know after the accident and with what happened to her brother, she was a wreck. I think she remembers me. I wave, she usually waves back."

"She does look like Christie," Lee said as he caught the last glimpse of the girl in the stands before the pitcher reappeared on screen. Christie is a very beautiful girl. She works at Mrs. Plennington's spa and is always very polite when I go in there."

"Hey, Lee, ever think maybe she still likes you? You should check it out. Talk to her a little more. Ask her out on a date." Reid said, as his waving hands emphasized each point of his matchmaking plan.

"Oh, I do not think I could. I have never been out on a real date."

"See, that's exactly what I'm talking about. I don't know any other twenty-one year-old that hasn't been out on a 'real date.' You should ask her out. But why do you go to the spa?"

"Sometimes Mrs. Plennington wants me to come over to tell her how things are going." He shook away the image from that afternoon again.

"Mrs. Plennington was my Mom's best friend; I guess she wants to keep an eye on me, make sure I'm doing okay."

"Hmm, I hear Audrey Plennington has been a very caring woman since her divorce. You're a good-looking guy, Lee, you know there is caring and then there is *caring*."

The image shot through his mind again. Did Reid know about that afternoon? Had he seen something in Lee that spoke about that afternoon? He looked at the TV not knowing what to say. Mrs. Plennington wouldn't say anything to anyone about that afternoon. Would she? But nothing had happened. He looked over at Reid whose eyes were now closed.

"Reid, I have to go. I can walk home."

"What? What time is it?" Reid looked at his watch. "Don't you want to watch the rest of the game?"

"The game is over."

"Okay let me get you home. Damn, that cable's something, isn't it?"

CHAPTER 14

Lee was careful not to wake his father who was asleep in the reclining chair. Lee sometimes thought his father found his only moments of peace in that chair. Tonight, by the time Jim Fitts cranked the chair forward and started to shuffle his socks across the floor, Lee was in bed. He would be free from his father's questions and jibes till morning.

With the faint light of dawn came the blaring clock radio, the clump, clump of Jim Fitts' feet as he rushed to shut off the news, and then, it would only be a short wait, Lee knew it was coming in the next breath or two – the smell of coffee. His father had not started at him yet, Lee's eyes locked on to the man he loved so much, hoping for a smile.

"Get fired yet?" his father asked without looking up from the bowl of flakes.

"No, I did not get fired. I still have my job with the Dan Calvert for Council Campaign. I only got to work half-a-day because of the rain, but I think they are still happy to have me as part of the team."

"If those people are that stupid I should vote for the other guy."

Lee usually said nothing after his father's first volley. He absorbed his father's words as he did the smell of coffee that hung in the kitchen. The door closed as it did every morning and Jim Fitts was gone to the bus, to the mall, to the thoughts of what might have been.

Lee said hello to Terri as he walked into the office. She scratched with the letter opener at her lopsided beehive.

"New day ahead of us," said Sanford as he shot in from the other room. "Each day, as we in the profession say, is critical as that big clock counts down to the Big E – *E for election* -- Day. Ready to go? You realize what's at stake, don't you? Can't lose the smallest opportunity each day presents. We campaign strategists know how important each and every day is, isn't that right Terri?" Sanford asked.

Terri Herman rolled her eyes and looked up just as her brother entered from his office. Andy nodded at Lee. "Looks like a nice day out there. Maybe we can make up for some of the time we lost to the rain yesterday."

"I can make up for that time, Mr. Herman."

"You can call me Andy; that will be fine. See me when you get back," the campaign manager said as he returned to his office. Lee gathered up his materials and new walk lists and headed for the stairs.

"Lee," Sanford called. "Come here a minute, pal. Look, now I know the boss said to try to make up for lost time, but don't rush it too much. What I mean is don't rush your delivery when you give your pitch to the people. As seasoned a veteran as I am, I find that if I rush too much, my delivery doesn't come off as smoothly as it should. And whatever you do, don't in haste get sloppy when you roll the handouts. And remember, get that tension just right when you put those babies in the door. Can you remember all this?"

"Yes, I will remember your important pointers."

Sanford put his hand on Lee's shoulder. "I think you're going to do okay, kid."

Lee had gone through ten walk sheets by noon in a neighborhood not far from the office. They were working-class households like the day before, but some of the people that came to the door, well, Lee wondered if he had never met them before and saw them at the mall, well, he wondered if he could tell if they lived in a working-class house or a nice house like his sister Ellie. Mr. and Mrs. Levin were just getting out of their car when Lee walked up the driveway. They both had gray hair and their clothes were very neat. Mr. Levin was about to grab some dry cleaning from the car, then turned and stood next to Mrs. Levin while Lee told them all about Dan Calvert. Lee knew that if he saw the Levin's in the mall and had never seen them before, he would certainly think they lived in a bigger house. They reminded him of Mr. and Mrs. Castle who lived next door to Ellie. The Levin's were not only very neat, they were polite and made Lee feel like he was doing a good job. They even said they had heard of Dan Calvert and that they might vote for him.

Lee thought if he saw Mr. Moreno at the mall that it would be easy to guess that Mr. Moreno lived in this neighborhood. Several stacks of newspapers in plastic grocery bags were heaped by a side door blotched with dirt and claw marks from some animal. He had a gray sweatshirt with Tweety Bird on the front and jeans that sagged in the seat. His hair was combed but it was not neatly trimmed as Mr. Levin's. But if Mr. Moreno had a good haircut and wore different clothes Lee wasn't so sure he would know where Mr. Moreno lived. Lee didn't know if he should walk up the driveway when he came to Mr. Moreno's house, but he did and although Mr. Moreno didn't smile, he listened patiently to Lee. When Lee finished, Mr. Moreno said thank you, put another bag of newspapers by the side of the house, and closed the door.

But aside from the Levin's, Mr. Moreno, a teenage girl who was watching her little brother, and the man with an oxygen tube in his nose who when he opened the door clearly was not happy, no one else on his ten walk sheets had been home. He was almost halfway through his supply of handouts. Just when Lee thought he was doing a good job he would have to run into the man hooked up to the oxygen tank. He asked Lee if he could read the sign. "No solicitors means no solicitors," the man said before slamming the door. Lee wasn't sure that he knew exactly what a solicitor was, but he didn't think he was one. Sanford hadn't said one thing about No Solicitors signs. Had Sanford forgotten, or did he think Lee could figure that out for himself, or was the man needing oxygen mistaken in thinking Lee was a solicitor? "Don't worry about that," Sanford said when Lee got back to the office. "Technically you're not a solicitor. You're always going to run into some old goat like that. Look pal, you're doing a good job; I should know, I trained you myself."

In the days that followed, Lee found that he was getting better and better at handling old goats. He also found that he had developed a system of rolling handouts that he thought was even faster than Sanford's and the voices of people as nice as the Aggarwal's and Levin's sounded in his ears long after he left their driveways. Sometimes those friendly voices stayed with Lee all the way home and even into the evening. When the voices were playing they could drown out his father's "They haven't let you go yet?" or "I'm telling you, remind me not to vote for that clown Calvert." The chorus of nice people was louder than the old goats and his father. The chorus was getting larger each day and the chorus was telling Lee he was doing a good job.

CHAPTER 15

"I want you to start telling people about the rally," Andy Herman said.

"I do not know about the rally," Lee replied.

"The sheet on the rally has been on the bulletin board in the main room for about a week. Everybody's supposed to read the bulletin board. I can't be spoon-feeding you Lee."

"You are right. I will read the bulletin board in the morning before I go out and in the afternoon when I come back. I will read all about the rally and everything else on the bulletin board so I know everything the Dan Calvert for Council Campaign is doing."

"Look, Lee, I didn't mean to jump on you, it's just that, well, you know there are a lot of things going on and we've all got to be on our toes. We've got a new handout that has all the info about the rally –next Saturday at Veterans' Park, two o'clock, ice cream, balloons, flags, the whole damn bit. Sanford is running this show and next week I just want you walking in the morning then coming back in the afternoons to help Sanford. In the mean-time, you make sure you let people know about the rally."

"I will let everybody I see know about the rally," Lee said as he walked into the main room to look at the bulletin board. It was all there, just as Andy Herman had said. Rally for Dan Calvert, Candidate for Council, two o'clock, Veterans' Park, RAIN OR SHINE. At the top of the sheet was a list of Dan Calvert sponsors serving on the Host Committee. There in the middle of the list was the only name Lee recognized; Audrey Plennington. The bolt rushed through his head: Mrs. Plennington standing in the room across from him, smiling. He hadn't seen Mrs. Plennington since that day; she hadn't been at church for the last two Sundays. He was relieved she had not been there. But now it seemed certain he would see her on Saturday at the rally. He thought briefly about asking Andy Herman if sponsors always came to a rally they were sponsoring. But that might have been such a simple question that anyone would know. Lee didn't want to get yelled at again. He didn't want Andy thinking; what? First, you don't read the bulletin board and now you're asking a stupid question like does a sponsor come to a rally he's sponsoring. Is this kid trying to lose the election of Dan Calvert to the council? But Lee couldn't remember when a question was so important to him. Maybe he could ask Terri. Maybe he could ask the question in such a way that Terri wouldn't think it was a big deal. Lee walked into the front office.

"I was just reading about this very interesting rally that Dan Calvert is having in the park next week. Do you know if someone who is sponsoring a rally usually comes to the rally?"

Terri looked up from her keyboard. She had so much work to do she thought, and now I have stupid questions. She glanced at Lee realizing the look on his face said that to him this question burned stronger than any feelings she might have about any of the paperwork on her desk. I told Andy this kid's not one hundred-percent right. Her ankles were swollen badly that day. The Motrin did nothing to help her shoulder. She knew she had eaten too much already this morning. It was a simple question. He looked so hopeful that Terri could help him.

"How the hell do I know? I'm not in charge of the damn rally. And you can bet your ass that's the last place in the world I'll ever be." She saw the hope drain from his eyes. She recognized she had responded with non-proportionate force. She forgot her ankles, her shoulder, that she had eaten too much. "Look, I told you I don't know, but I'll ask Andy, or you can ask Andy."

"No, please don't ask Andy," Lee pleaded as terror like a palsy took control of his body.

"Son-of-a bitch, all right I won't ask Andy. Don't come to me with any more of your stupid-ass questions; you hear me?" Terri knew for sure that he wasn't one hundred- percent. Sanford, Lee – her brother had her working with a couple of nut jobs. She went back to her keyboard and let out a sigh. There was no peace in Lee's walking that day. All he thought about was the rally. His steps up and down the driveways paced off his troubling thoughts. First, he now had another handout; that meant an extra step to putting the campaign materials on the door. But after the first ten houses, he had incorporated that step into his procedure as if he had had two handouts ever since he first started working for Dan Calvert. But his next two concerns seemed to get larger as the day progressed. The question of Mrs. Plennington, he knew she'd be at the rally; but what would she say to him? Would she treat him as if he had done something wrong? And then there was asking Terri Howard about if sponsors go to a rally. Lee knew she would tell her brother about the whole thing and even if Andy didn't say anything, he would probably think he had made the wrong choice in hiring Lee if he could ask such a stupid question such as does a sponsor come to a rally.

"Lee," came Andy's voice from the other room. "I need you to deliver something for me."

Lee looked at the envelope Andy handed him. It couldn't be true, but there was the name scribbled in red ink: Audrey Plennington. "You want me to deliver this envelope?" Lee said, his words ending in a plaintive rush of breath.

"Yeah, Audrey is one of our sponsors for the rally. She wanted some invitations that she could personally address. Just drop them off at her spa or fitness center or whatever she calls it. Is there some problem?" Andy asked as he adjusted the gold chain that had gotten tangled on the collar button of his golf shirt. The tight shirt made him look slighter than he was.

"Well, Sanford gave me a walk list for a new neighborhood. He thinks it's important that I get to as many houses as possible and well, if I walk all the way over to Mrs. Plennington's spa, I know I cannot get all my walk sheets done. I will be backed up for tomorrow and maybe even backed up for the next day and the day after that."

"Lee, look at me. Sanford works for me. I don't give a rat's ass about your walk lists right now. You two are going to be working on the rally. Remember the rally? This is what is important until weekend after next. Dan has told me himself that this rally is his top priority right now. I mean I guess I could tell him that you have a different opinion?"

Oh boy, Lee thought, now there's another thing to worry about. Mrs. Plennington being a sponsor, Terri telling Andy that Lee wanted to know if sponsors come to rallies, and now, Andy telling Dan Calvert that Lee didn't think the rally was a top priority right now.

"No, please do not tell Dan Calvert that I do not think the rally is a top priority." It was happening again, just like all the other jobs Lee had. He was going to get fired, there was always some reason. He just wanted it to be over so he could find Reid and get the landscaping job. His father would probably be happy, because he had said Lee would be fired. Now his father could tell him, "I told you so, I just don't know what took them so long."

Andy placed his hand on Lee's shoulder. "Hey, Lee, look at me. I'm only kidding. You got to lighten up. I mean you and Sanford are always so serious. Got to roll with the punches in this campaign business, always something new. Flexibility is key. Can you understand that Lee? C'mon, you're doing a good job. But flexibility; got to have it. Understand?"

"Yes, flexibility, flexibility."

"Now here, I told your friend Mrs. Plennington you'd bring this over this morning. She said she'd be looking for you."

Lee was out of the building quickly but slowed his pace as he walked the ten blocks to Mrs. Plennington's. He hadn't been fired and nobody at his other jobs had ever told him he was doing a good job. His stride acquired more confidence; he was propelled by an engine never felt before. Doing a good job; his father had been wrong. What would his father have said if he had been standing in the office when Andy said that? Maybe the old look would change, the look that might as well have been a punch to Lee's stomach. The look that said his father's life as a security guard living in a run-down bungalow was somehow Lee's fault. But Lee would be flex-ible, ready for anything if that's what was important to Andy Herman and that made Andy continue to think that Lee was doing a good job. He was afraid he knew, however, what "She'll be looking for you" meant." Maybe he was wrong. But he couldn't get Mrs. Plennnington mad at him. She was a sponsor of the rally. One word from her and it might be all over. "You're doing a good job" would be like a tattered flag flying in an abandoned fort.

This was the worst time to go to the spa, well maybe one of the worst times. The morning exercise classes were always full. But maybe it was bet-ter for him if there were a lot of women at the spa. Maybe that would be the time that Mrs. Plennington would be more business-like.

The disco bass lines joined the perfumed sweat that greeted him as he opened the door. Christie Veit was at the sign-in table, looked up briefly, but then returned to her conversation with someone who looked like a new member. Lee could see Mrs. Plennington was on the phone and he felt that at any minute she might turn and see him. The envelope containing the invitations was moist and becoming more so at the spot where it lay in Lee's hand.

"Lee?"

He turned and looked back at the counter.

"Lee, can I help you with something?" Christie asked.

He swallowed hard and looked at the woman who had grown from the school girl he had one time dreamed he would marry. He wondered what she would say if she knew he were doing a good job for the Dan Calvert for Council Campaign.

"I have, I have an envelope for Mrs. Plennington and she knows I'm bringing it over here this morning."

"I didn't know you and Audrey were such good friends," Christie said with an icy gaze.

Lee searched for a tiny lie that might help him, but as always, he could never find one. "I am a friend of Mrs. Plennington's because she is an old friend of my mother's."

"Hmm, did you have a nice visit at her house the other day?"

"My nice visit at her house the other day?"

"That's what she told the girls here, you were at her house the other day."

"I was at her house the other day because she said she had never had the chance to show me her house before and since I was all wet from walking in the rain, she could dry my clothes at the same time she showed me her house."

"That's very interesting, Lee. I guess I hadn't thought about you in that way for a long time," Christie seemed to realize she had said too much. There was a feeling now about Lee that she hadn't yet learned to handle; a feeling that she seemed to notice awakening the day that Audrey

Plennington spoke about Lee's visit to her house. "Anyway, I see Audrey's ready for you now."

Lee stared at Christie, but when she looked away it was like a phone connection gone dead. He turned and saw a smiling Mrs. Plennington waving him back to her office.

"Andy said he'd be sending you over. I haven't seen you for a long time, where have you been?" Audrey Plennington said as she leaned over to tie her sneaker.

"I have been out going to many homes and talking to people and giving them campaign handouts; I am trying to get them to vote for Dan Calvert. Andy Herman told me this morning that he thought I was doing a good job and . . . I am going to be helping Sanford Black work on the big rally."

"Slow down Lee, you're as enthusiastic as ever. Of course, you're doing a good job. I said you would didn't I honey?"

Lee hadn't even thought about telling his mother about his doing a good job. But it had been a long time since the last phone call and she was very clear: "Lee I think it's better for you that we not speak; maybe someday, but not now. Your father, well, I just think it's better for you, I love you honey, one day it will be much better."

Lee handed the envelope to Mrs. Plennington. "I'm sorry, the bottom is a little wet; I guess my hand was really sweating. These are the invitations you wanted, there are stamps in there too."

"Very thoughtful, very professional. Let me get a towel for your hands," Audrey said as she reached in front of him and drew a fluffy yellow towel from a neat pile. She stepped behind him and opened the cube refrigerator sitting on the floor in the corner of her office. She stepped to his side and nudged him into the chair beside her desk. "There, sit and relax for a while. You push yourself too hard sometimes."

From her seat at the reception desk, Christie watched the whirling Audrey Plennington move around Lee from every angle. The three-foot by four-foot window in Audrey's office framed her actions for anyone looking from the outside as a movie screen would to a theater audience. Christie didn't think Lee knew that he was in Audrey Plennington's movie. Christie had only worked at the spa for several months, but she knew clearly where her boss was going.

"I have to get back to the office, Mrs. Plennington, remember I told you all about my working on the rally?" Lee said as he placed the towel and water bottle on the edge of her desk.

"Oh yes, the rally. Did I tell you that as a sponsor, I've raised $3,000 for this rally?"

"Three-thousand dollars? You must be one of the best sponsors of the rally. Does Andy Herman know how much money you have raised?"

"Yes, he knows, that's why I don't think he'd mind if you were a little late getting back as long as he knew you were with me. She grabbed a skirt from the back of her closet and pulled it up over her workout shorts. She knew Christie was watching. Perfect. She hoped others were taking it in as well. "Lee, I'm going to run home. Get a quick bite of lunch – want to come?" She took a tiny perfume dispenser from her purse and three short hisses filled the room with a breeze swept from an orange grove peaked for harvest. It was the fragrance that would linger on his clothes when Mrs. Plennington would hug him after church.

"Oh, I have my lunch Mrs. Plennington. Yes, I have my lunch. Andy Herman lets me keep it in the small refrigerator in his office. He has a small refrigerator just like yours. I know I am going to have a lot to do when I get back to the office after I eat my lunch. Sanford might be looking for me right now, because he knows how long it takes to walk over here and get back." Lee could feel both hands starting to sweat and he reached for the towel.

"Honey, it's all right, please don't get upset. We'll do it some other time. Now take this water with you when you go. If I don't see you before, I'll see you at the rally. I'm proud of the good job you're doing. One day maybe we'll have longer to talk."

CHAPTER 16

"*H*ey *Wally, where's the warden . . . oh Hi, Mr. Cleaver. How are you this fine afternoon, sir?*"

"Damn, that Eddie Haskell, he never knows when Mr. Cleaver is around. This a funny show or what? They got all the old shows on the *TV Land Channel*. I'm telling you cable is the greatest. And you gotta see the other shows: *Bonanza*, Hoss and Little Joe, *I Dream of Jeannie* and those old astronaut suits, and *Andy of Mayberry*, did you know that little Opi is a famous director now? I can't remember what pictures, but he's bald now," Reid said as he twirled the remote in his hand. Eddie was getting the look from Mr. Cleaver and Reid laughed loudly but horribly out of tune with the laugh track.

"Boy, the Cleavers seem to be a very happy family and Mr. Cleaver always knows what to say to the boys so they understand what they are doing wrong. And Mrs. Cleaver cooks such nice meals and makes sure that Mr. Cleaver is not too hard on the boys." Lee said.

"Yeah, ain't no families around like that now. You don't think Mr. Cleaver fools around do you?

"What?"

"Just kidding," Reid said through a laugh. "They got *Green Acres* on next, but tell you the truth that's probably the *TV Land* show I like the least.

I don't know why, maybe that woman's foreign accent. Damn, we don't need no *Green Acres*. Ever see *Animal Channel*? Well, I guess we just missed a show about gorillas. Oh good, good, this show is about the animal police; they get calls about animals getting mistreated or somebody having a tiger in their apartment. These guys, got guns and everything and sometimes they bust these people who are mistreating the animals. Look at this idiot. Two hundred rabbits in that small house? Look at that mess! Damn right they should haul his ass out of there. They had this show on last night with this skinny horse kept out in the rain for months, didn't have anything to drink but some black-crappy looking water. One of the animal police asked the horse's owner if he would drink that water. Then they hauled that guy's ass off too. I'm glad there are animal police out there, but they're never going to be able to save all the poor animals. What's this? Professional pool; now that's what I'm talking about. Look at all the different camera angles, that bright green color. Damn this guy's gonna run the table."

"You really like cable TV don't you Reid?"

"Damn straight I like cable TV. The whole world comes to you right through that little wire over there. After a hard day of landscaping, me and my remote and that's all there is to it."

"How is your landscaping job going?"

"You know what? They may be making me foreman. My boss says I got what it takes. Maybe another month or so, he wants to see what jobs line up. What do you think of that? Me, a foreman, and another fifty cents an hour on top of that. Only problem we got so many of those guys from Mexico and Bolivia and those other countries, I have a hard time talking with a lot of these guys. Think they're here in the good old US of A that they'd want to speak our lingo, but most of the times they just blah, blah, blah, blah speaking that Spanish. If I'm going to be a foreman I'm going to have to know more than hello, good bye and you're a shithead. Hell, you know what, they even have a lunch wagon that comes around, all the signs are in Spanish, and it's got all the foods those boys ate back home in Mexico. But you know what? I ate one of those little biscuit pouches with the meat and potatoes in it. Not too bad. Luis bought it for me. Might even buy one myself, but I still eat from the other lunch wagon."

"Gee, a foreman. That is good Reid. You are doing good in landscaping. I found out today that I am going to be working on the big rally that is coming up for the Dan Calvert for Council Campaign."

"What big rally?"

It is the most important thing right now to Dan Calvert; we are having it in the park next Saturday. There will be a lot of his supporters and I think anybody can come and meet Dan Calvert, and I think there will be balloons, and refreshments."

"Huh, anybody can come?"

"That is what the paper on our bulletin board says and it is free admission. You should come Reid and you can bring the people at your work. They might like you better if you invite them to the rally; especially if you are going to be their foreman."

"Damn, free eats just cause someone wants to get elected to something. Yeah, I'll get my boys there, tell them that their foreman has some good connections and got them in the rally for free. They'll think I'm a big shot. What are you having to eat?"

"The paper says hot dogs, hamburgers, sodas, and I think ice cream."

"Ice cream!? I know my boys will like ice cream. And we can leave if the speeches get too boring. Just kidding Lee, just kidding. Don't worry about us, we'll be very well-behaved. Hey, know if there is going to be any cerveza at this rally? Damn, that's another word I learned, forgot all about that one."

"I do not remember seeing that. What kind of food is that?"

"Cerveza is Spanish for beer. Going to be any cerveza?"

"I do not think so Reid. I do not think Andy Herman would want any drinking at the big rally. I do not think you should tell anyone they can get cerveza at the rally."

"All right, all right, no cerveza. Ice cream will be fine for them. Know what I was thinking about yesterday, and I'm going to do it, damn, I know that's exactly what I'm going to do. I was thinking that if, not if, when I win the lottery I'm going to get a new TV, one of those big screen jobs. I mean I have this beautiful picture, but it's too small. I can't see the kind of complexion on those baseball players that I could when I was looking at that big screen down at the Best Buy. I mean if I'm going to have cable, I might as well have the clearest picture possible. When you look at that guy at bat on my set you can't see the stubble of his beard like you can on those big sets. And the damn sound is so much better – just like you're in a movie theater. Damn, if I win the lottery, I might as well get out of this damn room all together, move over to those Whispering Hills luxury garden apartments, sign says you get cable free with the rent. Yup, that's going to be the plan, and I'm going to win the lottery soon. Last week, I only missed by three numbers."

Reid was staring out the tiny window over the front door of the bar below. There was a lot of yelling in front of the bar, then a lot of laughing, then the slamming of car doors then a broken bottle. Always ugly noises in front of the Tammery Inn. He wouldn't have that at Whispering Hills where he would soon be looking for the instruction manual to see how to hook up his new, huge TV to the cable that came with his rent.

"I may go out of state if I have to," Reid said deaf to a new volley of noises from the summer street below. "I've been following the lotteries, and I think these people living in some of these other states have an easier time winning the lottery. I can feel that big screen remote in my hand. Hey, one day. You've got to have dreams. You have dreams don't you, Lee?"

"I do not know if I can dream hard enough to win the lottery. I have one dream, even though it is smaller than yours, a dream that came true that somebody told me I was doing a good job and not just telling me that to try to make me feel better about myself. I have always wanted to do a good job. But my big dream is that the person who tells me I am doing a good job is my father."

"Quiet down there, this is a residential area," Reid screamed at the noises outside.

"Shut up you moron, before we come up and beat the crap out of you," came the voice from the street."

"Idiots. Hey Lee, no offense, but I think I might win the lottery before that dream of yours comes true. Look, I know how you feel about your dad, although I don't understand why. I have no damn idea why. Who knows maybe things with him will change. But best I can figure, he had a dream too. I remember how he was about you before and after the accident. He just couldn't believe it was all over."

"My father thinks I can do something that I cannot do. I do not remember real good being able to do that."

"Oh, I remember. Damn, I remember and I don't think I ever saw anything like that. That leg of yours snapping around like some kind of whip, that smack against that air inside that leather, then the perfect end-over-end over the crossbar. Your dad had won his lottery. Damn, look at that picture. See what I mean? That batter's stubble isn't clear at all."

CHAPTER 17

The bobtail cat seemed to know that the orange of his coat was not the color it should be. He sprinted from the pile of decaying landscaping timbers where he would sit every morning and stopping short, twisted his leg back and chewed at his fur. He sprinted further towards the road and slammed on the brakes again, this time licking furiously at a black clump just below his chin. The cat would watch as Lee came down the street on his way in the morning to the Dan Calvert for Council office. Ever since that day Lee opened a sandwich bag containing leftover corn flakes and milk from his cereal bowl and placed it near the remains of a withered hedge, that cat would look for Lee. But then Lee stopped bringing food for the cat. It was the day after his father saw him pouring the remnants of his cereal bowl into a plastic sandwich bag. "What the hell are you doing? What? You're feeding a cat? Are you crazy? You think we have money to waste on sandwich bags and milk, and cereal to feed some flea-ridden cat? I see that damn cat and it'll see a rock flying at it." As he continued to look at the cat, Lee wondered how many times it would take the cat to figure out that it wasn't getting any more to eat.

"Lee, I need your attention pal, this is the big one coming up this week, I need you with me buddy," Sanford said.

"I am sorry Sanford, I was just thinking about the cat I see every morning."

"Lee, okay, let's forget about cats, we've got to think about dogs -- hot dogs, hamburgers, ice cream. What we do is going to make or break this rally; it's no simple matter getting all this food together. We have to get balloons, and some streamers, and those big black garbage bags. I've got to find out where to get those big black garbage bags. That's what I'm going to be working on first this morning and I need you to grab that Yellow Pages and put a list together of where we can get some ice cream and then I'll start to focus on that. This might get a little complex, and we have that calendar staring at us. Five days; Lee the calendar shows no mercy, got to remember that. Not many days to get this all nailed down. I've drawn up a battle plan with everything we need to get and do. It's going to be tough, but with a little grit and just keeping in mind how big this rally is . . . we'll do it. I've been in tight spots like this before and I think that's why Andy threw this baby into my lap. Let him work on the speech, and invitations, and sponsors and publicity; I think you and I both know what will make this rally a success."

They must think I am doing a good job, Lee thought, to have me working on this important project with Sanford. Lee also was relieved to know right off the bat where to find big, black garbage bags. They were right in the front window of Seedge's Hardware Store; the store window he passed every day on his way to work. But he thought he better put a list together anyway; that's what Sanford asked him to do and Lee had never worked on a rally before. He'd put Seedge's at the top of the list, this way that would be the first place Sanford would call.

"Got the hamburgers," Sanford said coming over to give Lee a high-five. Sanford lowered his hand before Lee fully raised his arm. "Yeah, got the burgers and that place has salads and drinks, sometimes things just fall into place. I decided to get the burgers before working on the black garbage bags. Sometimes have to switch tactics, switch them on a dime. I'll work on your list this afternoon. Who knows maybe I'll be as lucky with the garbage bags as I was with that other stuff. I've almost completed my schematic for the rally; we'll go over that before you leave today. Afraid I might be burning the midnight oil here if I'm to get all my planning done."

Lee didn't get to see Sanford's schematic until mid-week. The older man was totally absorbed in his charts, yellow-legal pads with broad black circles around broad black scribbling, and file folders each with information about different parts of the rally.

"Is there anything else I can do?" Lee asked.

Sanford took off his glasses and looked at Lee. "I wish you could," he said with a weight-of-the-world-on-my-shoulders sigh. "Don't get me wrong, you've been a big help Lee. I'll have to do this myself, see I'm crashing right now on the briefing Andy wants on where we stand. But first thing tomorrow morning, if you could get here a little earlier than usual, we're going to do a dress rehearsal. My list and schematic will be done and they'll only be one thing outstanding. Afraid I've left the toughest for last and I'm going to need you to come with me when we select the ice cream. Night kid."

Lee fingered the two twenty-dollar bills in his pocket. Tonight was shopping night just as any other time was when his father left the twenties on the kitchen table in the morning. But instead of thinking about Hungry Man dinners and other things he knew his father expected him to buy, especially unsalted peanuts, he thought about ice cream. As he walked into the store busy with shoppers on their way from work, he thought about the next morning. Suppose Sanford asked him a lot of questions about ice cream. Lee didn't buy ice cream. It was too expensive and even if it were free, he wouldn't be able to get home before the ice cream melted into mush. He realized he knew very little about ice cream. The ice cream was just on the other side of the aisle where the Hungry Man dinners were displayed.

He looked at the rows and rows of ice cream; different flavors, different brands, low-fat, no sugar, frozen yogurt – he stared at the ice cream cases and tried to remember as much as he could. The freezer doors opened and closed as Lee moved from one side to the other until he realized he was in the way of those shoppers wishing only to get their ice cream and go home and have dinner.

The next morning, he sat nervously at the table as Sanford laid his papers in front of them. Lee had a small paper in his hand with some information about the ice cream he had seen the day before. He didn't want Sanford to think he didn't know anything about ice cream for the rally, but he knew also that he would be embarrassed if he had to look at the paper if Sanford asked him a tough question. A question that Sanford probably thought wouldn't be difficult for most people.

"Here it is pal. The A-man signed off on it last night. This is my schematic; my blueprint for the rally. When I write my book on campaign strategy you can bet this baby will be in there," Sanford said as he pulled his chair closer to Lee. There it was, the layout for the rally: podium, chairs, sound system, banners, balloons, trash cans, food tables drawn neatly in pencil. Sanford had even drawn in a little compass at the bottom of the paper. Lee looked at the other sheets before him, one telling who was going to do what and another with a column of times down the left side and corresponding things that were to occur precisely at that time. From noon till two, for example, opening of reception/sign-in table to policing the grounds/litter pick-up beginning precisely ten minutes after the rally ended. Names of staff were listed next to the functions to which they were assigned. For the next hour Sanford took Lee through the plan which was part Napoleonic vision and part board game instructions for ages 4 years and older. Lee's eyes out ran Sanford's finger which tapped senseless every item on the sheets. When Sanford got to the last item he stared and tapped and then gave one slap tap that landed triumphantly on the paper. He looked up. "This is what they pay me for."

"Boy, Sanford that is great plan for the rally. Those are very neat boxes you drew and it is good that you drew that compass to show everyone that they will be looking into the sun at the end of the program so they can wear sun glasses."

"What do you mean looking into the sun?"

"Oh, all I mean is that everyone knows the sun sets in the west and that is the direction the podium is facing."

"Now listen here," Sanford said in a voice reserved for the worst blasphemer. "That sun setting in the west isn't always necessarily so, there are a lot of climatic and seasonal factors to consider concerning how the sun sets." He was starting to panic. His head started to throb as he thought about having to move the podium, and draw up a new chart and then have to present it to Andy who would ask him why he was wasting his time with a new chart. No. Sanford couldn't move the podium. If anyone asked he would tell them he heard it was going to be overcast on Saturday and thus he could place the podium in a more strategic position. "Didn't you think I already thought about what you just said?" Sanford asked Lee.

"I am very sorry; I guess I am wrong about the sun." Oh boy, he thought now Sanford is not going to be in a very good mood when he talks about ice cream.

"All right, forget it. We're all under a lot of pressure and I can see where it might cloud your thinking. Now, the one remaining item: ice cream." Lee gripped his paper tighter. "We're not going to do this half-baked, and I confess this is one area where I'm going to need some help. Lee tried to remember the way the different ice cream was lined up in the display case. "So, we're going to take a ride down to that Crample's ice cream parlor and talk with the manager, tell him what we're got in mind and get the ice cream that best suits the rally. I'm not going to spend a lot of time on the charts, but he's got to understand that we can't be taking any chances –*we need the right ice cream!* I know when I've got to consult the experts."

The store had just opened and an elderly lady in a white bib apron was filling napkin holders on the empty tables. "This is why I wanted to come now, too early for anyone to be eating ice cream," Sanford said in an aside to Lee. "Pardon me ma'am, I'm Sanford Black and I'm coordinating the rally on Saturday for Dan Calvert. Is the manager in?"

"Rally for who?" the woman said as she slammed a napkin holder shut.

"Dan Calvert."

"Never heard of him. Hold on," she said as she walked into the back.

"She obviously hasn't reviewed our campaign literature. Lee, run out to the car and get me a few pieces."

"Can I help you?" asked a man in a white shirt and white pants as he carried in an ice cream container from the back room.

"You the manager?" asked Sanford.

"That's right," said the man.

Hope this guy knows his ice cream, Sanford thought. "Good morning, sir. I'm Sanford Black. I'm coordinating the rally for Dan Calvert in the park on Saturday."

"Who?" the man asked as he lowered the container into the display case.

"Dan Calvert, he's running for council."

"Dan Calvert?" The ice cream manager glared at the campaign manager. "Say, you guys weren't out knocking on doors awhile back in the neighborhood up the street, were you?"

"No, why no. My associate and I work in the office; we're assigned to the office we do office work. Here, please take this flyer and here's one for you too ma'am."

"Well, I wasn't happy to hear that my father was getting disturbed by a couple of guys out knocking on doors. He's still very upset about my mother dying and all."

"And I can see why he and you would be upset. We'll report this as soon as we get back to the office. You have my apologies and you can be sure your father won't be bothered again." Lee stared at the napkin holder and was wondering to whom Sanford would report this when they got back to work.

"All right, so how can I help you?"

"Ice cream, I need ice cream for about one hundred people for our rally."

"Here's the price list and flavors are listed on the back," said the manager as he handed a white, business-envelope size paper to Sanford.

"Amazing, I mean, Lee look at all these flavors. This is going to be harder than I thought." Sanford studied the names trying somehow to find in a mind trapped in vanilla a way to process nonsense ice cream flavors. He realized he was looking at the list way too long. "Okay, so you're the expert, what type of ice cream would you recommend for our rally?"

"You want to go basic, go in vanilla and chocolate and maybe some Rocky Road or we got a couple of other flavors the kids might like . . ."

"Whoa, you're going to have containers of vanilla and chocolate next to each other. I mean, isn't there a subliminal racist message there? And Rocky Road, I mean come on, is that the type of image we want to create? Do we want to associate Dan Calvert with going down a Rocky Road? We're getting into risky territory. I mean ice cream makes a political statement. People start wondering about why we have selected a way-out flavor or some inappropriate combination and they're going to start wondering about what is in Dan Calvert's head."

As the manager's gaze shot to Lee, the door opened and the eyes of two elderly couples jumped to the beautiful poetry on the brightly-lighted board of ice cream flavors behind the counter.

"Look," the manager said, "I know ice cream, I don't know ice cream and politics, so why don't you just stay with vanilla. I guess you can't go wrong with all vanilla if that's what will make you happy."

"I thought right off you were an expert," Sanford said. "Just testing you. But don't underestimate yourself; you do know ice cream and politics. Lee do you have one of our flyers on the rally? Let's give one to, it's Mr. Snight?" Sanford asked as he read the name plate on the man's shirt.

"Yes, Al Snight."

"So, you'll get everything there when we need it?

"It'll be there; need payment the day before."

"Good man, Al. Got yourself a deal. Let's go Lee."

"That's how it's done Lee, there's no leaving things to chance, down the straight and narrow reduces the screw ups. Not that the old screw-up monster isn't always out there waiting for you. Now I know you probably think that old beast hasn't ever gotten a bite out of me, well, you'd be wrong, it did get me a couple of times, but that was a long time ago. Know what, we're going to get some whipped cream in those spray cans. I've always liked that aerosol whipped cream on vanilla ice cream."

CHAPTER 18

Lee was glad Ellie and D.H. were coming to the rally. Reid was coming too and bringing Luis and Lope from the landscaping crew. Rev. Warren Taylor was going to be there also. That was Sanford's idea. Can't hurt to start one of these shindigs with a few words from a preacher, Sanford said. Lee wasn't sure what Rev. Taylor would say, but probably something about the weather and nourishing our souls. Sanford had written a short speech that he had Lee give to Rev. Taylor. When Rev. Taylor started to read it, his eyebrows pushed so far up that his ears started to move. Maybe I can play around with this a bit, Rev. Taylor told Lee.

Lee paused that morning at the corner and realized right away that something was missing. It was the first time in the two weeks since Lee had stopped feeding him that the bobtail cat wasn't sitting by the pile of landscape timbers. Lee had his answer about how long a cat would come to the same place thinking he would get food: around two weeks. After two weeks, Lee surmised, somehow the cat mind figured waiting that same time, same place was a waste of time. He wondered if some cats waited longer and some not as long. Maybe they saw in the person that fed them something that set off some kind of clock that told them how long they should wait before they tried a different place, a place where someone else had something to feed a cat. Lee tried to imagine what there was in him that had the bobtail's clock set at two weeks. That bobtail was fat; he probably knew good places. He was probably eating better now than corn flakes and a bit of milk.

The office was busy. No one was canvassing; there was too much to do to get ready for the rally. "Less than twenty-four hours," Sanford kept saying over the heads of volunteers making phones calls to invite people to the rally. Lee had been at the copier all morning. Whenever the copier tired and jammed, whoever was using it would yell for Lee. Lee didn't take the bait from the copier's hieroglyphics of red signals and curse the machine as everyone else did. Lee had followed the directions the first time the machine jammed; he hadn't tried to rush to a quick interpretation of the red lights as others did. It became clear that if you rushed to interpret the squiggly lines in the red lights, the copier had you every time. But even when he followed all the directions in proper sequence, there were times that Lee couldn't get the machine to work. Then the repairman would have to be called and it would be hours before he would be done fixing the copier.

The morning of the rally was a gift from the weatherman. It was as if someone had stabbed a pin into the big bag of humidity smothering the town for the past two days. Blue sky and a lightly-slapping breeze had been outside waiting all along.

Lewis Talley's blue Ford 150 was beside the pavilion when Lee walked into the park. Lewis Talley was in his sixties, had gray hair and an athletic build. He was a Boy Scout troop leader, carried a pocket knife that was an orchestra of blades and snippers, and always knew the right knot for tying things down in his pick-up. He began volunteering for the campaign several weeks earlier and appreciated the way Lee listened.

"Lee, you're just in time, lot to unload and get set up," Lewis said standing in back of the pick-up among signs, a PA system, boxes of disposable picnic items, and cartons of campaign paraphernalia that he was handing to several other volunteers. "Thought Sanford would be here by now, but I guess as long as we have his diagrams and instructions we should be okay."

"Yes, I think we will be okay. Sanford gave me his diagrams and instructions too, but he told me to hold them close," Lee said.

"He told me the same thing," Lewis said, as he put his knife back on the clip hanging from a belt loop on his corduroy pants. "Wouldn't want this information to fall into enemy hands," he joked.

"My friend Reid will be here soon with his work friends, Luis and Lope, and they will help also," Lee said. "I see they are coming now. Let me go tell them what their jobs will be."

"Lee, my man, here comes the rescue squad. Lee, meet Luis Camero and Lope Alvarez. Luis and Lope, my best friend ever since way back, Lee Fitts," Reid said. "Now what do you want us to do to get this rally off the ground?"

"It is very nice to meet you, Luis and Lope. We are glad that you were able to come to our rally and help."

"Thank you," Luis said. Lope smiled and nodded.

"Lope don't speak no English, Luis, knows some, he usually translates," Reid said over Luis' translation. Lope spoke back a few shots of Spanish.

"What he say?" Reid asked.

"Lope said he's very happy to be at your big party," Luis smiled.

"Okay," Lee nodded. We should go help Lewis Talley."

By 10 o'clock, the area surrounding the pavilion looked like Sanford's diagram. Signs, banners, PA system, balloons, coolers of soda and water packed with ice, barbeque grills with coals heating up just the way Lewis' scout book said they should.

"All, you did a good job," Sanford said as he looked at the pavilion and then his diagram. "Yes, a really good job. Now, I need you to gather round. This won't take long, that's it, gather round. In less than two hours potential voters will begin streaming into this park and we have to make sure that when they leave they are rock-solid votes for Dan Calvert. We've got to make them feel welcome. We have to smile. We have to make sure that every one of their senses tells them that they're glad they came and that Dan Calvert is their man. Once we get those hot dogs and hamburgers fired up, well that's the All-American barbecue smell that puts everyone at one of these rallies in a good mood. And we've got ice cream too. Once they've had a chance to wash those dogs and burgers down with some of that ice-cold soda, then we open up the ice cream, then we've really got them. And I've seen Dan's speech, and let me tell you this, it's a doozy. I want everyone to be looking at Andy and when the boss starts clapping that's our cue. And some cheering, we need some cheering at those pivotal points. When Dan comes in we'll be playing the theme song from *Rocky* so we definitely need some whooping and hollering at that point."

Sanford went on for another ten minutes as if he were addressing the tattered peasants about to storm the Bastille. It was only when Lewis Talley said it was hot and everyone needed a drink that Sanford cut it off.

"Lee, come here," Reid said. "Is that character for real or what's the deal?"

"That is Sanford's plan for the rally, Reid."

"Damn, somebody better be assigned to watch that character. That guy's head's gonna explode."

Luis had just finished his translation for Lope.

Lope shot out a few words.

"What he say?" Reid asked as the three landscapers walked towards the coolers.

Luis looked around. "Lope said 'who is that asshole?'"

"Same in any lingo," Reid said as he nodded at Lope.

"Good crowd," Lewis said as he glanced at his watch. "It's a good crowd, Lee."

"Yes, it is a good crowd that has come to our rally. Thank you for helping me with this tape Lewis. Once we see Dan Calvert and Andy getting halfway down the walk to the pavilion we have to start the *Rocky* theme song."

"If you ask me, I don't know if I would be playing the *Rocky* theme song when they come walking in, but who am I to say?"

"It is a nice song, Lewis, and sometimes when I think about Rocky and the problems he had and how good he did, it makes it easier to go through the day with a better attitude."

"Maybe so," said Lewis. "Maybe so."

Just then, Lee saw Ellie, D.H. and his dad. Ellie waved and as they got closer, Lee saw that his dad was wearing his security guard shirt without the badge and tie, and the worn, gray polyester pants that Lee hadn't had time to iron. Ellie and D.H. knew how to dress for a rally.

"Lee, isn't it nice that Dad was able to come to the rally? When he called this morning, I told him D.H. and I were going and he insisted on coming," Ellie said as she held her arm around her father's waist. Lee knew the helpless look in his sister's eyes when their father's actions left her only with a forced smile as a response.

"Which one of these bozos is Dan Calvert?" Jim Fitts asked as he scoured the crowd.

His father's words made Lee's arms and legs lifeless. He tried to move his mouth to speak but the only words he heard came from Ellie.

"Dad, I told you coming over here how important this is to Lee. You assured me you would be on your best behavior." Ellie's voice lowered and as a trainer giving the reluctant lion one last chance to perform, she whispered to her father that they would leave if he didn't keep his word. His body jerked when she squeezed his waist.

"I told you not to do that," Jim Fitts said as he freed himself from his daughter's grip and sulked toward the coolers of soda. Rev. Taylor had seen everything; he turned away and walked quickly toward the pavilion.

"Why did you bring him Ellie?" Lee asked.

"He insisted, and I was afraid that if we didn't bring him, he'd get a few beers and come over himself."

"We'll keep an eye on him Lee, you just do what you have to," D.H. said.

"Thank you D.H. I have to watch for Andy Herman and Dan Calvert and start the theme from *Rocky* as soon as I see him. I have never met Dan Calvert so when I see Andy, I'm going to take a quick look at this poster just to make sure it is Dan Calvert then start the tape."

"You'll do fine Lee. We'll be over by the soda," Ellie said.

It wasn't long before Lee saw Andy's car. Andy got out, the other door opened. Lee saw the man with Andy and looked at the poster, then the man –*now*. Lee hit the button and the music started, people turned and some started clapping. Andy and the man with him started to wave. As Lee looked back to see the now cheering crowd, he saw Sanford running towards him, arms flapping fast enough for take-off. Then the one wing stopped and started a slicing motion across Sanford's throat.

"What are you doing? What are you doing?" Sanford said still doing the slicing motion across his throat."

"I am playing the *Rocky* theme song. You told me to play the *Rocky* theme when Andy and Dan Calvert got here."

"That's right," Sanford said hitting the button to stop the music. But for the love of God man, that's not Dan Calvert, that's his brother Dean Calvert."

Lee looked at the poster and then at the man with Andy. Same salt and pepper hair neatly trimmed, same sharp nose. It was the eyes, there was no way the eyes of the man in the poster were those of the man who had with Andy now reached the pavilion. Andy waved Sanford towards him and jabbed at the ground twice. Lee looked for Reid and Luis, and Lope. He didn't see them.

"No more *Rocky* theme song. Got it? No more! I'm going to wait for Dan and bring him in. Do not play *Rocky*!" Sanford said shaking his head gravely, as if the campaign had sustained a fatal blow.

"I will not play *Rocky*." Lee saw Reid and Luis and Lope. They were laughing. Lee wondered if he were still Reid's best friend, then saw Sanford trying again to initiate flight. It was Mrs. Plennington's Mustang. Unless there were another Calvert brother, Dan Calvert was sitting in the passenger seat with Mrs. Calvert in the back. They were soon in front of the pavilion. Mrs. Plennington waved. She wore a strapless dress with huge pink and blue flowers and a finely-textured straw hat with narrow ribbons matching her dress. Dan Calvert pointed her way as if to acknowledge that more eyes had been on her than on him.

Just as Lee wondered if he would actually get to meet Dan Calvert, Mrs. Plennington motioned to Lee to come over. Dan Calvert was shaking hands and back-slapping as he began to move into the crowd. When Lee reached them, she grabbed Dan Calvert's arm.

"Dan," she said, "Let me introduce you to Lee Fitts; he's one of the hardest workers you have and he's been out representing you exceptionally well."

"He has? Well then, Lee, put it there," Dan Calvert said as his hand darted out on its own looking for yet another shake to consummate.

Lee looked at Mrs. Plennington as if to make sure someone was witnessing this handshake. "I am very proud to be part of your campaign team," Lee said.

"Well, I'm proud to have you, Lee. If Audrey says you're doing a good job, that's a fine compliment. She's been a strong supporter." Dan

Calvert's hand had disengaged and it readied itself for –*zap* – it had found another hand.

Mrs. Plennington smiled at Lee and continued on with Dan Calvert while Mrs. Calvert advanced on a group by the barbecue grill.

"Looks like you finally got to meet the big man," Reid said. "What do we do if we want to meet him, just go up to him or what?"

"Yes, Reid, you and Luis and Lope should just walk up to him. I know Dan Calvert will shake your hand," Lee said as he looked at Dan Calvert whose hand was *zap, zap, zapping* like a machete through the brush.

"Okay, let's go," Reid said. "What's he saying?"

"Lope thought we should get something to eat first; he's afraid they're going to run out," Luis said.

"Tell him there's plenty of food, let's go shake hands first."

Lee looked for Sanford. He hoped he wasn't still mad about the *Rocky* theme song. Lee wasn't sure what he should be doing at this point in the rally. He saw Sanford over with Dan Calvert. It looked like they were discussing some papers Sanford had in his hands. Sanford seemed to be losing patience because Dan Calvert kept getting interrupted by other people.

"Lee."

Lee turned toward the sound of a voice he knew but had never heard that way. "Christie. It is good to see you; I am so glad you could come to our rally. I mean, I did not think you even knew about it."

"Oh, we had one of the posters in the spa window and every time anyone went into Audrey's office this week she was on the phone talking to someone about the rally. I can't stay long, but I thought I'd see if you were here and say hello."

A slight breeze nicked the edges of the leaves on the tree behind Christie. The wind fluttered against her hair and skirt.

"I am so glad you came. We have burgers and hot dogs and soda. Would you like some burgers and hot dogs and soda?"

"No Lee. I already ate. You wouldn't want me to get fat, would you? Why don't I take a rain check." She realized quickly Lee might not know what a rain check was. "You know, maybe I'll take you up on your offer some other time."

"I would like you to have a rain check. Does that mean we would go out on a date?"

The wind continued to flutter at her hair and skirt. "Yes," she said, just short of a giggle she had not expected. "We can go out on a date, but I have to run now. Call me at work."

"I will call you at work, Christie." Lee's eyes followed her quick steps up the path and away from the pavilion. Behind his back, Audrey glared. Lee thought this day, the day of the rally, might be the happiest day of his life.

"Can you hear me Lee? Lee?"

"I am sorry Ellie. I did not see you."

"I wanted you to know that Dad left. We wanted him to stay and drive him home but he said he wanted to walk. He really ate though, two hot dogs and two hamburgers. It was good to see him eat. But he was complaining to the guy serving the ice cream that they should have had other flavors besides vanilla. Matter of fact we heard several other people saying the same thing. It was good ice cream though. Was that Christie Veit you've been staring at?"

"I did not know I was staring. She wanted to see how the rally was going and she had to leave and she wants me to call her."

"Smooth operator there, Lee," D.H. said.

"I haven't seen her in a long time, She's a very attractive young lady. I remember you had a crush on her when you were in junior high school," Ellie said.

"She smiled at me first," Lee said. "And today she smiled at me the same way."

"I remember Mom really liked her and spent long hours at the Veit's house after Christie lost her brother. I'm sorry. I didn't mean to go back to that day. It was tough for all of us. That's why with Dad, I know how he gets sometimes. His world just changed so much that day and he's never been able to get back on his feet. He doesn't mean some of those things he says to you. He gets so angry; I don't know if he even knows how angry he gets. He has a son and daughter who love him. And I know he's drinking too much. His hand was shaking today when I held it. But Mom said his world was changing even before that day. Your accident just pushed him over the edge. I'm sorry Lee, I'm going on here. Sometimes it just comes out of nowhere."

"Ellie, I do not want to talk about the accident and hear about changes and how I am different now. You know it is hard for me to remember old things."

"I know, I'm sorry Lee. But, you did remember Christie Veit's smile." Ellie put her arm around her little brother. "Lee this is a very nice rally and you should have heard all the nice things Mrs. Plennington was saying about you and what a good worker you were. She said that right in front of Dan Calvert when she introduced us to him. We're going to go. Call me tomorrow."

"Are you going to listen to Dan Calvert's speech? I think he will be giving his speech very soon."

"No, we've got to get going. Love you Lee."

"Bye Lee. Don't eat too many hot dogs," D.H. said.

"I will make sure I do not D.H. Good bye everybody. Love you."

Towards the top of the field two boys throwing a football stopped so Ellie and D.H. could walk past them. Lee watched, noticing that the older boy threw a perfect spiral pass, and then another; all the passes were perfect. And when the other boy ran to catch the ball, the older boy's pass seemed lofted in a trajectory just like that of the rock Reid threw years ago when he hit the squirrel sitting in the oak tree just down the way. Reid said he never thought he'd hit a squirrel. The older boy threw several more passes. He could have wiped out all the squirrels in the park if he wanted to, Lee thought. Lee looked at his foot and then at the pavilion. Calculations started whirring inside his head.

"Amen," came Rev. Taylor's voice suddenly. Lee hadn't heard anything before that.

"Sorry, having a little trouble with the PA system," Andy Herman said, as Sanford fiddled with some switches on the control board. The theme song from *Rocky* blared out then cut off. Lewis Talley pressed several buttons and the sound system did what it was supposed to. Lee thought Lewis Talley might have learned that during all his years with the Boy Scouts.

Andy Herman welcomed everyone to the rally and then introduced a well-tanned man in a striped, short-sleeve shirt who read from a list of good things about Dan Calvert. The man said he knew Dan Calvert since when they were in kindergarten.

The man started clapping and said, "And now I'd like to introduce our next councilman, Dan Calvert."

Lee heard only applause and cheers. Sanford must have changed his mind. He had told Lee they would play the *Rocky* theme song after Dan Calvert was introduced.

Mrs. Plennington and the other sponsors were standing behind Dan Calvert as he walked up to the microphone. He waved to one side of the crowd and then to the other, then he started waving at will.

"Friends! Friends! Thank you so very much for an introduction as warm as our weather. I hope you get plenty of that good ice cream back there. Andy Herman, my good campaign manager here, has just told me that in response to popular demand, we've gotten some other ice cream flavors. Hope you enjoy them." The manager of the ice cream store was waving his scooper. Sanford just looked upward.

"Friends, I come here today asking for your help, not for me, but for our good city. I'm only the means to help our city and I want you to join me in never forgetting that. Your vote is not for me; it's for our city. My opponent has something different in mind. He wants you to vote for him. That's a major difference."

Dan Calvert seems to be a very unselfish man, Lee thought. He would rather have his supporters vote for the city instead of him. Lee was glad he was working for that type of man. Dan Calvert's subsequent words collapsed in Lee's ears. Something hard caught the muscle next to his shoulder blade and Lee grimaced as he turned around.

"And furthermore, friends . . ."

"Friends, my ass. Kick the ball, Lee. Go on kick the damn ball."

"Dad. Ellie said you left. Why did you throw that football at me?"

"Yeah, I left," Jim Fitts said as he half-staggered toward his son. Had some business to tend to. But walking back, I said to myself, I don't want to miss that clown Dan Calvin give his big speech."

"Dad, you cannot talk so loud. His name is Dan Calvert," Lee said, visibly anxious as several people near him started to stare at his father."

"Who gives a rat's ass what his name is?"

"And friends, your vote for me, I mean the city, the city will . . ."

"I'm just telling you one thing Lee. What the hell you looking at?" Jim Fitts snarled at an elderly man who quickly turned away. "I'm telling you one thing Lee, kick the football. I told those two boys over there that gave me the ball, that they'd see one hell of a kick. I know you don't give a damn about me. Everything I was doing for you and then all you would ever say after that day was you don't want to kick the football. I pleaded with you and all you ever said was no. Well, what about those kids over there. I told them they would see someone kick the football like they wouldn't believe. You going to make a liar of your old man? Go on, the older boy is all set to hold for you."

Lee froze, afraid even to try to work out the cramp in his shoulder. More people were staring. Mrs. Plennington looked at Lee; Andy Herman did also.

"And I know that with your support; well, we'll make a great team as we work to make this city a . . ."

"KICK THE BALL!!"

"That's a good one. That's the spirit. And that's exactly what I'm going to do. If you'll help me; if you'll hold that ball for me, I'll kick the ball right between the goal post and on to victory in November."

Rev. Taylor had reached Jim Fitts' side and began to place his shepherd's arm around a troubled member of his flock. It was a struggle to keep Jim Fitts steady, but the reverend's arm seemed to initially have a calming effect on him.

"Together we'll get that ball where it's supposed to go. Thank you. Thank you for your support." Dan Calvert was clearly fired up and so was the crowd. Andy Howard smiled and clapped.

"What's he saying?"

"Lope wants to know who the drunk was making the noise back there."

Reid turned. "Holy shit, it's Lee's father."

Reid moved quickly past people wearing Calvert for Council badges and toward his friend. Luis and Lope followed.

"Friends, friends, there's so much we can do if we work together, put our shoulders to the wheel and make this city a place to be proud of again," Dan Calvert said as he regained the crowd's attention.

Reid didn't want Jim Fitts to see him and Rev. Taylor seemed to have the situation under control. Reid knew that if Lee's dad saw him, Jim Fitts would start again. Reid stopped, ready to help if need be. Luis and Lope stood behind him.

"Jim let's take a little walk. I haven't seen you in so long. I think about you often and well, I'd like to catch up on things," Rev. Taylor said as he gave the stone-still Lee the slight "it's okay nod and wink."

"I've got nothing to say to you Warren. I think I made myself pretty clear about how I feel about you and your church." The sight of Warren Taylor had sobered up Jim Fitts much as if he'd been thrown into an icy pond.

". . . and thank you again for joining us today. It's on to . . ." Dan Calvert formed a wiggling V with his fingers, "Victory." The crack of Jim Fitts' outburst had melted away much like the remaining vanilla ice cream.

"Now Jim," Warren Taylor said as they headed in the opposite direction of those leaving the rally. "I know we spoke at great length back then and I thought you were beginning to understand, or least accept what had happened. Remember how we talked about the parents that lost their children that day? Remember how we spoke about your blessing, about how your son was spared?"

"Save your breath, Warren," Jim Fitts snapped as he stopped abruptly. "You don't know what I lost. Save your sermons for Sunday morning. They're worthless during the week when a man's just trying to get by." He brushed past his son. Lee had never seen his father's face as red as it was when his mouth spit those words at Rev. Taylor. Jim Fitts' eyes were open, but they saw nothing; not Reid, not the crowd, not Dan Calvert, not the boys who were again throwing the football.

CHAPTER 19

"And that guy screaming 'kick the ball,' well, I wish I could take credit for planting that guy in the crowd. What a great line, and Dan, like the clever orator he is, picked right up on it," Sanford said.

"Yeah, I thought the guy was some kind of nut at first. But it all worked out and Dan was happy, that's the main thing," Andy said as he sat down at a desk filled with folders, oversized charts, and proofs of newspaper ads.

Lee thought about the man asleep in his chair at home that Sanford and Andy were talking about. The chair cradled that man in a sleep that tried to repair the damage from the anger that controlled Jim Fitts' waking hours. Lee would not let them know the footnote to the rally was his father.

"Lee, thanks for your help. I didn't get a chance to thank you yesterday. One day, mark my words, one day you might be able to choreograph a rally. I must admit, yesterday was one of my best, a rally that sucked everyone into a perpetual vortex of political energy. Don't think you'd be stealing my ideas; you're welcome to them all. There's something about my rallies that is just pure genius. Just don't let the bad guys privy to the secrets of Sanford Black."

"I will not Sanford. But the person who plans our church's picnic must have found out the secrets. She always has people saying that was the best picnic they've ever been to. Her picnics have more people than the rally, and she has games and prizes, and all kinds of food, and singing and last year we had pony rides for the kids."

"Listen pal, meaningful political rallies are a lot more important than church picnics. Did you say pony rides?"

Terri Herman's Motrin was starting to wear off. She took a larger dose when Sanford was around, but it never seemed to be enough. Her stomach couldn't handle Sanford and a breakfast burrito at the same time. Andy Herman's sister got up and walked toward the rest room.

"Aw, forget the pony rides. Time for you to hit the streets again. Here are your new walk sheets."

Lee was glad to be out of the office again. The rally had kept him inside, away from the walking he loved. The outside was as welcoming as it had been the day of the rally. His canvas bag swung like a metronome as Lee hit the pace that sent electrical charges of euphoria through his body. He remembered that Mrs. Plennington told him once that she might hire him to take some of her spa clients out on his walks. Lee thought she might be kidding.

To get in as much walking as possible, Lee had decided to walk an extra block and then double back along the street that led from his house to the neighborhood where he would deliver his Dan Calvert for Council materials. If he walked just a bit faster, he thought, it wouldn't take more time to cover the longer route. Because he was walking so fast, he almost didn't see the crows – two big ones – by the pile of old landscape timbers. Both flew to a nearby branch as Lee passed and then they returned to something by that pile of wood. Lee turned and walked toward the pile; the crows retreated again to their branch. The orange fur below the eye was matted with coagulated blood. The crows had found the bobtail cat. There was a rock, small and gnarly like a potato that had been picked too soon, next to the head. Had the bobtail decided to return and give Lee another try? If not

Lee, maybe someone like Lee would come by and have something to eat. Had the bobtail waited just that extra second to see if what that person had in his hand was something the bobtail could eat? Lee put his bag down and moved the landscape timbers over the bobtail and then picked up handfuls of dirt and filled in the spaces so the crows couldn't pull at the orange fur anymore. The crows watched and then flew away. Lee knew he couldn't be sure; it could have been anyone. He would wait to hear if there ever was an "I told you I'd get him," when they were eating their Hungry Man dinners. But Lee thought how lucky a throw that would have to have been.

Lee threw the Hungry Man trays in the trash. There had not been a word out of Jim Fitts since the rally. There was nothing the next morning either. Lee watched through the window as his father disappeared behind the overgrown blue spruce that extended over the sidewalk. Vigilante bike riders and walkers had taken the matter into their own hands and twisted and snapped back the most restricting branches.

Lee studied his walk sheets as he began the mile trek toward his assigned neighborhood. He hadn't seen many people the day before. There was one grandmother who was having the inside of her house painted and had plenty of time to talk to Lee from her chair on the patio. She told Lee all about the painting. And when she was done talking about her house, she spoke about her husband who had died five years ago, and her daughter's knee operation. Finally, she asked Lee a lot of questions about Dan Calvert. Two streets over, there was a woman who came to the door with her little daughter. They were both wearing pajamas with short pants and Lee thought they should have put on bathrobes before they answered the door. The little girl wanted a Dan Calvert for Council badge and Lee gave her two. Several houses up, a middle-aged man pulling out of his driveway stopped to speak with Lee. But that was it.

He would finish the other side of the street and then he would eat his sandwich and apple. His bag had a large pocket on the inside where he kept his lunch. Christie Veit, Christie Veit, Christie Veit. He had wondered if she had been serious about going on a date with him; a real date not just talking in Mrs. Plennington's spa or someplace he by chance met her. But when she spoke to him on the phone, she said, "Yes, Lee I would still like to go out with you." He was going to meet her at the Peter Pan Diner at 6:30. As much as he wanted someday to ask Christie to marry him, a first date had always seemed as implausible as someday marrying her. He could be a good listener; a very good listener and if Christie wanted to talk a lot at dinner, he could be prepared to nod his head at the right time. But he knew Christie would ask him questions and he didn't know what type of questions Christie would want him to answer. Did she want to speak about Jim Fitts? Mrs Plennington? Reid? Dan Calvert? Lee thought he could figure out what to say, he just mustn't stare at Christie as he had at the rally. Did she know that stare said Lee wanted to marry her? It was foolish, Lee told himself, he and Christie getting married; as foolish as a date with Christie Veit.

Lee opened his wallet several times to make sure the twenty-dollar bill and the ten-dollar bill were still there. He loved the Peter Pan Diner, the little juke boxes on each table with oldies that played unabashedly just as if they were on the current charts. The refrigerated display cases, with cream pies and narrow layer cakes, stood in front of the window from which came dishes of heaping sandwiches, and platters of meat, potatoes, vegetables, and gravy waiting to claim every last bit of space on the servers' trays.

Lee looked around. There were no more tables and a line was beginning to form at the door. He was so glad he had gotten there early. Christie was probably hungry after working all day at Mrs. Plennington's spa. The line was getting longer and there at the very end was Christie. Lee held up his hand.

"Sir, I'll be right with you," the waitress said as she kept her hand at the center of gravity of a tray sprawling with cakes and pies.

Lee didn't hear her and Christie hadn't seen Lee. Lee began to wave more vigorously.

"Sir, please give me one second," the waitress said, her request as frosty as the dishes of sherbet on her tray.

Lee still didn't hear her, but Christie had seen Lee and was walking to his table.

"I'm glad you got here early," Christie said, as she began to take off her light, yellow sweater then stopped. "No, better keep it on; just as I remembered, this place has super AC."

"Would you like to go somewhere else?" Lee asked before he could think that he didn't know where else they could go that would be like the Peter Pan Diner.

"No, no, this is fine. I like this place."

"Okay, if you are sure."

"Yes, I am. I'm hungry too, look at all these things on the menu. They all look so good."

"I have been looking at all the things on the menu and also those same things as they come out on the trays. The food on the trays is just as good as the food they describe on the menu."

"That's good Lee. That's good. Now I'm even hungrier."

"I'm ready to take your order now sir," the waitress said.

"We may need a little more time," Christie said.

"I'm sorry," the waitress said as she looked at Lee. "I thought you were waving at me."

"Oh no, I was not waving at you. I was waving at Christie so she would know I already had a booth."

"Let me know when you folks are ready," the waitress said as she tucked her flapping order pad into her apron.

"I did not mean to confuse the waitress," Lee said.

"I'm sure it's not a problem Lee. What are you going to have?"

"I know what I am going to have: the meat loaf dinner with French fries and gravy on the French fries. Every time I have the Hungry Man meat loaf dinner I think about the meat loaf dinner at the Peter Pan Diner."

"Do you have Hungry Man dinners often?" Christie asked as if recognizing an integral part of a psychological profile.

"Yes, very often; every night. But we do not have meat loaf dinners every night. There are many Hungry Man dinner selections. My father likes the fried chicken dinner. He only eats the fried chicken dinner and the Salisbury steak dinner. And we have pie for dessert; at least for three nights a week, that is usually how long pie lasts. Our dinners are not long, because my father does not talk very often and then he eats his pie when he is sitting in his reclining chair. Sometimes, if the TV is not on too loud, I will hear him unscrewing the top to the wine bottle and then screwing it back on. But he does not like me being in the room with him watching TV. So, I walk after dinner. Then usually I go into my bedroom. It is really a converted storage area, but I have some nice posters up, and I read or listen to the radio. Now that I work for Dan Calvert, I bring home my walk lists for the next day and study them. I do not want to waste any time when I get into the neighborhood trying to figure out addresses. The Dan Calvert for Council team is expecting me to get my work done on time every day."

Christie realized that questions she had about Lee's father should wait. Something about Lee tonight, something about him that made her smile at him as she had ten years ago on the school bus. She wasn't sure if she had meant to send that smile, but it was gone, delivered by the Motown sound of the Four Tops singing "*Sugar pie, honey bun. You know that I love you. Can't help myself . . .*" Lee recognized the smile instantly. They both turned their eyes down to their menus.

"Everything looks good Lee. What did you say you are having?"

"Oh, the meat loaf special. It would not be dinner to me at the Peter Pan Diner if I did not have the meat loaf special."

"Well, I'm going to have the grilled chicken salad platter. I must admit, the meat loaf sounds good, but must watch my figure, don't want anyone at the spa saying that I'm getting fat."

"You have a very nice figure."

"Why thank you Lee, I'm glad you noticed."

Lee wasn't sure if he should have said anything about Christie's figure. He didn't know what to say.

"Ready?" the waitress asked as she flipped a page on her wrinkled order book. She scribbled out some codes for grilled chicken platter and meat loaf dinner and left.

"Lee, it sounds as if you like your job."

"Oh, I do, we are all working very hard. My two bosses, Andy Herman and Sanford Black, do not think anything can stop Dan Calvert from winning the election. Dan Calvert gave a very nice speech at the rally. I am sorry you had to miss that."

"I don't know, Lee. I know you are a very loyal Calvert supporter, but, well let's talk about something else."

"It sounds as if you have some questions about Dan Calvert. I am not allowed to talk to people about Dan Calvert's position on the issues. But, I could get Andy Herman or Sanford to tell you everything about Dan Calvert."

"That's just it Lee, there are some things about Calvert that I'd just as soon not think about. I'm sure there are a lot of people who forgot about the things Calvert did a number of years ago. People were so confused by Calvert's lawyer, who made what was a right or wrong thing into a mishmash of twisted facts and statements that they lost interest and Calvert came away looking as if he hadn't done a thing. My father worked with Calvert's brother . . ."

"Do you mean Dean Calvert? He was at the rally first."

"Yes, Dean Calvert. He used to laugh when he told my father about how his brother never got into any trouble. And at the same time, he would tell my father about all the things his brother did and what a smart businessman Dan Calvert was. It was a big joke. Calvert had gotten such great press, picture in the paper, all kinds of community awards for making space available in several buildings he owned for homeless shelters, low-cost housing and neighborhood clinics. When I read about Dan Calvert, I thought he was one of the greatest men there was. But then, according to what his brother told my father, a development company out of the blue offered Calvert a huge sum for his properties. He accepted on the spot and told the charities some ridiculous story about how with the proceeds from the sale of his properties he was going to get them even better facilities. He never did. He kept stringing them along. The money he got from the sale, his brother said, more than made up for the tax write-offs he lost when he kicked the charities out. I'm sorry Lee, maybe I shouldn't have told you all this. The only reason Calvert is going to win is because his opponent hasn't been able to raise any money. He's no match for all the slick handouts Calvert keeps turning out."

Lee thought about the campaign literature he had in his bag. Anyone reading those brochures would certainly know that Dan Calvert was a decent man, the best man for the job. It said so right there in all the campaign material and there were quotes from real people that had the nicest things to say about Dan Calvert.

"Lee, are you all right?"

Lee looked down at the meat loaf dinner the waitress had placed in front of him. Was someone going to tell him now that there was something they hated to tell him about the meat loaf? "Christie is everything you said true? I mean are you sure what you said is true? It is just very hard for me to believe that Dan Calvert would do something like that."

"Yes, it is true. I'm sorry Lee." She had only meant for Lee to know the truth about Dan Calvert. She thought he deserved that. But the truth in this instance was a wrecking ball into the refuge that Lee had constructed around himself. He was doing a good job. Andy Herman had told him so. Sanford too had encouraging words. Could he ask them about Dan Calvert? He trusted Christie, but maybe she was wrong. But she seemed very sure, he thought. Maybe it wasn't any of his business what happened a long time ago. Maybe Dan Calvert had been confused, maybe he was really trying to help people. Lee looked at his plate. The meat loaf special didn't look special any more.

"I shouldn't have said anything, Lee. I'm sorry," Christie said. She placed her hand on his forearm.

Lee looked at her hand, then into her eyes. He cared about what was important to her. He cared about her. He would always remember how he felt on his first date with Christie. "I am glad you told me these things. I have walked a lot of miles thinking I was working for a very good candidate. I do not know if I can work for someone like Dan Calvert after hearing the true facts you have just told me. I brought enough money for dessert. Would you like something for dessert or do you want to leave?"

"Why don't we go? I'll drive you home. We can talk more in the car."

The radio in Christie's car was tuned to an easy-listening station. She turned the volume down. "Lee, why don't you try to forget about what I said in there. The campaign is almost over. Just finish it out. You seem very upset. I don't want you quitting or doing anything you'll regret. She placed her hand on his forearm again and the movement sent a faint swirl of her perfume his way. He placed his hand on hers and she felt the shudder move through his body. Christie's eyes were on the road ahead, Lee's moved slowly from Christie's collar to the front of her blouse to the slender belt on her navy blue shorts. She felt another shudder as she pulled her hand away to make the turn down Lee's street.

"You know Reid Fletcher?" Lee asked, the sight of his street sign vaporizing the pastoral scene his mind had begun to draw of Christie and him in a place where there were no angry fathers or complicated truths.

"Yes, I know Reid. I run into him every once and a while. Why do you ask?"

"He does not live far from here. It's two streets over. He has a very nice room over the Tammery Inn and he has cable television. He has told me that I can come over any time. Would you like to go to see Reid? It is not far."

"I don't know Lee. I don't know Reid very well."

"That does not matter. I know Reid would like to have company. He can be very funny when he is watching his cable TV. It is a very good picture." He was hoping Reid was home. Lee wasn't sure if he could work for Dan Calvert any more after what Christie said. He might need that landscaping job.

"Here is the Tammery Inn and there is the light that is on in Reid's room. We can park over by the back."

"It's pretty dark back here."

"Reid says there are some young punks around here, always throwing rocks at light posts. Reid says if he catches those punks they will be sorry in a way they never even thought about. I am not sure what Reid is going to do to them, but I would not want to be them."

"Lee, I don't think this is the safest place to be. We need to get inside," Christie said as she walked toward the doorway Lee had pointed to earlier.

"You are right, this is not a safe place to be."

Two men in T- shirts, grimy jeans, and untied work boots came out of the Tammery as Christie and Lee were arriving at the stairs leading to Reid's room. The two men turned on unsteady legs. Lee knew they weren't looking at him.

"Hey sweetie," the fat one with a tiny chin called over. "Dump that jerk! Come on with us; plenty of room in my truck."

Lee stopped.

"Lee, don't stand there. Come inside right now," Christie said as she opened the door. "I don't mean anything against Reid, but I really don't care for this place."

"I'm sorry this has not been a pleasant visit for you so far Christie. We will not stay long at all and I will ask Reid to walk us back out to your car. He may have a flashlight so we can see in the dark." Lee rapped on the door.

"Who is it, man?"

"Reid, it is Lee and I have Christie Veit with me."

"Hold on man, I'll be right there." One chain slid off its track then a bolt disengaged from the door jam. "Hey come on in; Christie, Lee, how you guys doing? Lee, man I was going to call you," Reid said hurriedly. Christie and Lee's eyes were fixed on the far side of Reid's room. "Yeah, yeah, I was going to call you. It happened just like I told you it would. I won the lottery. I thought I might as well treat myself."

"How big is that screen?" Lee asked.

"Forty-six inches. Yeah, they got this baby over here pretty quick. I bought it this afternoon and now it's up and running."

"Boy, look at your cable TV now. Those faces are so big. Look at that picture. That is some picture, Christie. And especially since there is not much space left in here. When you are up so close, everything seems so big."

"Yes, that is some picture, Lee," Christie said, seeing in him a boy she might have to take care of forever.

"Boy, Reid, you always said you would win the lottery and you did. You must be very proud of yourself. How much did you win in the lottery?"

"How much did I win? Well, I, I have to see. They have to figure out all the taxes and everything. I guess it will take a while to figure out."

"Reid, look one of your favorites is coming on, *Mr. Ed*. Reid loves *Mr. Ed*. Come on Reid, show Christie how you do it."

"No, I don't think she wants to see that."

"Oh, I know she will love it, come on, you do it great."

"W-i-l-b-u-*r-r-r*."

"Hear that Christie?"

"Yes, Lee, that's a pretty good Mr. Ed impersonation."

Lee's finger went quickly to his lower lip as he thought what else Reid's winning the lottery might mean. "Does this mean you have so much money that you will be quitting your landscaping job?"

"Quit, how can I quit? I didn't win enough money to stop working forever. I don't want to lose that landscaping job. Damn, they already laid off two guys. Luis and Lope might be next soon. No, I'm not quitting my job. My lottery money will just be like a rainy nest egg or whatever that is."

"So, they're not hiring any more people at your landscaping job?"

"No, I just told you they're laying people off. Some contracts fell through or something."

"Do you want to watch any more cable TV, Christie?" Lee asked.

"No, it's very nice, but I think it's time for us to be going. It's a work night you know."

"Yes, it is a work night. Reid could you bring your flashlight and walk us to Christie's car?"

"Sure. Let's go. I'm going to get those punks one of those days."

"You probably will, just like you won the lottery," Lee said.

"Hey guys," Reid whispered. "Me winning the lottery; I want to keep that just among us for now, okay?"

"Yes, that is okay with me Reid. Is that okay with you Christie?"

"Yes, Lee, that's okay."

CHAPTER 20

Lee was very concerned about what Christie said about Dan Calvert. He had listened very carefully to Christie and he could understand why she didn't like Dan Calvert. It sounded as if she had all the facts and from people who would know about what had happened. He also thought that Christie didn't like his working for someone whom she believed had done bad things. But he didn't know what to do. If he quit, where could he work? Reid told him the night before that there were no more landscaping jobs. Mrs. Plennington would be angry with him; she would be very disappointed and he didn't know if she would tell more people that he had been at her house alone with her. His father, well, his father would give him another "told you so," but his father had been acting strangely since the rally: he wasn't yelling or saying mean things. He seemed mostly to be ignoring Lee. Maybe his dad was sorry for yelling "kick the damn ball, kick the ball." Maybe his father was taking a breather, his anger being strengthened as a hurricane passing through tropical waters replenishes its fury.

But the truth was Jim Fitts knew it was over that day at the rally. His anger was gone; carried away with his vanishing dreams by the football that had hit his son in the back and then rolled towards the two boys from whom Jim Fitts had taken it.

"Feet nailed to the floor? You've been standing in that same spot for twenty minutes and staring at the wall," Terri said, annoyed that Lee was blocking her view of the hall.

"Someone told me that Dan Calvert might have done some bad things and I was thinking about that," Lee said in a rush.

"Tell me something I don't know," Terri Herman said. "Everyone knows that Dan Calvert is a real piece of dirt. Kicked the damn homeless out of those buildings and came up with some bullshit scheme to tear those buildings down. My brother told me all about it when he first said we were going to work on the Calvert campaign. When I asked him why we would work for Calvert then and not someone else, Andy smiled, shrugged his shoulders and said "six-to-one-half-dozen-to-the other, but Calvert's the one that's willing to pay what I'm asking."

"So, Dan Calvert did those bad things?"

"Would you please get the hell out of the doorway? I just told you he did. What the hell do you care? You're getting paid, aren't you?"

"I am, sorry I have been standing by the doorway and staring."

"You better get your ass out there and start ringing those door bells. I don't give a damn about Dan Calvert, but we damn well better win this election." Terri moved the glasses down the bridge of her nose, her mouth stretching into a smile. "Andy and I get a nice fat bonus if that jerk wins."

Lee remembered them all. He thought if he hurried, he could finish by the end of the day. He'd talk with Andy later at the office.

He didn't take long once their doors opened. The people that smiled at him when he first visited smiled at him again. The grumpier people were no more pleased to see Lee than when he had first knocked on their doors.

"I've never heard of anyone doing that before," said one of the smilers.

"That was very nice of you to come back," said another.

"That's a new twist," an old grumpy man said as he hurriedly closed the door before Lee had finished speaking.

The last house he visited that day was the Aggarwals. K.S. Aggarwal smiled politely as her elderly father stood behind her with an impassive look. A Dan Calvert for Council sticker was on the glass pane next to the door.

Lee took the deepest breath of the day. "Hello Mrs. Aggarwal. Hello sir. Do you remember me? My name is Lee Fitts and I gave you that Dan Calvert sticker."

"Yes, I do. I showed my husband the brochure you gave us and he said that we would vote for your candidate," Mrs. Aggarwal said in an accent that tapped out each syllable precisely. She looked at Lee as if to ask what further business they needed to transact.

"That was very kind of you and your husband." Lee paused. "I came here to tell you something that is not easy for me, but I am not going to vote for Dan Calvert. I have found out things about him that make me believe he is not a good man and that he should not be elected. I do not know all the details, but I think it was more important to him to make money on a deal that left some really needy people with no place to live. I do not think he cares about those people; he was only thinking about making money. I wish I knew more, but that is all I know. But it is enough for me to know that I cannot vote for him. I have spent the whole day going to the houses of everyone I told to vote for Dan Calvert and letting them know of this new development."

Mrs. Aggarwal looked toward the other room. An impatience to attend to things in the other room overtook her formal smile. "I will tell my husband about these things, but I am not sure I understand why you are telling me these things."

"Thank you for listening to me Mrs. Aggarwal. I wanted you and your husband to know that I think I gave you wrong information when I was here before." Mrs. Aggarwal's father nodded approvingly at Lee.

Andy Herman was on the phone. Sanford was in the back room staring motionlessly at a chart on the wall. There was no one else in the office. Lee unfolded a chair and waited for Andy to finish his call.

"You did what?" Andy Herman asked, his eye brows exploding upward. "Are you kidding me?"

"No, I am not kidding you. That is what I told the people."

"Why you dumb shit. Are you out of your mind? "I'm giving you five seconds to get your ass out of this office. I don't give a damn if Audrey Plennington got you this job or not. Wait till I tell her about her nice young man who she was sure would do such a great job. I'll get you Fitts. Now get the hell out of here before I . . ."

"I am leaving. I do not want to work for the Dan Calvert for Council team any more. I believed the brochures I was handing out." Lee stopped at Terri's desk on his way out. "I walked fast because I wanted to tell as many people as I could about all the good things Dan Calvert was going to do. You tricked me and I tricked those people. That is why I had to tell them the truth."

"I told you to get the hell out of here," Andy Herman said.

As Lee strode away, Terri took off here glasses and looked at her brother. "I told you he wasn't right," she cackled. "That nut, I wish I could have seen the look on those peoples' faces when he started to tell them that what we know all too well, that Dan Calvert's a no-good son-of-a bitch."

"That's helpful Terri, oh that's very helpful right now. Sanford, get in here!"

"This is a new one boss. Got nothing in my playbook for this one. I didn't tell him to do this, you know. You know that, don't you?" Sanford cowered.

"Yeah, I know that Sanford, but you're going to fix it. I want you to go to every house on his walk sheets and fix it."

"But how do I do that?"

"Fix it!"

"Okay, okay. That's why I get paid the big bucks. There's got to be someone here for the toughest job. I can handle it. I can handle it boss. Let's see, I know. I'll say it's part of our opponent's dirty tricks campaign. Yeah, that's it. Our opponent hired some creep to go around acting as if he were a very sincere person telling the unvarnished truth about Dan Calvert so the voters wouldn't be fooled. Yeah, I'll put this whole package together, we'll have these people back supporting Dan in no time. I'll . . ."

"Just fix it; I don't need to hear all the horse shit."

CHAPTER 21

Ellie's kitchen was like the one she and her brother had known as children. The same blue and white curtains hanging on the window; the refrigerator with an armor of magnets sprouting homey aphorisms or Bible passages; vases of artificial flowers shooting colors across the spotless white counter tops; a large wooden container brimming with kitchen utensils; and the aromas announcing that Ellie had prepared, almost subconsciously, every meal exactly as her mother had taught her.

"Lee, I guess you did what you had to. I must admit I never cared much one way or the other about Dan Calvert, but when you started working for him I guess I tried to see him in a new light. Are you sure you are all right?"

"Yes, I am all right. I was a little scared when Andy Herman started screaming at me and using bad language. There was nothing I could do about anything at that point but leave the campaign office. But now I do not have a job. That is not a very good thing because now there are not even any more landscaping jobs."

"Did you tell Dad yet?"

"I did not tell Dad yet because he left early this morning. Dad has been very quiet since the rally. And one more thing, Dad left fifty dollars on the table to go shopping with. He scribbled a note "use the extra ten to get yourself some pie or chips." Dad has not yelled at me since the rally; he has been different. He still is not home on Tuesday nights so I do not know if I will see him tonight."

Ellie smiled and sat down at the table across from Lee. "I told you that you should come over here on Tuesdays for dinner. D.H. normally has to travel early in the week. So, you see you'd be keeping me company. You can walk over if you'd like, and I'll drive you home. We can even stop at the grocery store on the way home so you can do your shopping."

"I should have listened to you Ellie. I like Hungry Man dinners, but it's like Mom's cooking when I come over here and you always have much larger portions than Hungry Man."

She let pass his comment about their mother. "Well, maybe one day, we can get Dad to come over. Maybe things might be different than they've been."

Lee put the plastic grocery bags on the table and read the scribbled note that Reid had left in the door. "Didn't know when I would see you next and didn't want you to make a trip to my room at Tammery for nothing. I had to move. My new address: Apt. 170 B, Hickory Hollow Luxury Garden Apartments. I don't have a phone yet, but try to come over tomorrow after four so I can show you the new digs. Reid."

Lee knew where those apartments were. They were brand new; they had those red and white flags in the garden with the beautiful rock wall. There was a big sign that said "Last section of units now available." Reid must be doing very well in his job to be able to move into Hickory Hollow Luxury Garden Apartments Lee thought, and on top of that he won the lottery.

"Hello Christie," Lee said before the phone went dead. He played with the clip at the end of the wire on the receiver that frequently came loose, and got Christie's voice back although there was still an intermittent crackle.

"Lee, can you hear me?"

"Yes Christie, I can hear you. I am holding the wire on the receiver so there is not so much crackle on the line."

"Well, I guess that's a little better. I tried to get you earlier."

"I was at Ellie's for dinner and then she took me to the grocery store so I could do my shopping and then she brought me home. I am unpacking my groceries."

"Do you want me to call back?"

"No. I am glad you called. There is something I have to tell you. I do not work for the Dan Calvert for Council Campaign any more. I lost my job because I went back to every house and told them I did not think Dan Calvert was a good candidate and that I would not be voting for him. You were right about Dan Calvert. Terri Howard also said he was no good."

"Lee, I didn't mean for you to lose your job. This is horrible. I mean I'm sure there is something wrong with all these candidates."

"But what Dan Calvert did was bad."

"What Dan Calvert did was bad, but Lee, what are you going to do? I want to help you find something. I'll look in the paper tomorrow and talk to some of the clients at the spa that I know. We will find you something Lee."

Outside of Ellie, there was no one else in the world who spoke to him with the caring that Christie did. "Did you know that Reid moved? He moved to Hickory Hollow Luxury Garden Apartments. He would like me to visit him tomorrow night. Would you like to go with me?" Lee realized that this might qualify as his second date with Christie.

"Well, do you really want to go?"

"I think that Reid wants to show me his new apartment, it is Apartment 170 B."

"All right Lee I'll go with you. I can pick you up at your house."

"I have an even better idea Christie, I can walk to the spa and wait outside until you are done with work so you do not have to go out of your way to pick me up."

"Okay, Lee I'll see you tomorrow, outside the spa. Are you sure you're all right, I mean with everything that happened today?"

"I am okay. I did the only thing I could do."

"I'm proud of you Lee. We'll get everything taken care of."

CHAPTER 22

"Dad, I need to speak with you before you go."

Jim Fitts turned just as he was about to open the door. Lee told his father what had happened. The impatience and intolerance usually quick to overcome his father didn't appear.

Jim Fitts put his lunch bag in his other hand. "That's pretty damn funny," was all Lee's father said. He wasn't yet prepared to say more. Lee watched as his father walked toward the small crowd waiting at the bus stop to go to work.

Lee walked all day, looking constantly at his watch to which he surrendered all freedom. The watch flashed off seconds as if they were minutes. The watch would give him plenty of time to think about the Dan Calvert Campaign, Mrs. Plennington, his father, Reid, Rev. Taylor, Ellie, his mother, and Christie. He wished he could make the watch shoot to five o'clock so he could see Christie right then. He knew the watch would laugh at him. It was a different story when Lee was walking from house to house handing out Dan Calvert for Council Campaign material. Lee didn't need any special dispensation from the watch then. Lee knew what he had to do, and he could always do more than he had to. Maybe that had made the watch mad. Maybe that was why the watch had slowed down today, just at a time when Lee needed it to go fast.

Lee walked to Ellie's, but she wasn't home. He walked toward Hickory Hollow Luxury Garden Apartments and found 170 B. Several men in green T- shirts with yellow writing stood on self-propelled lawnmowers that whirled across stretches of the new lawn. He would know now exactly where to go when he came back with Christie. He walked across the street that led to the Aggarwal's house. Lee froze, but quickly recovered and ran. He didn't think the man approaching the Aggarwal's house had seen him. It had been Lee's experience that Sanford didn't see much around him. What would Sanford say to the Aggarwals? Sanford always spoke about his long years of experience and his playbook. Lee hoped Mrs. Aggarwal's father wouldn't think he had been wrong to give that I-approve-of-what-you've-done look to Lee. Lee knew he could never be the political pro that Sanford was.

Lee stopped looking at his watch. There was no hope now. The time piece was holding on to the seconds even longer. The lunch lines were long gone when he ordered his burger, fries, and chocolate shake. He found a bench in the park where the rally had been and began to eat the only meal he would have that day. Before he left home, he set a place for his father at the kitchen table. Beside the plate, Lee left a note saying he would be back probably before nine. Maybe his father wouldn't mind eating his Hungry Man dinner alone. Lee would find out after Christie brought him home.

It was four-thirty. The watch started to work as it should. It took Lee twenty minutes to get to the spa. He looked in the window and saw Christie. She waved. Was it Hi? Was it I'll be right out? No, it was go away. Her hand started pointing faster and it was pointing away from the spa. But it was too late and Christie turned away and walked toward the far end of the spa.

"So, I see you've found a new friend, Lee," Audrey Plennington said as she finished tying a wrap-around skirt that left a small portion of her flat stomach visible below her taut exercise top. "I guess I wasn't your type."

"Mrs. Plennington, I did not know if I would see you. I do not know what you mean about type."

"Oh, you know very well what I mean," she said in a tone designed to make Lee as uncomfortable as possible. "When were you going to tell me?"

Christie reappeared to the window. "Do you mean about asking Christie out on a second date?"

"Oh, I knew it. You'll never know how much better you could have had it with me. No, I was wondering when you were going to tell me about what you did with the Calvert campaign. Lee don't you understand anything? Do you realize the position you've put me in? I got you the damn job. You know that."

Lee had been hit by both barrels: Mrs. Pennington's "type" statement and then the "hurt look" of one "whose act of kindness" is completely unappreciated. He wondered if he would be safe if he ran all the way to 170 B at Hickory Hollow Luxury Apartments.

"Audrey, I've got to take Lee home," Christie said as she appeared at his side and guided Lee's shaking arm.

"I bet you do," Audrey said.

"I was trying to wave you away, I didn't think you saw her coming," Christie said as she started her car.

"I did not see her coming because I was looking only at you. And then Mrs. Plennington started raising her voice and looking at me as if I had done something very wrong. I could not get my breath when I opened my mouth to speak and then I did not know which of her questions to answer. My head is still tingling."

"Lee, it will be all right. Don't think about it anymore," Christie said as she turned into the Hickory Hollow Luxury Garden parking lot. She placed her hand on Lee's and he relaxed his grip on his thigh.

"Christie, what do I do about Mrs. Plennington? I do not want her to be mad at me. And she said I didn't think she was my type and I did not understand."

"She said that?"

"Yes, she did say that."

Christie turned off the engine and looked at Lee. "Lee, I would stay away from Audrey for a while. I've seen the way she looks at you. She wants to be more than just a friend."

"Mrs. Plennington was my mother's friend and she used to stay with me so my mother could go out for a while by herself when she got very upset."

"I know she was your mother's friend. And I'm sure your mother appreciated having Audrey there to watch you. We can talk about all this some other time when you're not so upset. I just think it's better that you leave her alone for now. Come on, let's go see Reid's new apartment."

The warmth of her hand as it grasped his reminded Lee that he and Christie were on a date. If there were types, his boyhood heart told him that Christie and he were the same. She swung their hands in small back and forth motions as they walked.

"Here is Reid's apartment, 170 B," Lee said as he rang the bell.

Reid Fletcher opened the door. Cracked motorcycle boots with heels worn well past hope for repair lay to the side of the door. Reid's Calhoun Community College Volleyball Club shirt was caked with what had to be more than one day's worth of dirt and sweat stains. "Damn, I forgot all about asking you to come over today. I meant to get cleaned up, I just forgot. I'm still trying to get the TV hooked up. Come in, come in."

"This is a very big apartment," Lee said as he looked at the freshly-painted walls and the wood-patterned linoleum. "It is much bigger than your old apartment."

Christie's gaze darted from cardboard boxes to lawn chairs in front of the TV to an old bedspread hanging in the front of the window to a kitchen counter with an open chips bag and a half-empty package of bologna.

"Much bigger? Of course it's bigger. That old place was much too small for my TV. And when I bought the theater sound system, well, it was like the guy at the store told me, the acoustics were crap. That's why I had to move. And know what, I get cable free here with my rent, premium channels too. It's a bit more than I was paying, but you're either going to have cable TV the right way or you might as well forget about it. And two bedrooms, can you dig that? Luis is living here for a while and will help with the rent. Lope left, went back home to Ecuador or Bolivia, I keep forgetting. His mother was sick or something. He said he was coming back. Who knows?"

Reid's new apartment had to be very expensive Lee thought to himself. Christie wondered how substantial the lottery winnings were.

"I got these speaker wires all messed up last night and only get this tinny sound. This home theater system is supposed to make it sound like the explosion is going right through your body. The guy at the store said they're coming out with a new system that's like a punch right in the gut. I know I'm going to have to get that one soon as I can. I don't know how I'm going to keep up with all this new stuff. I think I almost got it, just another minute or so. You guys get some chips and soda from the kitchen then come sit in the chairs. They're exactly where they need to be to get all the special effects."

"I'll get the things from the kitchen," Christie said.

"Hey Lee, my man," Reid whispered as Christie walked into the kitchen, how you two getting on?"

"Well, we are on our second date."

"Second date. That's good, Lee, real good. She's a nice-looking chick and I think she really likes you."

"I like her too."

"Chips, soda, guess we're ready for the big show," Christie said as she placed the bag, a soda bottle and three tea cups on a snack tray between the lawn chairs.

"Go on, go on, you and Lee sit in the chairs, this will just take a second to get these last wires figured out," Reid said.

Christie flinched as the first swoosh punched from one speaker to the other in a fast-paced cascade of sound too loud even for Reid.

"Sorry," Reid fidgeted with his control panel. "Okay, damn, feels just like that Tyrannosaurus is about to squash you like a bug doesn't it, Lee?"

"Yes, that looks and sounds very real to me. This whole apartment is shaking."

"That's the whole point. You get the cable TV, then you get that big screen TV, and this sound system. And you wait till your brains get blown out."

"Reid!" Christie admonished. Do you need to be so graphic?"

"What did I say?"

Christie shook her head as Lee wondered if it were wrong that he was enjoying Reid's TV system so much.

Lee had no idea an hour had passed. Christie's tap on his shoulder went unnoticed amidst the pulsating sounds of screaming dinosaurs. A second, harder tap got Lee's attention and she pointed to her watch. Reid was only physically in the room. The rest of him was on the screen running with the others from a diving Pterodactyl.

"I think we have to go at this point, Reid," Lee said. "Reid, I think we have to go at this point," Lee said louder.

"What? Yeah, okay. Guys, mind if I finish this?"

Lee and Christie waved as they left. Reid stuck up his hand, but he was already back in the chase.

As he approached the door, Lee saw a small cardboard box containing papers, bills, tattered envelopes and other items that were probably important to Reid. That is, if he even knew they were there. There was one green envelope that caught Lee's eyes. The envelope was more dog-eared then he remembered but it had the same LF that Lee had written on it before he started putting into it the money his mother would send him.

Christie tugged at his arm. "Lee, is there something wrong?"

He looked at her and then turned to look at Reid who was now entirely at the mercy of his big screen, cable TV home theater system.

CHAPTER 23

Christie Veit's brother, Sam, was one of the strongest sixth-graders in the school. He was fast, and had exceptionally good hands. As a starter on the football team, he seemed always able to pull the football out of the air. He had dark brown eyes notched under mischievous Peter Pan eyebrows. His light brown hair had blonde streaks in the sunlight. Christie had the same features, but her long hair accented soft curved angles in her face while her younger brother had already begun to develop the clipped angles of a maturing natural athlete. The day before the accident, Christie had called Sam over to the sidelines and whispered something in his ear. He turned and pointed to Lee. She quickly pulled her brother's hand down, and Lee didn't see her again until the bus. That was the bus ride home where Lee got the smile he still carried with him. Christie was sick the next day and wasn't on the bus, but she was occupying Lee's thoughts. It happened so quickly. Lee saw Sam thrown back, but thought if there was anyone who could squirm free, it was Sam. The fierce rush of colliding steel and collapsing seats, however, was too much even for Sam. His skull had been shattered and the light brown hair was wet with blood. It was one of the last things Lee saw.

As they rode in Christie's car, he wondered if they would ever talk about that day. He wondered if he could tell Christie or anyone about the green envelope he saw in Reid's apartment.

"Where would you like to go Lee?" Christie asked as she turned on the wipers. "I guess we don't want to be out walking around too much in this. Starting to come down pretty hard."

"No, we do not. We will get all wet and I do not have my umbrella. But I do have money for burgers."

"Lee. You paid last time. I'll get the burgers tonight. We'll order at the drive thru and we can go to my apartment to eat."

Lee had only been alone with a woman at her home once before. Christie's suggestion was like a package that he hadn't ordered arriving at his door. Was it a gift from someone or something bad? "Okay, we can eat our burgers at your apartment."

They took short, choppy steps on the sidewalk watching not to slip on the wet stone being pounded by rain. Christie held on to Lee's arm as they turned the corner leading to a small awning over a door at the bottom of a half-dozen steps. The rain pelted the metal awning as Christie shook the wet key chain before opening the lock. Lee huddled over Christie and a wrinkled wet bag not designed to shield burgers and fries from such a storm.

Christie turned on the light. At once, an apartment as warm and comforting as its occupant offered Lee refuge from the storm. Nowhere near the size of Reid's living room and with none of the modern fixtures of a luxury apartment, Christie's home bore the trappings of a basement finished well before she was born. On one side, a crude stone wall was painted a faded yellow, while the rest of the walls were adorned in a tired wallpaper. A half-dozen posters in thin, bright blue frames hung above a loveseat upon which was spread a multicolored Afghan. Christie turned on a portable stereo console that shared a table with a small-screen TV. She lit a candle and the scent of cinnamon and apple wafted over Lee. As he turned his gaze to Christie, Lee realized there was nowhere else he'd rather be.

"Diet Coke good for you?" Christie asked as she looked into the refrigerator.

Yes, Diet Coke is good for me," Lee said as he dabbed at his wet hair with the small towel Christie had handed him.

They sat at a small kitchen table of unfinished pine and ate a dinner of rubbery burgers and crusted French fries. Lee looked down as he ate. He was not sure what he should say to Christie; he never thought he would be in her apartment. He had never even pictured where she lived. If he had a map, he would mark where she lived so it was clear to him where the center of his world was.

"You're awfully quiet, Lee."

"I did not want to disturb you while you were eating."

"I don't know that I would call this eating," she said as she pushed away a carton still almost full with fries.

"I am sorry that the burgers and fries are cold. I can eat them cold, but I know they taste better when they are hot."

"I am not really that hungry. I had a large salad for lunch and I usually pack a piece of fruit and a bag of nuts so I have a snack before I leave work."

"That sounds like a very healthy diet Christie. I am sorry I suggested burgers."

"Oh, I thought when you said it that it sounded like fun. It's no big deal, Lee. Know what? Saturday night, I'm inviting you over for a nice home-cooked dinner. That is, if you're free on Saturday night."

Lee wondered why Christie would think he wouldn't be free on Saturday night. "I am free on Saturday night and I would like to come here for a nice home-cooked dinner."

"Very well, we're on for Saturday night," she said as she cleared the table. "Lee, I hate to shift gears so quickly, but would you mind if I took you home now, I have class tomorrow night and a paper to finish."

"Are you going to school, Christie?"

"Yup, one more semester of community college and then I have my associate degree. My adviser says that with my grades, I should be able to get some good financial aid to go to state."

"Go to the state university? Isn't that far away?"

"I guess about three hours."

Lee knew that was taking the interstate. If he walked there he would have to use all those streets that went through towns. If he walked nonstop, it might take him as long as a day to get to the state university. Maybe he could hitchhike, or go by bus; there had to be a bus. "Christie, I can walk home, the rain has stopped and I do not want you to waste time if you have homework."

"No, Lee it's not a problem, come on let's go."

"No, I am walking and I do not want to say another word about this thing."

"Are you sure?"

"Yes, I am very sure."

"Okay Lee. You remember, dinner Saturday night, okay? Say about seven. Do you want me to pick you up?"

"No, that is very nice that you offer, but I would like to walk to your house for dinner."

"Okay, Lee. I'm looking forward to seeing you on Saturday."

Lee smiled as he looked down. He saw it when he turned toward the door. There on a small table in the corner was a photo of Christie and Sam. He stopped.

Christie put her hand on his shoulder. "Good night Lee," she said realizing how they were bound by that photo.

"Good night Christie."

CHAPTER 24

A flutter of leaves blew across Christie's windshield as she waited at the light only several blocks from Audrey Plennington's spa. She closed her window and turned up the heat. Most Halloween decorations were gone, but over-ripe pumpkins remained in front of several of the houses she had passed. Inviting targets those pumpkins. She remembered how much trouble Sam had gotten into when he and two of his friends were caught smashing a neighbor's pumpkin. The neighbor wasn't angry; his was a "boys will be boys" attitude. So long as they cleaned up the mess, that was the end of it for him. That was not the case with Christie's parents. Sam was grounded for two weeks and lectured to every night about how wrong it was to smash that pumpkin. Was someone else's property, have to respect other people's property. You can't do things like that. If you get away with this, next thing you know, you'll try something worse. We have to punish you. It's because we care. Because we love you. You'll thank us one day when you grow up. You'll remember this so you can teach the same lesson to your children when they do something wrong and they will do something wrong. It will be your job to teach them right from wrong. That's what Christie's parents said. That was Sam's last Halloween.

Christie used to resent those that had been spared in the accident. But she had come to recognize that it was not the survivors' fault. Christie had no answer for why Sam's ever-challenging voice was one that had fallen into eternal silence. Lee had been spared, and it was her purpose now to rescue the broken survivor still held prisoner by the monster that had risen that day and killed her brother. Her two dates with Lee were her opening gambit.

The tiny, ornate bells Audrey Plennington had installed on the front door sang a tinny harmony as Christie walked toward the back room where she and the other two spa employees had small lockers. Thoughts of her recently completed school paper gave way to a mental list of the things she needed from the store for her dinner with Lee. She looked forward to the weekend's special sense of release that some students felt was a God-given right. When she turned on the light switch in the back room it was as if Audrey's voice was also connected to that switch.

"Good morning, Christie," she said. "I meant to speak to you yesterday, but I guess you and Lee Fitts were in a hurry to get somewhere." She paused. "I've been considering several program changes at the spa; I'm always looking to improve the quality of service. Well, as you may know, and I knew they'd never make it in this area, that franchise fitness club is closing and two trainers from there approached me recently. They've been working together for years and outlined a program that I think our clients will just love. Even better, when word gets out about the kind of things these two gals have to offer, I think the sky's the limit for new clients. But, Christie dear, and here's the rub, I can't hire these two trainers without letting someone on our current staff go. I've tried to look at it from all angles, but it keeps coming back to that same premise. I'm afraid I'm going to have to let you go and that's only because our other gals have been here longer than you. And Christie, please don't think this is any reflection on you. The senior citizens' programs you've been working on have been a real hit, but I think I'm going to try to take the spa in a new direction, exercise with a bit more edge and slinkiness to it. But Christie, once we get these new programs up and running, and I'm confident, very confident they'll be a big hit, we'll be able to bring you back, you have my word," Audrey Plennington said in a manner that evoked the misplaced piety of medieval clergy sentencing heretics to a fate from which everyone knew there was no appeal.

"So, I'm to leave?" Christie asked calmly

"I am so sorry my dear, I wish there were some other way."

"When do you want me to leave?"

"Oh now, don't you worry about having to rush, we'll be able to keep you on for another two weeks. And don't you hesitate to let me know if there is anything I can do to help you find something."

Christie felt Audrey's hand move toward her shoulder. There was power in that hand that was meant to humble and intimidate. Audrey Plennington didn't have to say anything further.

During the remainder of her shift and then on the ride home, Christie tried to control her thoughts which were now bobbing frenetically within her head. Christie had no other income, she had student loans, she had rent. Her car was paid off, but she had insurance premiums to pay. The job at the spa allowed her to get to her classes on time. Whenever something went wrong, and things now had gone very wrong, she felt the paralyzing helplessness that brutally seized her when she lost Sam. That feeling, like a dormant virus just waiting for its cue, gave her chills and a blinding head-ache tearing at the back of her eyes. When she got home, she undressed, went to bed, and prayed for sleep.

The alarm shook her as morning trickled through the curtain on the small basement window. She got through all her classes and sessions of personalized instructions at the spa. She didn't tell anyone about her leav-ing and it appeared Audrey hadn't shared that news with anyone either. At the end of the day, she went home, changed into over-sized sweats and ate a spinach and tomato salad in front of the small TV. She played again the phone message Lee had left: "Did she want to go for a walk? She did not have to if she did not want to. But it sure looked like a very beautiful night for a walk." She felt stronger, but Lee would have to wait until tomorrow.

Lee Fitts watched the phone, the clock, and the moon. Until one of them said differently, it was still a beautiful night for a walk. Of the three, the clock was the meanest; stealing seconds, then minutes, then hours from a night he had wished to spend with Christie.

As it got later, not only did Lee not expect to walk with Christie that evening, but the clock, gobbling more and more time with its greedy sweeping hands, told Lee not to expect a call. Lee hoped she still planned to have dinner with him. He had bought her a Lalique crystal dove. He had seen that dove in the jewelry store window everyday he walked to work at the Dan Calvert for Council office. It was the first time he took more than fifty dollars from the envelope containing the money his mother sent him. With two hundred dollars less, the envelope was noticeably thinner. He wondered how big Christie's smile would be. He knew he would have a big smile if she ever gave him something as beautiful as the Lalique dove that was now in a box under fancy gold wrapping paper and a tan lace bow. He thought about his envelope and the one just like it that he had seen at Reid's new luxury apartment. He wondered why he didn't ask Reid about it that night he and Christie visited the apartment. He was glad now that he hadn't because Reid must have taken it by mistake and would have been embarrassed if Lee brought it up while Christie was there.

After Lee and his dad moved to their tiny house, Reid had helped paint Lee's bedroom so that awful greenish wallpaper with the tiny winding rows of never-ending roses was covered up once and for all. The two boys had to move and cover the bed and small dresser and Reid had spilled the box into which Lee had put a lot of odds and ends including the oversized envelope with the money his mother had sent him. Reid had asked if he could have several of the old sports magazines Lee had in the box. It seemed very simple: Reid must have gotten the envelope mixed up with the magazines. "Oh, yeah, I found it," Lee thought Reid would have said, "It was right in there with those magazines. What's so important about that envelope anyway?"

Yet, when Lee asked Reid about the envelope, Reid said he hadn't seen it, but would look around and let Lee know if the envelope were mixed in with the magazines. It was the worst that Lee felt since his mother left home. From some town probably very far away, she had mailed out four ten-dollar bills every month. His mother had made sure she had done that for her son every week, beginning a couple of years after she left. Lee was so upset those first two weeks after he couldn't find the envelope that he lost ten pounds. All the kindness contained in those envelopes he received every month was gone. How could he do that to someone who had faithfully showed how much she cared for him. But now he had found the envelope. He knew how careless and sloppy Reid could be. Lee tried to imagine how big a smile Reid would have when told that the missing envelope wasn't missing anymore. Tomorrow would be a great day. First, he'd go to Reid's luxury garden apartment and then later he would go to Christie's for dinner and give her the dove. Lee stood in front of the bathroom mirror. The first big wide smile was Reid's when Lee told him the envelope wasn't lost any more.

CHAPTER 25

"See if you can find a place over there to sit. Move some of those boxes, I think there's a folding chair in there somewhere," Reid said as he closed the door.

"Reid, your apartment is getting very crowded, it looks like you got a lot of new things for your TV," Lee said as his friend got back to studying some instruction manual.

"Lee, this isn't a TV, this is a premier home theater, you wouldn't believe all the features on this baby – it's not just cable TV anymore. And I can't help it, every time I go into that store the salesman has something new he's waiting to tell me about. Says my system won't be anything without it. The next thing I know, I'm in the checkout line then I'm home with another empty box and another instruction manual to figure out. But look at those babies, look at all those flashing colored lights and digital displays."

"Reid, you may be running out of room for your premier home theater."

"I know, that's why I had to ask Luis to move out, I may need his room for some of the new components. You think I may have to move out? Don't think that hasn't crossed my mind, that's why I'm keeping all the boxes."

"I have one question for you, isn't this rent very expensive and Luis is not here now to help with the rent? I know you won the lottery and all, but still."

"Don't think I'm not troubled every day by how expensive it is to live here. And I just ordered a new premium monthly package from the cable company. Damn, it's not easy having a premier home theater. People just don't know."

"Reid, I have very good news for you. Do you remember when I lost that envelope with all the money from my mother in it? I think I have found it. I was not sure the other day, but I know that has got to be my missing envelope."

Reid's head shot up as Lee walked over to the box that the other day contained Lee's envelope. There under some Styrofoam and other packing materials was the envelope.

"Here it is. Just as I thought, when you took those sports magazines, the envelope must have gotten mixed up with them."

The pages of the instruction manual fluttered as it fell from Reid's hands. "Wait Lee, I can explain."

Lee tugged at the corner of the envelope. It was clear that the envelope was considerably thinner than when Lee had last seen it.

"Lee, I can explain."

"What happened to all the money in my envelope?"

Reid stumbled on one of the boxes as he walked toward Lee. "You got to let me explain. The morning after I brought those magazines home, I picked one up and out fell the envelope. I didn't know what it was, but it wasn't sealed and when I opened it, well, I can't remember ever holding that much cash. Please believe me, my first thought was that I had to call you and tell you that I had your money. Then I got involved doing something else and a few days passed and I was at the store with those big-screen TVs staring at me and I thought I could just borrow some, pay it back, then call you and tell you I found your envelope. But then the cable TV, it, it got worse and I couldn't handle it anymore. It was always something else, always something else that guy at the store showed me. I, I couldn't control myself. I needed room, more room. You see the problem I'm facing now, you said it yourself, I may have to move to someplace bigger. That costs money you know."

Lee opened the envelope. There were three ten-dollar bills remaining. "Reid my money is almost all gone. You won the lottery, why did you have to take my money?"

"I didn't win no lottery. That was a story. What did you expect the first thing people would ask? Reid, where did you get the money to pay for all this? I have dreams though, Lee, I know I'm going to win the lottery someday. But, it's over, it's over big time. I can't meet next month's rent, not by a long shot. Lee boy, my head's swirlin. I'm going to have to sell all this stuff. I'll give you all the money I get from it. And I'll pay you back every last cent of all the money that was in the envelope. I'm sorry Lee, I thought I was going to give you the envelope back. It just seemed like you weren't using it. But I'm sorry. What kind of guy am I who would steal his best friend's money?"

"It is okay, Reid. You have always been my best friend. I can see what the cable TV did to you. I think you are finally over it. I have to get ready to go to Christie's."

CHAPTER 26

"This is very good sauce on the chicken, Christie," Lee said as he brought the last forkful to his mouth.

"It's my mother's recipe. It's on a little wrinkled piece of paper in my cook book. It's really easy to make, but it looks kind of special."

"It is special. It is a special sauce."

"I'm glad you like it Lee."

Lee put his fork down, picked up the napkin from his lap and tapped at his mouth. He looked down at the plastic grocery bag that contained the most expensive thing he ever bought. Christie had asked about the bag and Lee simply said it was a surprise for later. He had thought it out as carefully as he could. He did not want to give Christie her gift when he first came in. He didn't know what he would do if he sensed she didn't like it. He was afraid he might start shaking and have to go home. There was nothing more important in the world to him at this point than to have Christie like the crystal bird in that box in that plastic grocery bag. He didn't know if this was the right time, but with all the talk about special, he thought this was the time.

"I have a gift for you Christie."

"Oh Lee, that wasn't necessary."

He pulled the box out of the bag. His hands brushed against hers as she took the package.

"This is some gift wrapping, exquisite! I hate to ruin it." She carefully pulled the paper back and stared at the writing on the dark gray box. "Lalique!" She pulled the snug top off and her mouth opened wide as she looked at the crystal bird nestled in gray foam rubber. From where he sat, Lee tried to see if the bird was as beautiful as he remembered. Christie had it out of the box by then and the dove, reflecting the flames from the candles, was more beautiful than ever.

"I hope you like the . . ." Lee started to say.

"Lee, this is the most beautiful thing I have ever seen. I love it. But this is probably so expensive. I don't know if I can accept this. I don't want you to spend that much money. I don't think I can keep this. You should save your money."

"But I did save my money. I have saved my money for a long time. I wanted to save it for something special. And you are very special to me and now that you like the crystal dove, I know that I was very wise to save my money."

"Lee, you are very special to me. You're very kind and very caring." She held the solid glass bird in her hands, then placed it on the table. "It's beautiful. It may be the nicest gift I've ever gotten."

"I know it is the nicest gift I have ever given."

As she came around the table to get his plate, she kissed him on top of the head.

"Thank you." Lee wiped his sweaty hands on the sides of his pants. "Now, for dessert. I baked some snickerdoodle cookies to go with some nice vanilla fudge ice cream."

"I have had vanilla fudge ice cream but I have never had a snickerdoddle cookie."

"Snicker*doodle*. Just wait, I think you'll really like them."

By the end of dessert, Lee had eaten five cookies. He thought about what a good cook Christie was. Christie was good at anything she wanted to do. "I think I took too many snickerdoodle cookies. I did not realize how many I have eaten."

"I have plenty. I have to confess," she smiled. "I didn't bake them just for you. My church is hosting the homeless shelter this week and I signed up to bring in dessert for tomorrow."

"I did not know that churches had homeless shelters. My church does not have a homeless shelter."

"Well, I didn't explain it very well. Our church doesn't have an actual shelter. There are about ten churches involved and each one hosts the shelter for a week. At the end of the week, usually Sunday night, we move all the cots and supplies to the next church. The shelter opens at six o'clock for dinner and closes at seven the next morning. Before the people leave they get breakfast and we make them a bag lunch so they are getting three meals a day. People in each of the churches sign up for what types of food they'll bring and then we have another sign-up sheet for people to volunteer to be night-time supervisors who spend the night at the church. I feel very good about what we're doing. There was a mother and father and their three-year old daughter who had been sleeping in their car. They are very polite and so appreciative of the help we're giving them. The father had a tumor in his stomach that burst and he was laid up for six months; lost his job and they couldn't make the rent payments. The mother had a part-time job, but it didn't bring in enough money. Know where they lived? The luxury garden apartments; they lived in the building across from Reid. Now? The father goes down to the diner parking lot every morning. Sometimes there are twenty, thirty men waiting down there hoping that some contractor has some work for them like landscaping or some other odd job that pays about five dollars an hour off the books." She paused as she eased the pile of dishes into the sink. "Some people at the shelter look at me as if I should have an answer for their problem. Some look at me with like a snapshot smile; like they have to give me at least some type of smile if they're going to use the shelter, but seems they've stopped looking for answers long ago."

Lee waited for more of the story but saw that Christie was staring at the stove. "That is a very nice thing that you and the churches are doing Christie. I have seen those men at the diner. I did not know they were looking for work." Christie had come through for him again. If he had to, he could wait at the diner in the morning and even if he didn't work every day, it would be enough, at least for now. "Christie, can I help out at your church? I would like to help, maybe there is something you could find for me to do."

Christie turned from the sink and wiped her hands on her short blue and white terrycloth apron. She smiled. "Meet me here tomorrow night at 5:30 and you can go with me up to the church. There's always something to do."

"I will be here at 5:30." He looked down at the crystal bird invested with a life of colors woven from the candle's flame.

"I think my beautiful dove will stay right where it is, Lee. It brings such a regal presence to the room. It could be a centerpiece in even the most ornate palaces."

Lee watched as Christie placed the glass bird in the center of the table. He imagined her in the most beautiful palace, but couldn't imagine her being more beautiful than she was as she stood before him. He told her that she looked tired and that he should leave so she could sleep and not be tired for work the next day. Christie sat down and told him about how she didn't fit into Audrey Plennnington's future business plans. Lee looked back at the bird not knowing what to say. Christie told Lee not worry, she'd find a job. She knew she'd find a job. At least that is what she told Lee because she saw the frightened look in his eyes as he tried to hide inside a Lalique crystal dove.

"I have more money, Christie, if you need it."

"I'll be fine Lee. I promise, I'll be fine."

Lee knew that Christie, even though she didn't have a job, was the type of person who was much happier receiving the crystal dove than an envelope filled with all the dollars that his gift had cost.

"Thank you for my very special gift, it will always remind me of you," she said as she reached up as Lee was trying to put on his coat and kissed him on the lips. His arms were frozen at his side in his half-on, half-off coat. He wasn't sure, even if he had been able, if he would have put his arms around Christie. He continued to think about that as he walked home.

CHAPTER 27

Reid Fletcher knew he was early and stood behind a tree across the block from the Fitts' house. The door opened and Jim Fitts, lunch box in hand, began walking down the street towards the bus stop. Reid started to move from behind the tree then quickly retreated as he saw Jim Fitts stop and look over his shoulder. Lee's father shook his head and continued down the street. Reid was now going to have to wait until the bus came, which he did.

Lee recognized Reid's knock, with the quick follow-up, and sometimes a further rap-tap. "Reid, I cannot walk any faster to open the door. I need more time to get to the door."

"Sorry, I'm sorry. I just wanted to get in as soon as possible so your dad didn't see me. Hey, got news for you. I sold all that TV crap. I mean I didn't realize how much it controlled me. It was like it hypnotized me and I just did whatever it told me to do. I sold it all; one big package, it was the best offer I could get, to the manager of the apartment. He's got his own apartment on the complex; actually, it's bigger than mine. He knew he had me over a barrel though and I didn't get near what I spent, so here's one-thousand and I'll have to work out something to get the rest back to you."

"Lee looked at all the money Reid had just placed in his hand. His mother had worked hard for the money that was missing. Yet, he had learned to live without any part of it. There were two other crystal doves in the jeweler's window. He could buy them and give them to Christie and have enough left to take her out to dinner at a very fancy restaurant. He could tell her he won the lottery. He could give the money to his father and tell his father that it was from the lottery. His father was changing, ever since that day at the rally for Dan Calvert. Lee's father didn't shout at Lee anymore; he didn't make fun of him. He even had smiled at Lee on two occasions and he left extra money for Lee to buy groceries. But Jim Fitts seemed to stay away from home more. There were more and more nights that Jim Fitts stayed out and stumbled around after he had come into the house. Lee told his sister Ellie about their dad's behavior. She said she would talk to their father, but she hadn't yet. It seemed to Lee as if she were afraid to confront him, especially if he had stopped being as mean as he had been to Lee.

"Did my dad seem okay when he was walking to the bus stop?"

"What, your dad? Yeah, seemed like he always is. I just wanted to make sure he didn't see me and have another nuclear explosion. So, listen, I got more news. I got my old apartment above the bar back. They couldn't find anyone who wanted to rent that rat trap. They even knocked off ten dollars a month in rent, but if they found me hooking into their cable TV again they'd kick my ass out. So, I'm back where I started, all's right with the world. Things have changed big time at work; no more layoffs. Even with winter coming, the weather's been warm and we got plenty of landscape work. I want you to let me know if you want a job, I can get you one now no sweat."

"I might need a job. I might also go down to the diner and wait with the others."

Lee told Reid what Christie said about the diner and the men that waited there for work. He also told Reid about the church's homeless shelter and how he was going there that night with Christie.

"Listen, you want to go to the homeless shelter, that's your business, but stay the hell away from the diner. You don't want to work for any of those guys who come to the diner looking for workers – they're bad news, man. A lot of time they never give you the money they say you'll be getting. And some of those guys that wait down at the diner have gotten beaten up a couple of times if they complain too much. No, keep your ass away from the diner. Hey, I got to get back to work, I just wanted to give you your money and let you know I moved. Come over some afternoon this week, let's talk about everything and you know what, don't be rushing things too much with Christie. But you come over this week; we'll talk."

CHAPTER 28

St. Luke's Church stood on a hill at the end of a winding, gravel drive. Lee had never been there, but Christie was expert at negotiating the turns. There were a dozen cars in the parking lot and lights atop the church building which amid the woods looked like some type of frontier outpost.

"That's the parish hall," said Christie as she shifted the large tin of snickerdoodle cookies she held in her arms. She pointed to the A-framed sanctuary which with the other building formed an L shape around a small courtyard. "Over there is where we're building the new parish hall. It's going to be great; we'll be able to do so many things." Lee looked in the direction of a sign that was now only slightly taller than a massive tangle of vines.

"That is a nice place for the new parish hall. You will have a very nice view of the main road and people down there will be able to watch as the building is being built. Well, maybe not when the leaves are on the trees."

They walked down the gravel path alongside the parish hall, toward a door in the middle of the building. Lee saw the sanctuary door open and several people walk inside. The rushing light framed a small birdbath and several small bushes in the courtyard.

"I know our church is not much to look at; in fact, when it was built twenty-years ago it was supposed to be a temporary building. But there are a lot of good people here. And did you know that we never lock our sanctuary? Anyone can go in there to pray at any time of day."

Lee thought for a moment. "That must be very convenient. I mean if you need to pray in church, you do not have to worry about not fitting it into your schedule. But suppose someone breaks something or steals something?"

"It's never happened."

Lee began to worry about the people driving below who might see the new parish hall being built. Maybe they would want to break into the new building and then if they saw the church and found it unlocked, well, then there would really be a problem.

Christie waved Lee into a crowded kitchen where she placed her cookies on a small table with the other desserts for that night. Organized, purposeful women, the kind usually running church functions, coordinated the warming of casseroles in the double oven that had once been in someone's home kitchen. Several teenagers were tossing salads in large bowls, next to several loaves of bread that had been put into baskets.

In the main room, the homeless sat at ten folding tables with white paper tablecloths. There was a couple with two young children, two women with toddlers, several middle-aged women. The rest were men; in ages ranging from early twenties to, well, to Lee they were old and gray, their leathery faces with lines as deep as those on a pumpkin. Lee thought about which ones he would have guessed were homeless if he had seen them walking around at the mall. None talked; they turned occasionally towards the kitchen, waiting anxiously for whatever emerged that was hot and filling.

Lee recognized one of the men bringing a steaming casserole bowl to the first table. It was Mr. Cantoli, one of the greeters at his church. He realized then that he hadn't seen Mr. Cantoli in a while. That was very strange.

John Cantoli, with his crisp Windsor knot in his tie; white, starched shirt, trousers with a razor-edge crease; and sturdy tie shoes with a buffed polish was a fixture at Lee's church. The John Cantoli in front of Lee now was thinner and his gray hair longer. He wore jeans, a flannel shirt, and well-worn sneakers.

"Lee!" Mr. Cantoli said with a hearty fellowship that Lee had not heard before in the voice of the older man. "It's good to see you again, Lee. What are you doing here?"

"Hello Mr. Cantoli. It is good to see you also. I am here tonight with my friend Christie Veit. She was telling me about the homeless shelter that her church helps with and that is why I am here tonight to see how the shelter helps the homeless people."

"Hello Christie. Yes, I've seen you in church, but we've never actually met."

"I do not understand, Mr. Cantoli, Christie does not go to our church. How could you have seen her in our church?"

"Lee, I go to St. Luke's now; Christie's church. Our church, Rev. Taylor; don't get me wrong, that church and my good friends still mean a lot to me. But, for some time I was getting the feeling that I needed more, that I wasn't doing enough to immerse myself into words that I would hear every Sunday at church. I have a friend a couple of houses down from me who goes to St. Luke's. He was involved in more projects and activities with the church, you couldn't believe it. And I had heard that people around town knew about St. Luke's and what it did to reach out to the needy. So, when my friend invited me to go with him to church one Sunday, I did. From that day forward, I knew that St. Luke's was the place for me. Heck, I'm involved in more activities and groups than you can shake a stick at. But each hour gives me a feeling that come Sunday morning, well, the words during the service just wrap me up in their arms."

"So, you do not go to our church anymore?" Lee asked as if he needed to find out if it were still okay for him to attend his church and to continue to believe that Rev. Taylor knew everything there was to know about Jesus.

"No, Lee, I go to St. Luke's now. But don't think that your church isn't right for you. You have to be where you're comfortable."

Lee was thinking just that, maybe Mr. Cantoli and Christie knew something he didn't. Maybe he should join St. Luke's. He wondered if he could do that right then. Yeah, he was sure he could that tonight. Wait a minute, came his voice from when he went to Sunday school, you can't leave your church. What would your parents say? What would your sister Ellie say? What would Rev. Taylor say? What would Jesus say? Lee never even thought about people going around switching churches. He had been taught the way of his church. Maybe Mr. Cantoli would come back.

"Another course ready to go," a middle-aged woman in a bulky tur-tle-neck sweater and jeans called out.

"Come on Lee, let's go, we need to get the hot food out on the table," Christie said.

"I'm glad you're here tonight, Lee," said Mr. Cantoli. I know you'll get a good feeling by helping out."

"I am glad I am here also, Mr. Cantoli."

Lee placed a steaming bowl of beef stew in front of the man. It was hard to tell how old the man was. His blue knit cap was stained and the part hanging over his ears was frayed. His puffy eyes atop a face partially hidden by patches of unruly whiskers wouldn't let the bowl of stew out of their sight. The layered odds and ends of clothing which he had chosen not to remove gave him an amorphous shape, much like that of Lee when he was a youngster and his mother would wrap him to death in layers of winter clothing before he could play in the snow. As he pulled back after serving the stew, Lee was careful not to disturb the man's crutch; a crutch of chipped, weathered wood with layers of dirty tape and foam wrapped around the top. The man's leg hung at an unnatural angle below the knee. Lee thought at that moment that no one in the world deserved that bowl of hot stew more than the man with the crutch. Lee felt good that he had given the man that bowl of stew. Maybe that was what Mr. Cantoli meant. Maybe Lee should join St. Luke's. He looked at Christie. She was beautiful; she seemed to be even more beautiful as she served that hot beef stew. He wondered what else he could do for the man with the crutch. If he brought the man home to his house to have a warm place to stay and have plenty to eat, maybe Lee might even feel better than Mr. Cantoli regardless of all the hours he devoted to St. Luke's programs and activities. Lee forgot to tell his father about the man with the crutch who was now sitting at their kitchen table. It was not a pleasant sight. Lee was glad he hadn't brought the man with the crutch home.

"We're doing good work here, Lee," Christie said as she rinsed the last of the dishes and handed them to Lee to dry. She rolled up the sleeve of her sweater and reached into the deep stainless-steel sink of soapy water for the drain stopper. Before saying anything, Lee reached for a dry towel for Christie and when he turned to give it to her, found she had stepped toward him. His hand with the towel had not expected to land on her breast.

"I did not mean that Christie. I did not mean that Christie." She would never let him join St Luke's now. She might never even speak to him again. She might scream. The old man with the crutch might start hopping toward Lee and swinging that old wooden crutch.

Christie's smile disarmed the bomb that was about to detonate in Lee's head. The old man with the crutch was still eating his dessert of apple pie and Redi-Whip. "Thank you for the towel, Lee. Let's see if there is anything else we need to do, but I think we can go home." Her glance turned toward the old man with the crutch. His profile, even camouflaged by the wiry, uneven beard, and the lines and swelling that homelessness had branded on his features, was one she had seen before. She walked toward him even as he scraped the last bits of pie from the plate with his fork. It couldn't be but it was. Photos, video footage, and even the image of the man emerging in a wheelchair from the courthouse, raced through her head carried by a flashing current of hate and vengeance much like that which might flow through the brain of the most ardent Nazi hunter who had finally cornered his prey.

"Speakes. Damn you. It's you, isn't it Speakes?" Christie yelled.

The old man turned his head. He dropped the fork and with a powerful push off on his good leg, stood and grabbed his crutch. His only glance back, one of fright, was at Lee. Everyone in the room froze, looking at Christie and then at the old man furiously limping out the door.

"Speakes," Christie said in a voice smothering in sobs the last letters of the name that had tortured her for almost ten years. She looked at the door, but the bus driver was gone.

CHAPTER 29

"Speakes? Nelson Speakes the damn bus driver?" Reid Fletcher asked as he put the last of the cartons down near the window facing the street. Without the oversized TV and home theater paraphernalia, he realized he didn't have much in the way of belongings to bring back to his room above the old tavern. "What the hell would Nelson Speakes be doing at the homeless shelter? I thought they sent him to prison."

"Nelson Speakes was in prison. Christie said he got out of prison two years ago, much sooner than expected. I know it was way sooner than my dad thought. But no one could find him and I know Ellie said she and my dad asked a lot of people. I think there were a lot of people that wanted to hurt Nelson Speakes because of what he did. When my dad saw him on TV one time coming out of the court house, he yelled that he was going to rip Nelson Speakes out of that wheel chair and beat him over the head with the wheel chair."

"Well, that dumb bastard killed a lot of kids and others got hurt real bad. You remember much about that day, Lee?"

"I do not remember much about that day. Christie talks a lot about it, because of her brother. She tells me about everything that happened that day. Then when I am by myself and some thought about that day jumps into my head, I do not know if I am remembering things about that day or only remembering things that Christie has told me about that day."

Reid looked at the emptiness in Lee's eyes. "That son-of-a bitch messed you up Lee. Damn, I shouldn't have said that. I'm sorry. You've always been all right in my book; you've always been my best friend and always will be. What did you say to that old, crippled bastard? Did you feel like punching him or something?"

"He was out of the room so fast I did not know what to think. The only thing I could think about was Christie. She was hysterical. She just stood there sobbing. Her face was buried in her hands. Mr. Cantoli came over to help, but she just kept screaming: 'He killed my brother. Speakes the bus driver killed my brother.' I ran outside thinking that was what Christie wanted me to do, you know, find Speakes. But when I got outside, there was no trace of the bus driver. I went back inside and Christie was still sobbing and Mr. Cantoli and some woman were trying to comfort her. And I thought Christie would probably want me to find out where Speakes stayed, so I asked some of the homeless men. One told me that Speakes lived near some old camp in the woods behind the library; he said he would take me there if I wanted him to. Then the man with the boniest face I have ever seen told me no one was at that camp anymore and that he had never seen Speakes before. Another man with what would have been the boniest face if it had not been for the man I just told you about said he too had never seen Speakes before. Most of the homeless people stopped looking at Christie and went back to finishing their dinner. So, we never got any information about where Speakes was staying. Mr. Cantoli drove Christie and me back to Christie's house in her car and the woman at the shelter followed behind in Mr. Cantoli's car. I stayed with Christie for a while. She stopped sobbing but did not want any of the hot tea I made for her. She just said how much she hated Speakes; that he had killed her brother and then just kept saying how she couldn't believe that we were actually feeding him, helping him at the shelter. I did not know what to tell her, other than maybe he had gotten what he deserved. That he was a crippled old man, homeless, with no one to care for him. And that I thought that was what she told me the shelter was for; to help people even if it meant people like Speakes. Maybe the other people at the shelter had done something terrible at one time; there could be no way we could find out. But if these people had done something bad, they seemed to be suffering enough now, without us trying to make them suffer more. That is what I told Christie. I do not know where all those words came from, but she stopped sobbing. She held my hand and said she couldn't think any more and would have to go to sleep. She seemed much better when I saw here the next morning."

"So Speakes is still out there somewhere?"

"I guess, but I do not know where. I have not told my sister or my father about seeing the old bus driver. I know my father would start yelling at me for not catching Speakes and I think Ellie might be upset if I told her about that night. I think it is better to just forget about him. Christie is doing much better. She even got her old job back at Mrs. Plennington's spa. Mrs. Plennington told Christie that there had been a change in her plans for Fitness Fling's future and that she had found a place for Christie in these new plans. She was even going to give Christie a raise in pay. The first day Christie went back to the spa, the elderly ladies told her that they had gone to Audrey Plennington and told her that if she didn't bring Christie back they were going to cancel their memberships and make sure no one in their families, any of their friends, or anyone else they could think of, came to Mrs. Plennington's spa. Christie was laughing when she told me this, but she said she has been careful not to have Mrs. Plennington see her laughing, because sometimes she just didn't have the best feeling about Audrey Plennington."

"Lot going on in your life since I last seen you, buddy. Going to be working anywhere?"

"I am not sure. I guess I have been thinking a lot about Christie and when you gave me my money back, I guess having that if I need it, I have not been thinking too much about getting a job. But I know that I should."

"Told you, just let me know, cause I can always put you to work. This landscaping work is really taking off around here. I even been thinking about opening my own business. Damn, I learned all about this business, I could make a real killing and I know how to talk with all these immigrants; my boss doesn't even try. Without me, yeah without me, I think he'd be in deep doody. But I need some, what they call start-up capital and maybe even a partner. I got a truck already. I know it's not the best, but I can rent other stuff I need. Way I been figuring it, with a couple of thousand dollars, the next landscaping empire is born."

"I do not think I can give you that money now Reid. You are my best friend too, but I do not think I can give you that money now. I am trying to save my money. I know I have to find some job, but . . ."

"I wasn't even asking about your money," Reid said surprised that even before he had finished his prepared vision of the next landscaping empire, his friend had known exactly where the discussion was leading. "I hadn't even thought about your money." Reid said, in feigned indignation. "All I want you to know is that if you need a job, I got one waiting for you."

"You have always been my friend, Reid."

"Damn right, I've always been your friend." Reid reached into one of the boxes for something that had caught his eye. "Don't know how this ended up in there," he said as he tossed the Wilson 2000 football to Lee.

"I have been looking for this; I knew I had a least one left."

"Yeah, maybe you should start practicing again. Want to make your Dad happy? Start slamming that pigskin through the uprights if you can. So, what is going on with you and Christie? I mean are you going with her or what?"

"Yes, I think I am going with her. I think. I like Christie very much and she is always very kind to me. I am going to see her tomorrow night."

"That's good, man. That's good. Bring her next time you come over. You guys are always welcome."

CHAPTER 30

"Christie and I are going to the movies this afternoon. I cannot be late to the movies. What time will you be here?"

"Lee, you have to stay at the house until I get there. D.H. and I should be there in ten minutes. You must stay at home until we get there. I have something very important to tell you," Ellie Wilson told her brother.

"If this is so important, you can tell me now. I cannot be late for the movies. Christie really wants to see this movie. Tell me what is so important."

Ellie fidgeted with her hair band and rolled-up the sleeves of an oversized sweatshirt. She had just finished making spaghetti and had started to run the water for her shower when the call came and now for a moment thought only of how she would make the unwashed image reflected in the sun visor mirror more presentable. She pulled herself back to her brother's question. As her throat tightened, she fought to retain a patina of assurance in her voice. "Lee, I am asking you. Please do not leave until we get there."

"Ellie, I hope this is important. I am supposed to be going to the movies with Christie."

Ellie placed the cell phone on the console and took her husband's hand. She held on to his hand as memories of her father floated through her head. The other girls were laughing too and their fathers were trying to be as patient as Jim Fitts as they assembled pieces in the birdhouse kit. Her Brownie leader was busy preparing refreshments at the other picnic table. Ellie and her father finished first and as he handed her the birdhouse, he kissed her on the forehead and told her how happy the birds in their yard would be to have this fine new house.

She had had her driver's license for one day. She told her father she would back the Jeep out of the driveway, but she had neglected to adjust the mirrors. With more acceleration than she anticipated from the pedal, she slammed into the pole holding Lee's basketball net. Her father came to her first before inspecting the damage. You all right? he asked. Daddy, I'm so sorry, I didn't mean to. He went back to look at the bumper and the pole. Ellie, we all make mistakes, just have to make sure you learn from them.

The Friday afternoon she found out she hadn't made the cheerleading squad till that point had been the worst, the absolutely worst time of her young life. She had made the first two cuts and was sure she had done much better than usual in the final routine. That was what made it more unbearable. She knew she had done well; better than the two other girls that made the squad. That's what some of the older cheerleaders had told her. They didn't understand why Ellie didn't make it, but they were on to other things. People don't make the cut. That's the way the world works. The girls told her it's a shame she didn't make the cut, but having paid their condolences they just left her and expected her to just carry on. Her father managed to get off work early that day and stayed with her through the night telling her every possible way a father could that things would be all right, that things happen for a reason, that he was very proud of her, and that she brought so much joy to him and to her mother. The medicine of the next morning's light picked up where her father's words had left off. Getting down from her bed, she placed the comforter on him as he lay asleep on the floor next to her bed.

"Ellie, El," D.H. said as he slightly shook his wife's arm. "Ellie we're almost here. I know you want to collect your thoughts, you know, what you're going to tell your brother."

She looked at her watch; a few minutes longer than the ten minutes she told Lee. He was standing outside the door and looking down at his watch several times as Ellie with D.H. not far behind, approached the front step. D.H. watched as her words turned Lee into a trembling little boy. His sister put her arms around him and they walked quickly to the car.

The Locust Shade Mall wasn't really a mega-mall. But it was the mall that everyone in town, or for that matter in the county, knew you were talking about if you were to say "I'm going to the mall." It wasn't very upscale: corrugated siding on the outside with groups of colored flags mounted along the roof. The one-story structure housed about eighty stores. Signs with faded flowers hung from the ceiling to tell you that you were either in Neighborhood 1, 2 or 3. Jim Fitts worked in Neighborhood 2, at Cutuli's Jewelry Store. Cutuli's carried an inventory appealing to shoppers to whom a big jewelry purchase usually meant several hundred dollars, tops. Still, there was a counter with several trays of items costing as much as five-thousand dollars. Security Guard Jim Fitts usually stood between that counter and the entrance to Cutuli's. That's where he was that afternoon when two Orientals, that was the term the store manager used, with shaved heads, earrings and baggy jeans, rushed past him or almost past him. Maybe Jim had picked up some police skills after being a rent-a-cop for almost eight years. Hearing Cutuli's manager yell, "Stop him! Stop him!" Jim reflexively reached for the second Oriental. He got a good grip on him, which surprised both Jim and the man in his grasp who was markedly displeased that the old rent-a-cop had done what he had done. "Let go of me, you dumb shit," the second Oriental said as he whipped around and plunged the serrated-edge of a combat knife first into the upper-right section of Jim's groin and then a little lower into the top of Jim's upper thigh.

The amount of blood spurting out surprised the attacker who hesitated a half-second before turning and running in the opposite direction of his companion. Jim fell to his knees. His head was light as he tried to stop the bleeding with his hands. The manager was soon holding several polishing towels on the wounds as the assistant manager dialed 911. Jim fell back on the floor as his head and hands began to tingle furiously. Jim's eyes locked on to the security camera above. The camera recorded his eyes closing as paramedics reached his side.

CHAPTER 31

Lee listened to the doctors describe his father's condition –grave, but they thought he'd pull through, they had stopped the bleeding. Ellie asked most of the questions. Lee said nothing. He watched Ellie's reaction to what the doctors were saying; something about the first stab wound slicing what he thought they said was the femoral artery and the second hitting something they thought might be like a vascular mass, but they weren't sure why there would be a vascular mass at that site. The younger doctor had that look in his eye that said even though the situation was bleak, somehow, he was convinced that his doctor skills could fix everything. The older doctor did not have that look in his eye. Ellie and D.H.'s questions had shifted early in the conversation to the younger doctor, and his colleague realized that.

If it had been up to Ellie, she never would have made the call. She had done it for Lee; for some reason, she thought it would comfort him. "Lee." She tried to temper the harshness she felt slipping into her voice. "I tried to reach Mother. Maybe I shouldn't have. Anyway, I just got some robot voice so I don't even know if this is still her number; it's the cell number she got just before she left. I found it on some piece of paper in my purse. I don't even know how it got there." That was all she told her brother. There was still no reason for him to know that their mother had left an envelope with a short note and her phone number for both of them before she left.

"That was a very good idea to call Mother. A very good idea and we are very lucky that piece of paper was there."

"We've got to get back inside now," the younger doctor said. "We'll call right to that phone over there when we've finished."

Lee wondered how long that would be. He could see that Ellie and D.H. were wondering the same thing as they glanced at the phone next to the nurse's station; but no one asked.

"Dad will be okay. He'll be okay Lee," Ellie said. "Have you eaten today? Have you eaten anything today?"

It seemed to Lee a reasonable question for reasonable times. But he didn't know how he could think about eating under the circumstances. Maybe Ellie was trying to make it seem for him a reasonable time even though their father was in critical condition in the operating room on the other side of the very wide doors. "I ate my cereal this morning, but I am not hungry now. I am not hungry even though that is all I have had to eat today. El, what happens if Dad is not all right? What happens if . . ."

"Lee," Ellie said, so as to stop her brother from raising the subject that a normal brother wouldn't address. No one normal would discuss that; they might think it, but they wouldn't ask it out loud, especially not when the younger doctor had that "I'll be able to handle this look in his eye." That was the look that Ellie and anyone normal in her spot would expect. Save my father, Ellie's look had told the young doctor, much as if he had been a lifeguard at the beach and she pointed to her father in distress out among the waves. He'd bring her father back safely. "Daddy's going to be all right. If you don't want anything to eat, let's go over to the couch." Ellie pulled change from her pocket, shook her head, and walked to the phone.

Lee and D.H. sat on a couch whose springs and strappings sagged considerably from many hours of supporting troubled families and friends. D.H. stared at the corner around which his wife had disappeared to make her phone call. Lee started to think about another reasonable thing: he had to get in touch with Christie. He was already late. Christie was so kind, but how would she feel about Lee not being where he was supposed to be. He looked at his watch. The movie they were going to see would start in five minutes. He wished he had Christie's pager number. If she went into the movie, he wouldn't be able to reach her for hours. Maybe she wouldn't go to the movies. Maybe she would go to his house. Maybe she would think something happened to him. Lee pictured himself being operated on in the room behind the very wide doors. Maybe she would call the hospitals and ask if Lee had been admitted. He knew somehow Christie would find him.

Lee looked up as tired nurses with coats and carry bags walked past them. "I gave your message to my relief," said the nurse to whom Ellie had spoken about a possible call from Marian Fitts. "You all look very tired; you've been sitting there a long time. Why don't you go downstairs and get something to eat?"

"We will," Ellie said. "Thank you for all your help."

"Really, get something to eat," the nurse admonished from behind the closing elevator doors.

There were three elevators across from the waiting area and the doors were opening and closing much more frequently now during the early minutes of evening visiting hours. Rumpled, dripping umbrellas and wet jackets, to which paper visitor badges refused to adhere properly, told of a rain storm that must have punched through the afternoon's blue sky. Each succeeding elevator unloaded passengers who were more drenched than earlier visitors. One said, "they said possibility of brief showers, they didn't say nothing about no monsoon."

Lee watched the patchwork of puddles grow in front of the elevators. A custodian came with a mop, planted a yellow, plastic sign warning in English and Spanish that the floor was wet, and began to mop. The wet visitors still came and the floor sprouted more puddles and the custodian came back with his mop. Lee looked at the visitors' facial expressions and mannerisms and tried to determine if the patients these visitors were coming to see were sicker than his father. He gave up; the people who had been caught in the nasty rain storm appeared preoccupied with how wet they were.

When the doors next opened, only one visitor emerged. Christie, her brown hair soaked, saw Lee and began to walk towards him. He knew they were tears, not rain drops that she wiped from her eyes. He stood first, then D.H., then Ellie.

"I am so sorry, so sorry. How is your father?" Christie asked as she clasped both of Ellie's hands.

"We haven't heard anything for the past several hours," Ellie said as she began with great precision to describe their early conversation with the doctors.

"I knew you would find out where I was," Lee said. I worked it all out in my head. How many hospitals did you call before you found us?"

"The whole horrible thing was on the local news, the whole thing about your father. They caught the men that did it. I was at the movies and I waited for a while. Then I went to your house. Then I went home again, and back to your house, and that's when I heard in on the radio. It was the whole story and they gave the name of the hospital. I came right away."

Ellie and D.H. sat down. "Thank you for coming, Christie," Lee's sister said. "This is all just too much; you never think something like this can happen to your own. I mean all the things in the police blotter section of the paper; I feel lucky it's not us. But then, what happened to Daddy is just so much worse. Why couldn't we have just had our car broken into or even if someone had to rob us at least not hurt us? I mean, we shouldn't even be having anything happen to us after what we've been through." Lee, D.H., and Christie looked at Ellie, nodding up and down as they did. This was not a question you answered any other way. Ellie and D.H. stared at the double doors beyond which were Jim Fitts and the young doctor.

Lee helped Christie off with her jacket. The rain had penetrated through to the shoulders of her blouse. "I will be right back," he said. He brought her a handful of brown paper towels. Christie blotted at her face and hair and the back of her neck. "I am sorry you got so wet coming to the hospital."

"The storm is bad Lee. It's amazing that they caught those guys on a night like this."

"My father tried to stop them. He could have looked the other way. I remember him saying when he first took that job that for what he was getting paid he wasn't going to be a hero."

"The radio said he really went after the guy, Lee."

"I hope my father will be okay; that is the only thing I want right now and I have been praying really hard. I have been praying also that my mother will come to us."

"Want to walk a little Lee? Just down the hall a bit."

"Okay, yes, we can get some exercise."

"Lee, I was talking to my parents yesterday. They keep telling me they're coming to visit, but I knew when they moved they wouldn't be back. But I told them about you and how we had been out a couple of times and that we were going to the movies tonight."

"I'm sorry I made you miss the movies, Christie."

"Lee, don't even say that. That's not what I meant. I was talking to my parents and they said you were always a very nice boy and to say hello. I felt happy when I was talking about you, I just wanted you to know. I'll help you through this Lee. While your father's in the hospital, when he comes home, just tell me what I can do to help. I know if something awful happened to me, I wouldn't even have to ask and you would be there ready to help with anything I needed."

They stopped at the end of the hall and as they turned to walk back, looked into a room where a patient lay expressionless as the laugh track of an old sitcom blared away. Christie took Lee's hand in hers and they walked back to join the vigil Ellie and D.H. were keeping. Her hand was like his but so different. He felt the thin bones in her hand tighten. He wanted to be with her forever. Her words, as he pulled every probable meaning from them, could sustain him against anything. At least that's what he thought until they reached the end of the corridor. Even the lovely weight of Christie's words couldn't plumb the deepest reaches of the debilitating fear Lee felt that night. His father, that was his father in there behind those closed doors. Those doors sealed shut any way of knowing if the young doctor had enough skill and luck to overcome seconds of senseless slashing or if those seconds -- one, one thousand; two, one thousand; three, one thousand – would be like those that had thundered from nowhere to show they could take out a school bus if they wanted.

The custodian had been back again with his mop. He saw the floor dry, but decided to dab at a small area anyway as if he didn't want his trip to be for nothing. Deciding there was no further need for the yellow plastic sign; he picked it up and walked back down the hall.

The double doors opened and the young doctor walked out; drained of a lot of the energy he had had four hours earlier. Ellie, helped up by D. H., scanned the doctor's face which showed no emotion until one of the determined steps of the young physician slid across the custodian's recently swabbed tile.

"Damn," the doctor said as he caught himself on the type of handrail that wends its way along every hospital corridor wall. "Sorry, I didn't mean that. Actually, I have some encouraging news. The doctor turned his neck and stretched his back. "Yes, given everything we're working with, it's good news. We've stopped the bleeding in the femoral artery. We used a few staples inside and more outside. It should hold; we'll have a better idea in the morning. In the other area, just above the groin on the right-hand side, that's a little more complicated, but I think it's going to be okay. There was a lot of bleeding there. See, your dad in that area has what we call an arterial venous malformation or AVM; it's a vascular mass so it's full of blood. Not sure really what causes them, most likely congenital and often as with your dad you don't even know you have an AVM, especially if it's small; but your dad's wasn't small. We can't cut out something like that; we wouldn't be able to stop the bleeding. What we do and it took pretty well in your dad's case, is patch with a special glue so that the blood flow to and from the AVM can be stopped. We were lucky that the wound only slightly nicked the mass; I think the glue's going to hold there too. If the cut were a little bigger we would have been certainly faced with a much broader range of problems. But I think we're okay; I think he's going to be okay for now. I'll be in to see him in the morning; we'll have a much better idea at that time."

The young doctor, Lee looked at his name tag which had been a blur earlier, Dr. Kevin Centers, had come through. Skill and luck had come out of another corner to trump the seconds of slashing. Dr. Centers looked tired.

"Is our father going to pull through, Dr. Centers?" Ellie asked. Lee looked at his sister. Hadn't she heard what Dr. Centers said, all the things Dr. Centers said he fixed?

Dr. Centers seemed to be looking too long for his answer to Ellie's question. "I'm going to see him first thing in the morning. You have to know how fortunate we are that the bleeding has stopped. I can only tell you we will know better in the morning."

"Thank you, Doctor," Ellie said hoping but unable to find more of an answer in his smile before he walked away.

The nurse had waited for her cue and she filled quickly the emptiness left by Dr. Centers' departure. She handed Ellie a sheet with phone numbers and hospital procedures. "I'll be here the rest of the night, till eight tomorrow morning. My name is Susan and I'm one of the CCU nurses." Lee looked at her name tag: Susan Andrews, R.N. "I want you to know that we have one of the best critical care units around. I'll keep a close eye on your dad. Call the number at the top of the sheet if you want to see how he's doing. Ma'am someone just called for you; but it was a very bad connection, I could barely hear her; bad static on the line."

"We're going to go home now," Ellie said. "It was probably my mother; I'll try her when we get outside." The elevator door opened. Lee scuffed at a wet spot on the floor until it was dry. He walked Christie to her car and she hugged him. He watched her headlights skid across the puddles in the parking lot, then turned and walked to his sister's car and got into the backseat.

"Lee, it's going to be all right," the big sister said to her little brother. "Geez," you think you'd be able to get through to your mother the one time you needed to. I was making spaghetti when all this happened. At least we'll have something to eat when we get home. We all need something to eat. D. H. has a trip tomorrow morning, but Lee, you and I will go first thing tomorrow morning back to the hospital."

CHAPTER 32

D.H. and Lee had gone to sleep and Ellie sat at the table staring at the dinner dishes. She lifted the glass of wine to her mouth and took three swallows. She grabbed the phone on the first ring.

"Ellie, were you trying to reach me?" Marian Fitts asked.

Is that all she could say?

"Ellie, are you there?"

"Mother, Daddy is in the hospital. He was attacked; stabbed with a big knife. He's lost a lot of blood and is in the hospital. He's in critical condition. I thought I should let you know," Ellie said fulfilling in her mind the last vestige of responsibility she had to her mother.

"Ellie, what are you saying? When did this happen?" Marian Fitts asked. "Are you and Lee all right?"

"Thanks for asking mother. Lee and I are all right. He's asleep right now," Ellie said as she looked up the darkened staircase. She had tried, but had not been able to prevent a faint note of sarcasm from shading her response.

"What did you mean by that Ellie? Is that tone really appropriate at a time like this?"

"I don't know what tone you're referring to mother. I think the nurse on CCU is the person you should speak with. Do you have a pen?"

"If that's the way you want it Ellie. I don't know why you've been so hard on me for all these years."

"Oh, I think you do."

"You know I had to leave. You know I had no choice, and you know how hard I tried. And you've told Lee not to call me, haven't you?"

"Here's the number mother." Ellie finished speaking, waited several seconds, and hung up.

Marian Fitts lowered the phone and looked at the clock on her stove. Maybe her daughter was just tired. After all, if the clock said 9:10, it had to be after midnight where her daughter was. She hadn't expected her daughter to be so short with her. Marian's slender fingers reached over to the Mr. Coffee and she poured herself a half-cup. She thought of Ellie and what Audrey Plennington had said some four years ago, the last time Marian had spoken to her. I can't get over how much Ellie looks like you, Audrey said. She has that cute, narrow nose, and those full cheeks she still highlights with that apricot blush just as you used to do. She's thin too; but you can tell there's a nice little figure there. And Lee has grown up to be such a fine looking, young man. Audrey Plennington had been such a good friend. Marian wasn't sure why, but they had seemed to just drift apart. But even Audrey agreed that Marian was right to leave if that's what she felt she had to do. Audrey Plennington had known all too well what Jim Fitts had turned into. Marian missed hearing from her friend. Rev. Warren Taylor became the main link to news about her family; at least until several months ago when their conversation ended on a decidedly sour note. He became impatient with what he called her flimsy reasons for not wanting to come back to her family.

"Coming up we've got the Turtles, Paul Revere and the Raiders, and one I know you're going to really like from the Byrds," said the classic rock DJ. Marian stared out the window, high above the trees, and looked into a weave of smoky trails brushing a faded blue sky. There was no scale she could establish in that sky. She saw Jim Fitts in that sky, looking at her, then he was gone. Would he be gone now forever only to be seen in the sky? The DJ was back with the music he had promised. She remembered how she and Jim would sit at the kitchen table reading, writing out bills, pouring more coffee into their cups, devouring in their desultory talks a small morsel of an idea that to them seemed important. The same music was playing back then. She wondered if Jim listened to it any more. Having more than one chair at the table made a big difference.

Jim had made her laugh. He was the disciplinarian, but the children didn't fear a vicious hand; although there would at times be some memorable swats to the bottom. Ellie and Lee feared most the look of grave disappointment on their father's face when he learned of something they did that they knew was very wrong. Wrong was something that the family could absorb with barely a ripple. But very wrong was something that produced a look on their father's face that made the children wish they could go back in time to stop the egregious act that they couldn't believe they had actually committed. Marian's "Look how much you've upset your father," shot into her children like a paralyzing dart. Jim's disappointment would lead him to say things, she would say things, Ellie and Lee would say things and the appetite of the fire spreading in the house would seem unquenchable. Eventually the flames would die down. The damage wasn't as bad as anticipated, but it would take a while, sometimes several days, for the smell of smoke to be gone from the house. Marian and the children looked for the all clear signal; the look in their father's eyes that showed his disappointment was gone. There was no better father in the world than Jim Fitts when the disappointment in his eyes was gone. There was no better husband then either, Marian thought as she laid her head in her arms not far from the cup of cold coffee and pile of mail on the table. As much as she wanted to sleep and thus be even farther from what Ellie had told her about, Marian Fitts knew she had to call. She brushed her eyes and dialed the number.

The nurse spoke slowly, her voice halting unexpectedly only to start up again as she interspersed technical terms with language a non-health-care professional could understand. She provided Marian with all the details that Ellie hadn't. "Your husband," the nurse said, "is still officially listed in critical condition. I'd say his condition has stabilized, but he's sustained very serious wounds; very serious."

"I'm not close by and I'm trying to think about travel plans," Marian said. "Do you think it might be possible, maybe some time tomorrow, to speak with my husband?"

"Mrs. Fitts," the nurse paused. "That's something that I'm not qualified to say at this point. We would have to check with Mr. Fitts' doctor. But let me say this. From what I've seen today, it will be awhile before Mr. Fitts will be able to speak with any one. Is there a number where the doctor can reach you?"

"Well, let me think about my plans. I'll call back later in the morning. Thank you very much."

During the past five years, Marian had gradually come to distance her-self from that painful moment that seemed at first to choke the very life from her. While her best thinking, her best rational thinking had led her to that decision, it had not made the moment any less painful. But since she left her husband, a husband who by that time bore no resemblance to the husband with whom she used to share the kitchen table, she had struggled and successfully found firm ground to replace the quagmire into which she had been sinking. She, too, had felt the same cannon shot to the stomach upon learning what happened to Lee; but nobody, nobody except Audrey Plennington recognized that. Even Rev. Taylor seemed more concerned about Jim Fitts and Ellie. When the good pastor finally recognized what was happening, Marian was too far gone, her husband's abuse began to terrify her. Ellie knew only bits of what was happening to her mother. Her mother had to understand, she said that this was all just too much for Daddy. When he looked at his son, when he thought about what was left of the son he had known, Jim Fitts could unload his torrent of rage at anyone. At times, Marian thought he was going mad. But there was never that look in his eyes toward his children regardless of how much he yelled at them. The look was reserved for her; his eyes told her what his mind was thinking when it would get crazy. She could never feel the hurt he did; how dare she even think she could, he wouldn't stand for it. Rev. Taylor began to see the danger she was in. Ellie too looked for some way to rein in her father. Ellie and Rev. Taylor had answers for her, but no way to stop the abuse. Marian never returned that afternoon and Ellie told Lee she never hated anyone more than her mother. Lee wished only that his mother hadn't left. Rev. Taylor thought Marian's leaving was not the most constructive thing to do. He would come to see in subsequent conversations with her that Marian had no choice.

Marian knew she didn't have to make the decision yet about flying back to be with her family. She still had to talk with the doctor and she would touch on some of the past problems so as to open the door for him to say, "Maybe, if that's the situation, it might not be best for you to come back at this time. Given Mr. Fitts' condition, it might be too upsetting for him." But the doctor didn't say that when they spoke. It was her call, her family's call, even though he understood what she was saying. She looked at the stainless-steel toaster. Nothing fancy, it toasted two slices of bread. She leaned over and in the curved corner was her reflection just as if she were looking into a round glass Christmas tree ornament. What would seeing her husband again be like? There would be no purpose in telling them she was coming.

CHAPTER 33

Rev. Warren Taylor handed the driver twenty dollars and watched as the man pulled a wad of well-worn bills from his pocket to fish for two singles. The twenty was placed where the twenties went and before the driver began fishing for two singles, Rev. Taylor told him to keep the change and got out of the cab. The cab pulled out from underneath the canopy over the hospital entrance.

Rev. Warren Taylor had on his game face, or as he used to joke with himself, his collar face. When people he didn't know looked at his clerical collar, then made eye contact with him they would find a Mona Lisa half-smile. Even on a morning such as this when, his car, after five-hundred dollars in repairs refused to start; when he was forced to pay his monthly offering for the first time in two installments because his younger brother required another new and costly medicine; when again he was suffering from a headache after his morning Bible readings, even on such a morning the half-smile was on good and tight.

"Yes, it is a beautiful morning," he responded to one of the elderly volunteers who handed him a visitor's pass. He listened carefully as she pointed a shaky finger up, left, right then left again. "Don't take the first elevator, that's the wrong one. You want the second elevator."

"Second elevator, thank you very much."

As he got out of the second elevator, he saw Ellie, Lee, and D.H. standing in front of a nurse with a clipboard. Ellie saw him first and motioned for him to come over. "This is our pastor, Rev. Taylor; he's known our family for a long time," Ellie told the nurse. "I'm so glad you came, Warren." D.H. held his wife as her voice trailed off into the beginning of a sob.

"I'm sorry I wasn't here sooner. I didn't return home till late last night and got your message then. I knew it was too late to call and when I didn't get you at home this morning, I just came over here. I'm so sorry about what happened to your father. I can't imagine what you're going through. Were you able to get in touch with your mother?"

"My mother knows," Ellie responded coolly.

The nurse opened the huge double doors and disappeared into the CCU. The others walked over to the waiting area and sat. Ellie meticulously described the events of the day before and her father's condition when they left him. She went on for ten minutes. Lee said nothing and didn't take his eyes off his sister. He was glad she was repeating the story because he wasn't sure he remembered all the details.

"And the nurse just filled us in on where things stand this morning," Ellie said. "They're having a little trouble with the bleeding and may have to inject a little more coagulant into the artery. He was in quite a bit of pain and still very groggy, but she said we can see him in a few minutes. We can't stay in there long. The nurse thinks we can go in again in a couple of hours." Lee's head moved up and down and his sister finished the definitive summary of where things stood.

"Lee, you doing okay?" Rev. Taylor asked.

Lee looked at his sister as she smiled at him. "Yes, I think I am doing okay. I want to see my father and I have to ask him if he needs anything from home and I have to make sure the house is clean for when he comes home. I have to find out if he will be able to sit in his special chair in front of the TV and I have to find out if he needs something special to eat when he comes home and I have to ask about all the things I need to do to take care of my father when he comes home."

"Those are all good questions, Lee. I'm sure the nurse and the doctors will be able to answer your questions. I want you to know that you and your family won't be alone; you have a lot of friends at church who'll help you through this."

The double doors whirred open and the nurse with the clipboard smiled as she invited them into the land she knew was medicine's last hope. "Make this just family for now, so it's not too much for your dad. I wouldn't even tell him I was out here," Rev. Taylor said, remembering the unpleasant discussion he had with Jim Fitts at the rally. "I'll talk with him later when he's a little more awake." Rev. Taylor watched as the double doors whirred shut behind the Fitts family.

Jim Fitts's eyes were closed. By his bed was a bank of piggybacked monitors speaking in a foreign language of lights and beeps. Lee looked at the man in the bed. Plastic tubes carrying oxygen disappeared into his father's nostrils and a tube with several valves was taped to a pale, slightly bluish arm that had never to Lee looked so thin. Ellie called to her dad in a hushed voice and as his eyes opened she brushed and patted at the unruly gray strands on his head.

"Ellie?" pealed her father's unsteady voice.

"Yes, Daddy, I'm here and so is Lee and D.H."

"Lee." As he called his son's name, Jim Fitts tried to stem the tremble in his mouth and the welling in his eyes. Ellie was quick to wipe away the tears trailing down his face. "Oh, Lee," Jim Fitts said as a series of sniffles and gurgles preceded a deep sob as he inhaled. "I am so sorry for everything. It was never your fault. I realized that. Did you see how over the past months I realized that? But I never told you." Lee's father looked at the ceiling and stopped talking as abruptly as he started. The nurse put down her clipboard and listened carefully to what the monitors were telling her: "You better get them out of here."

"Why don't you let your father rest a little more; maybe it would be best if you'd step into the hall for a bit."

Ellie wiped Lee's tears with her hand and unable to hold back any longer, embraced her brother amidst her own jagged sobs. "Lee, it will be all right, Dad will get better. We'll take good care of him."

"He never left us, Ellie," Lee whispered into his sister's ear.

"I know Lee. He never left."

Rev. Taylor awaited the travelers emerging from behind the whirring double doors. The nurse waved as the doors closed.

"How's Dad?" Warren Taylor asked.

"He's, he needs some sleep. The nurse said he needed some rest and that we should come outside for a while," Ellie responded.

"He started to cry, Rev. Taylor. My dad started to cry and he told me he was sorry, that it was not my fault," Lee said.

"Your father loves you very much, Lee. He loves you too Ellie. I could always tell that even when we had discussions that were, er, heated."

"He never left us. He could have run away. If he really felt the way he acted toward me, he could have eaten his breakfast in the morning, go out and catch his bus for work and just never come back," Lee said.

"That was a wonderful thing your father said to you, Lee. If it came late, I'm sure he is very sorry. I know how these years have been rough for you. I've prayed for you every day since the accident. I asked God to let us understand His way and to bring you and your father back together in a manner that was even more loving and caring than you had known. You and your family have been in the prayers of many people."

The Fitts family remained in the waiting room. Warren Taylor would be back at his office, he said, if they needed him.

Rev. Taylor's younger brother weighed more than four-hundred pounds. He would be ashamed if his parishioners ever saw him screaming at his brother; his big, fat brother who did nothing about his weight. Diabetes, skin disorders, swollen joints, an overtaxed heart were aliments that required many pills and doctors' visits which his brother couldn't afford. Rev. Taylor's savings were draining quickly; he had never planned for a brother who required such care. Rev. Taylor knew that someone had to yell at his brother; how else was he going to learn that if he didn't do something about his bad health he was going to die? He was also going to drain dry the meager savings of a frugal, already sacrificing member of the clergy.

Realizing he left his cell phone in the car parked at home, the distraught clergyman headed for the pay phone off the hospital lobby. Dialing, he hoped his secretary had arrived in the office. She'd have to drive over and pick him up; he found he had only a dollar in his wallet.

The phone rang and a long description of the church as a place of good fellowship and worship preceded the hours of worship and announcements concerning important upcoming activities. He left a message that he was still at the hospital and would try back later. He went outside, thought about walking, but it was just too far and he didn't want to have to answer questions about why he was walking along the highway. He stood on the sidewalk staring into the parking lot as if he were trying to make out a ship far offshore in the fog.

"Rev. Taylor?" He turned. "Rev. Taylor, I don't know if you remember me. My name's Christie Veit, I'm Lee's friend."

"Oh yes, I remember," but he couldn't remember from where. "It's good to see you again. Yes, very good to see you. I've just come from being with Lee, and his sister; and her husband's upstairs as well."

"I thought he'd be here. I tried getting in touch with him all last night and this morning and figured he must be at the hospital."

"Yes, yes, Lee's upstairs. I'm sure he'll be glad to see you, can always use a good friend at a time like this." He continued to stare into the cars as if one would recognize who he was, that he needed a ride, and would drive up to the curb so he could get in.

"Rev. Taylor, are you waiting for someone?"

"Well, not really, I mean, well, I couldn't get my car started this morning, so I took a cab to the hospital and I tried to get through to our secretary at the church, but she's not in yet. So, I'll wait a bit and try her again."

"Let me give you a ride. The church is only a few miles away. I can drop you off and be back in no time. It's not as if Lee were expecting me at a particular time."

"No, I couldn't impose, Christie, but that's very nice of you to offer."

"Please, I insist. I know Lee certainly would want me to take you if he knew you didn't have a ride."

Rev. Taylor, rescued from the cold, harsh desolation of the street that was the traveling buddy of those with no money and no one to turn to, said "Maybe I will take you up on your kind offer."

The growing warmth of the heater in Christie's car chased the chill from both his body and his thoughts. They were out of the parking lot and he would soon be within the protective walls of his office.

"Have you known Lee long?"

"Yes, we've known each other since middle school." She quickly added," but recently Lee and I have become good friends, I guess closer."

Warren Taylor hesitated then realized it was an important piece of information. "So, did you know Lee before the accident?"

"Yes, I did and Lee knew my brother Sam Veit."

The name sounded very familiar to him, he was sure he had seen it in one of the newspaper stories. "Pardon me for asking, but was he one of the ones that was . . ."

"Yes, Sam was killed in the crash. I could never bring myself to call it an accident because the bus driver knew exactly what he was doing; there's no doubt in my mind. But, and I'm sure this comes as no surprise to you, eventually everyone gets what they deserve. A while ago, at the homeless shelter we have, I mean that our church, St. Luke's, has I saw an old man at the shelter. He was in sorry shape and had a makeshift crutch for his bad leg, but I recognized him. It was Speakes, the bus driver, but he got out and got away. For days, I thought about how badly I felt that he got away; I'm not sure what I would have done to him, but I wanted to hurt him. I think I'm over it, I mean I'll never get my brother back, and you can see what's happened to Lee, but Speakes got what was due him. He's a crippled old homeless man and judging by what I saw he's pretty sick. There was terror in his eyes when I started yelling at him." Christie took a deep breath and scrunched her lips as she put on the turn blinker. "Still doesn't look like there's anyone here."

Rev. Taylor shook his head. What a coincidence, he thought, but then what does that word mean to the Lord. "Christie, it's all coming together now. The crash was so long ago, and I had forgotten the bus driver's name, but when you said Speakes and homeless and the man's physical condition, well, I remembered. I'd say maybe a year ago, it was a cold afternoon, late in the day, I was getting ready to go home. I was going to lock the sanctuary door, then it opened and three men walked in. They were shivering, poorly dressed, and one had a crutch similar to the one you described. He asked if they could stay in the church for just a while to warm up. There was no room at the shelter, he said. I told them of course and went to get some food from the pantry. When I came back, that man was in the front pew, kneeling in prayer. One of the men, pointed to the pew and asked me to pray for the man with the crutch; he called him Speakes. Said he was a really good man. He would always be on the lookout for those homeless having a particularly rough time. He spends just about all of his monthly disability check on others. But Speakes's health was getting worse especially with the freezing cold. I did pray for Speakes and after an hour or so, they left."

Christie lowered her head into her hands, then looked to the sky. She had her answer about Speakes and thanked the Lord.

Warren Taylor placed his hand on hers and looked at the empty church parking lot. He scanned his memory for a Bible verse or some pithy commentary that could respond appropriately to Christie's story but nothing came to him. "Well, I'm sure Margaret our secretary will be here soon. But you were a real lifesaver Christie, I should say. You go to St. Luke's, we just had someone transfer to our church from St. Luke's. His name's Clement Ezzer. Do you know him?"

"The name doesn't sound familiar right off, maybe if I saw him I'd recognize him."

"Sure, I'm sure that might be." Warren Taylor thanked her again and got out of the car. He watched as she drove to the end of the driveway and turned into the traffic heading toward the hospital.

Christie was back in the hospital parking lot in less than fifteen minutes. Much more crowded now, the only vacant spot was the one she had pulled out of when she drove Rev. Taylor to church. It had been a short trip according to the odometer, but had covered much ground in terms of what she had discussed with Warren Taylor. Her brother, Speakes the bus driver, Lee; that had been a lot to unload on the reverend but he was very understanding. She was glad that someone like Rev. Taylor didn't seem to have any problems of his own; must be because of his deep belief in God.

Lee stood in the gift shop, his back was toward her and she said nothing as she walked over. He was staring at a tabloid on the rack. "EXTRATERRESTIAL FOUND LIVING IN WHITE HOUSE -- Has Secretly Recorded Private Presidential Conversations of the Past Fifty Years," screamed the headline. Below was a photo of the back of what looked like a person in a reptile suit with a pointy head. In handcuffs, the creature was being led away from the White House by policemen.

"Lee," Christie said.

"I did not see you there Christie. I am glad you are here. I have been with Ellie and D.H. upstairs visiting my father. Ellie said I should come downstairs and get something to eat and I was just reading the newspaper. I did not hear about the problem in the White House and the television has been on the whole time we have been in the waiting room. Maybe this story came on when we were in my dad's room."

"Lee," Christie said in a voice she might one day use to tell her children there was no Santa Claus. "This newspaper just makes up stories. There is no truth to them. The readers laugh at them. They're supposed to be funny."

"But Christie, that story is in the newspaper and there is a photo of the White House and if you look at the smaller photo, there's the tape recorder that the alien used to listen in on the presidents' private conversations."

"Lee, why don't we get a sandwich and go outside. I saw a couple of picnic tables near the parking lot and the sun's come out; looks like it'll be a nice day after all. Don't worry about the newspaper; I'm sure the White House can handle whatever comes up."

Christie listened carefully as Lee told her about his father. He knew his father would get better. She told him how happy she was that his father had such kind words about Lee. Yes, my dad and I are going to be fine now. Once he gets better, we will be able to do a lot of things together. I am going to take very good care of him. I know Ellie will help too.

"Lee, I saw Rev. Taylor earlier when he was standing in the parking lot. I gave him a ride back to his office. We started talking about Speakes, and Rev. Taylor said he saw him about a year ago with some other homeless men who said Speakes was a very caring man who went out of his way to help the homeless. They asked Rev. Taylor to pray for him, because he was doing such kind things and his health was bad. Lee, I don't think I can hate him any longer. I need to move on, and be thankful that God is using Speakes in this way."

"I cannot hate the bus driver. I cannot hate. I saw what hate did to my father."

Lee's wisdom cleared a path for her. She looked up at the buds bursting into a green fizz of shoots that by late spring would form a canopy of leaves shielding the weathered picnic table from the summer sun. She smiled at him, knowing that he too had moved on.

"That looks like a good sandwich Lee, they gave you a lot of turkey."

"Yes, they did give me a lot of turkey. She gave me more turkey than the man in front of me. Maybe that was because I smiled at her."

"Lee, you weren't flirting, were you?" Christie said. She sometimes forgot and didn't calibrate her humor for Lee.

"No, I was not flirting, Christie. There is no one I would ever want to flirt with except you. I mean, you know what I mean, I really like you."

She was about to apologize for the joke; she had not meant to embarrass him, but she saw an unexpected opening, and something deep within her took over. "Lee, do you really like me, or do you love me?"

He looked at her and stopped chewing. He put down his sandwich.

"Will you still be my friend if I say I love you?" he was finally able to ask.

Her response was quick. "Yes, Lee I will still be your friend, but I hope you will see me as more than a friend because I love you."

"I do love you Christie." His look was as trusting as when he had been reading the story about the interloper in the White House.

"There, we both love each other," she said through a smile as the sun skipped from behind a stray cloud.

"What does this mean Christie?"

"I guess it can mean whatever you want it to," she said in an unexpected coquettish flair. Even with Lee she thought her declaration of feeling for him didn't need a dictionary.

"I hope it means we will spend a lot of time together, does this mean also that we will get married?"

"It might, Lee. People who love each other often get married. Do you know me well enough to marry me?"

"I love you, Christie."

"But do you think you know me well enough to marry me."

"I know I love you and would like to marry you."

She wondered how they could ever get married. She wanted to go to school. He didn't have a job. He was now going to be caring for his father. Yet, she was so drawn to him; he was something left of her brother. And she loved Lee. The seedling of her feelings as a teenager, much like the budding flowers around her, took its command from the spring. She had never felt that way about anyone else. She may have thought she had, but each time she had been with Lee, since the first time those months ago when she saw him at Audrey Plennington's spa, he was defined by the strongest of feelings; what so many refer to dismissively as puppy love. She thought at that moment that there was nothing at any age more romantic than puppy love.

"Let's just be in love for now," she said. She held his hand and after glancing behind lifted it up and kissed it. "You need to get back to your dad and I've got to get ready for work. I'll call you later tonight."

"Good bye Christie." Lee walked toward the hospital wondering what he was supposed to do now that he had told Christie he loved her.

CHAPTER 34

Jim Fitts had asked the nurse to close the blinds. At least as he looked through half-open eyes at the late-morning sun he thought he had. He'd asked her to turn off the light across from his bed; or was he going to ask her? The first face he saw in the recovery room said the burn on the back of his throat was normal, from the tube the anesthesiologist uses, only lasts a short time. He asked for a lozenge, or had he asked the nurse who came to him after he took the medicine? Percocet, he remembered the name because of how the nurse placed so much stress on the first part of the word. This nurse had an orchestra conductor's baton in her hand that waved in a smooth rhythm to choruses of Percocet, Percocet. His once-throbbing sur-gically-repaired areas were soothed by the calm buffeting of the sea against his inflatable life raft. From his count, he had been afloat for three days. Ellie, Lee, and D.H. sometimes pulled beside him in a twenty-four-footer. They'd talk for a while. Jim enjoyed their company; then they said they had to go and the boat throttled away leaving Jim to float again by himself. He remembered telling Lee that everything was fine; they'd be all right now and he hoped his son would forgive him. Lee yelled back from the depart-ing boat that he would. Then the throbbing started again.

Jim Fitts' thoughts turned to what were his first minutes of off and on consciousness in the hospital. "Shit," he remembered hearing the surgeon say. Then it was just a blather of incomplete sentences. "Mr. Fitts, we're going to stop the bleeding first, then we're going to close . . . and the artery should . . .. We're also going to have to fix this vascular mass by . . ." He shivered as they daubed at the blood that caked the lower part of his body. The shivering got worse. He never felt anything warmer than the blanket with which someone covered him.

Jim Fitts opened his eyes as she called to him; it had become routine since his surgery. He told the nurse that yes, his name was Jim Fitts. Having heard the password, she began her work in the sleepy light of night time in a hospital room. She took his blood pressure, pulse, and drew yet more blood. He wondered against the clang of her tools, why each nurse asked him his name. He knew his name and they must know his name. She handed him a tiny paper cup containing two small white pills that his entire body waited impatiently for him to swallow. "Anything I can get you Mr. Fitts?"

"A lozenge; a lozenge for my throat."

"I'll see if I can find one. I might have to call down to the pharmacy. I'll have to see if anyone's down there."

The small white pills bypassed the usual controls in the cockpit. Jim felt his legs and arms, then his head and back rise from the mattress. Even with the pills, his leg still throbbed. He'd have to ask for more pills. He started again to float in that small raft; the warming sun and the small lapping waves embraced him. Lee was in his own boat this time, and father and son spoke against the idling engine. Their words were loving and clear. It would be different this time, Jim Fitts said. All he wanted was to have his son there to talk to. Lee called for someone. Jim saw Marian Fitts standing next to Lee. She was as beautiful as the day he fell in love with her. Lee helped his mother into the raft with his father. The waves soaked through the bottom of her sun dress. Jim and Marian Fitts looked into each other's eyes.

"I shouldn't have left," she said.

"No, it was my fault; it will be better now." His head shot up from the bed. Marian Fitts, his wife. Had anyone told his wife what had happened to him? As his thoughts clanked unsteadily back to his first days in the hospital, he seemed to remember asking someone if they had called his wife. Maybe he had told them not to call his wife. He would have to ask someone in the morning. He wondered if she would come if she knew. He closed his eyes, laid his head back down, and traveled again to the open waters.

The ocean below basked in the morning's first light as the 757 turned up the coast. They'd be landing soon and the peace she knew during her string of cat naps was pierced by the cabin lights. The pilot's voice, split by static, announced landing information and Marian Fitts sat up as she readied herself for a day filled with painful uncertainty.

She looked into her purse to find the rental car information and she looked at the envelope she had for Lee. It was addressed and stamped a day earlier; before she had decided to go to her husband and her children. She could still mail it to Rev. Taylor as she had done with the others. Maybe she would hand it to Lee. Maybe he would need more than the usual forty dollars, but as she looked into her wallet, she saw there wasn't a whole lot more to give.

She pulled her small flight bag briskly through the terminal. Welcoming faces lit up as long-awaited travelers were spotted. There were no hugs for Marian and she thought more than briefly if she should inquire about seat availability on a flight there and then that would bring her back to her small apartment. Once in the car, she felt more at ease. She buckled her seat belt and flipped her hair back as she looked into the visor mirror. Her plan was to go right to the hospital. It was less likely that Ellie would make a scene there. She was sure her daughter and son would be at the hospital; but if not, she figured they would return shortly. Maybe she should call

Rev. Taylor. Maybe he could be there to back her up. He could tell her children she had no choice but to leave. It seemed to her that her story, her true story, would seem so less convincing with Jim Fitts in critical condition. Their poor father almost died and now their mother finally shows up with some sob story? Marian Fitts could leave. She'd see her husband first; but she could leave right after that if she had to. She could slip back into her rental car and drive back to the airport. She would have a gin and tonic on the plane and assure herself that she had done what was right, and at no little cost considering the lost day's wages, the airline ticket, the rental car. She had done what was right and would be back soon in the only chair at her kitchen table. She had become resigned to what seemed the impossibility of getting her family back.

Lee was alone in the waiting area when the elevator door opened and his mother stepped off. They looked at each other, chipping away at more than ten years-worth of features they hoped would bring them to images they remembered. Slow steps took her to him. She now had to look higher to see his eyes. "Lee," she said as she embraced him and her voice cracked. He put his arms around the woman he had known all these years solely through the envelopes containing four ten-dollar bills.

"Thank you for the money, Mother. I have saved most of it. It was very nice of you to send me the money and I did as you said, I did not tell Dad or Ellie about the money you sent me. I did not know if you would come to see Dad."

She stepped back letting her hand slip down the side of his arm. The way he spoke, the way he looked at her; she had deceived herself all these years and had remembered him the way she wanted to. All her husband's taunting, his screams calling his son a quitter, a coward; all Jim Fitt's dark psychology and relentless bullying hadn't brought back the son that left them that day. "Lee, I am here because I thought it was the right thing to do. I wanted to see your father and I wanted to see you and Ellie. That's why I'm here, Lee."

"I am glad you are here mother. It has only been three days, but it seems to me much longer that Dad has been in the hospital. The doctor and the nurses say he is getting better and that they see progress. But the doctor said Dad is still in the woods; that he is not out of the woods yet. He was more awake this morning and when I took his hand, he closed his eyes and smiled and said 'Lee, remember what I've told you since you were a little boy? Always have a nice firm handshake; that's very important in the world.' He spoke those words very slowly. That is the most I have heard him say since he has been in the hospital."

"Where is Ellie?"

"She will be here soon. She had to go to the store with D.H. before she came to the hospital."

"Lee, maybe I'll go in to see your father now. I might have to leave soon and it's probably best that I see him now."

"Mother, where do you live? You never told me where you live."

"No, I never told anyone where I lived. Rev. Taylor probably figured out from the post mark on the outer envelope when I mailed you your money. It was better that no one knew; maybe it still is. Come, let's go see your father, we can talk later."

The hospital-clean smell hung like a veil fluttering in the air of taut hope found in every CCU room. Marian looked at the monitors and they looked back at her, their electrical breaths never losing a beat. This world belonged to the monitors; they discerned truth in the CCU in a fashion that eschewed bedside manner. If they had to, they would erupt into a spasm of lights and alarms and quickly-changing numbers with no care for how the truth, sometimes the deadly truth, was received. With their report that modern medicine was failing at the hands of some superior force, the monitors would suck up all hope in the room. Marian Fitts had better understand there was nothing special about her husband, the monitors would call 'em as they saw 'em.

She looked at her husband. Jim Fitts was sleeping, paler and thinner than she'd ever seen him. This was the man from whom she told those who cared, that she had to leave? She stood back as Lee reached gently for his father's shoulder and whispered something into his ear. His father's eyes opened.

"Yes, she is here right now. She has come to see how you are doing. She must care about you very much if she came here to see you. Mom, come over here."

Marian half-stepped to the side of the bed as Jim Fitts' head tilted forward. There was no expression on his face. "Jim, Oh Jim, I can't believe this happened." She reached for his hand and held it. Jim Fitts smiled as if not remembering that his wife had left him, as if he didn't know that his son hadn't sent a ball through the uprights in more than ten years. Then his focus sharpened and he withdrew his hand.

"Why are you here? Why have you come back?" came the words that crawled from the dry walls of his mouth.

"I can leave if you want me to, Jim. Would you feel better if I left?"

"No, no he does not want you to leave, Mother," said Lee as he rushed to save his dream of his parents reuniting from the same quick spiral of misunderstanding that had driven them apart.

"Lee, son, I am talking to your father. This is something only he can answer."

Jim Fitts said nothing, then grabbed for Marian's hand as tears made their way down the side of his face. "I'm sorry. I'm so sorry for everything. I want you to stay. I want you to stay." She reached for a tissue and blotted his eyes.

"I didn't know you were here Mother. You never said anything about coming," Ellie said as she moved to the side of the bed. "I don't think you should be applying so much pressure to his hand." She removed her father's hand from her mother's grasp. Ellie established quickly, by checking the monitors and smoothing the bed linens, that she was in charge of her father's recovery.

"Ellie, I have very good news for you. Mom asked Dad if he wanted her to stay and Dad said yes."

"I'm sorry Lee but I don't know why I would think that was good news. And I don't want to discuss anything that will get father upset. You know we've been able to do without her help and I see no reason why that would change."

His parents' quick exchange had patched up everything as far as he was concerned. Ellie's words were like a brick through the front window of the new house Lee saw himself and his parents living in.

"I'm sorry I didn't let you know I was coming. My plans were uncertain, but I won't be here long. I think I'll go downstairs for a while, get a cup of coffee."

Jim Fitts caught his wife's glance. He had told her he wanted her to stay, but now she was leaving. "I told her I was sorry," Jim told his daughter. "I don't want her to leave again."

"She'll leave just as she left us before. You never left us Daddy."

"She was right to leave. You all were right to leave if you wanted to. I told Lee I was sorry. I did things and said things." The Percocet pulled the covers over his head. If his daughter said anything, it was in a foreign language.

Lee followed his mother to the elevator. "You said you would come back."

"I'll be back," Marian Fitts said as she smiled. "What do you want me to get for you downstairs?"

The elevator door opened. "I just want you to come back."

"Here's my jacket. Hold it. You know it's too chilly outside for me to leave without my jacket."

Lee walked back to his father's room. He felt the years that hadn't been as he held his mother's jacket. It was going to be different now. He knew what his mother and father had said to each other. Ellie hadn't. Maybe she would understand once she saw mother's jacket.

CHAPTER 35

"So, your dad's been in the hospital for three days now?" Reid Fletcher asked. "Damn, this is a pretty good tuna fish sandwich for coffee shop food."

"Yes, today will make three days that my father is in the hospital," Lee answered.

"Man, I still can't believe this whole thing. I knew there was something wrong when I couldn't get in touch with you for so long. Don't worry Lee, we'll get you through all this. And now that your mother's back; are you really glad your mother's back?"

"Yes, I am very glad. I am going to see my mother tonight when she comes back to the hospital. I do not know if she will stay. I know my father and I want her to stay, but Ellie is still very mad."

"Yeah, I know that has always really rubbed your sister the wrong way. I mean, I'm not a member of the family, but your father got a little out of control sometimes."

"Things are going to be better now Reid, and if my mother stays, things will be a lot better. I will just have to talk to Ellie."

"Yeah, talk to your sister. I mean, those years are long past, man. Start fresh, that's the best way to do it. And your dad's going to recover just fine. You know, when I was waiting for you this morning, I was reading the paper and it's amazing what happens in the world of medicine. I mean you just never know what's going to happen. They had this woman who was in a coma for ten years. The doctors said nothing could be done. The daughter was talking about how the doctor said she should think about pulling the old plug; just let her go. Well you know what? The daughter is sitting by her mother's bed and all of a sudden, her mother's eyes open and her mother starts moving her fingers. Ain't that somethin? I mean they wanted to pull the plug. Hey, I'll tell you about another thing I read in the paper, you know that guy you used to work for, Dan Calvert; the guy that lost the election? They arrested his ass. He has some company that was buying up real estate through some phony program using government loans. He was supposed to fix the property, something to help poor people with their rent. Well, seemed the money he was getting wasn't doing what it was supposed to be doing. His lawyer said it's a misunderstanding. Those guys always say there's a misunderstanding; I mean what else are they going to say?"

"Dan Calvert, arrested?"

"That's what the paper said. They had someone, I think it was his campaign manager, who said he was shocked to hear about the charges and if it was true, it could have a negative impact on Dan Calvert's future in politics."

"Christie was right, now I know she was really right."

"Well, I didn't like that guy too much when I met him that time at the rally. Something about him just wasn't right; his handshake or something."

"You did a lot of reading in the paper this morning, Reid."

"I try to stay up with the news whenever I can. Hey, when I spoke with Christie she said she had been up to some state university and that's why she wasn't home when I was first looking for her. What's that all about?"

"Christie is a very good student and her professor at the community college thinks she can get a scholarship to the state university. When I spoke to her on the phone this morning, she said she had some very good news and would tell me all about it when she came to the hospital tonight."

"State? That's like five hours from here. Where the hell does that leave you? I mean you and Christie been kinda tight lately. She's gonna be a long way away, man. And you know, lot of guys at that school. I mean, you never know what happens in a situation like this. She could become a changed person."

"There is a bus that goes from here to the state university. I have not told Christie about the bus yet. I was going to surprise her. I would take the bus to the state university every weekend. That is my plan I am going to tell her."

"I think you're missing the big picture here, man. Your plan might work for a while, but it's gonna be big bucks. I mean, bus fare, got to find some place to stay, and you have to eat."

"I can bring some food from home. I can make small portions and have it last the whole weekend."

"Lee, you're still missing the big picture. You have to get a snapshot in your mind of what I'm saying. Christie's going to have all these college friends, they're all going to have something in common and then they'll all have degrees so they can get some big- time jobs and there's gonna be guys going to hit on her. I don't see you in that snapshot."

"I will be in that snapshot. Christie said she loves me, and I told Christie that I love her."

"But that's before she gets up to state; it'll be a different ball game, man."

"I will be in your snapshot," Lee shot back.

"All right, all right, calm down. Damn, look at me; I'm supposed to be here trying to comfort you because of your dad and everything. Lee, I'm your friend. I just don't want to see you get hurt anymore." Reid paused and took the deep breath he thought appropriate for the important information he was about to share with his best friend. "You know, there was this guy once at work, he was a smart guy, always reading the newspaper or some magazine. I was talking to him at lunch one time, and I think he got this from one of his magazines, but this is what he told me. He said it was the best advice he'd ever seen. Ready for this, listen carefully: '*It's a big universe. Only live in as much universe as you can handle.*' And this was a smart guy, so you know this is good advice. I'm just trying to help you man. Don't go getting into things in the universe you can't handle."

"Reid, I know you are my friend. But I will be in your snapshot."

"Okay. Look, I got to go. I told them I'd be a little late, but I gotta go," Reid said as he took a last swallow of coffee and picked up the check. "I got this. Have a truck load of bushes waiting for me. No rain, and they got us planting bushes. Damn bushes are gonna die, just like last summer during the drought when they had us planting bushes. Look, call you man. You know if there's anything I can do, let me know."

Reid put his arm around Lee then walked out of the coffee shop.

As Lee turned he noticed someone from his canvassing days. She was pushing a stroller carrying a toddler wearing a neck support.

"Hello, Mrs. Aggarwal," Lee said.

Mrs. Aggarwal stopped. "Hello, why you're the boy from the election."

"Yes, that is right. My name is Lee Fitts. I was at your house during the campaign for Dan Calvert for Council."

"I remember well. My father, my husband, and I were very impressed with your honesty."

"My boss was not happy. He fired me. But I thought it important to do the right thing."

"Doing the right thing is very important, Lee. What brings you to the hospital?"

"My Dad is here. He was trying to stop a robbery and he was stabbed. He is in critical condition."

"Lee, I am so sorry to hear that. If we can help in any way, please let us know. I am usually at the hospital on Tuesdays and Thursdays for Raymond's treatments. Raymond has muscular dystrophy but he's making some progress with his therapy here and at home."

Raymond had been looking at Lee. Something in that look made Lee want to do something to help the boy. "Raymond is a very handsome little boy. Thank you for offering to help my father. Is there something I can do to help you with Raymond?"

Mrs. Aggarwal thought about that; at times, she could get desperate. "Lee, I might take you up on your kind offer. Raymond has someone who helps him with his exercises at home, but sometimes she cancels on short notice and I can't get off work. My father is at home, but he can't do these exercises with Raymond by himself. It would be so nice if . . ."

"I would be glad to help, but I do not know how do to those exercises."

"Oh Lee, that would help us so much. They really are quite easy; my father can show you."

"Okay," Lee said as he began to write his phone number on a scrap of paper.

"Thank you so much, Lee. You're a fine boy."

He smiled, and waved good-bye to Raymond.

Lee headed toward the elevators through the lobby's morning hustle-bustle of visitors, incoming patients, discharged patients being wheeled to the front by volunteers, doctors trailing other doctors, flower deliverymen, technicians pushing carts of medical devices, nurses in flower-covered smocks and a nervous air that said anything could happen in a hospital, that's why there's a chapel.

Jim Fitts smiled at his son and Lee took his father's outstretched hand. His father's face was clean-shaven and the part in his still damp hair reminded Lee of how his own hair looked when he first went to Sunday school. Jim Fitts' pillows had been fluffed and his bed linens neatly tucked. Anyone listening to Jim and his son talk would detect no hint of how things had been during those years which as Reid said were now long past. Jim spoke of the sunlight through his window and of telling the nurse about how good he felt to be alive to see the sunlight. Breakfast had tasted good to him. The eggs were a little cold but the tea was hot. Jim Fitts asked Lee why his mother had come to the hospital. He asked his son a lot of questions about Marian Fitts. He asked in that tone Lee heard in his head when he thought about Christie. Jim Fitts closed his eyes. He opened them again when he heard his daughter's voice; he knew instinctively not to ask any more questions about his wife. Ellie adjusted the pillows, smoothed the blanket, and rustled up her father's hair. His hair never looked that way, she told Lee in an annoyed tone, even though she realized that the nurse meant well. Lee watched as his sister got up to pull the curtains. Jim Fitts pulled on the straw his daughter put against his lips. He drew and then stopped. He needed sleep. The nurse helloed as she put her clipboard on the bed: tubes, check; IV, check; monitor's electrical faces, check. She picked up her clipboard and left, her high-pitched thank you dissolving slowly behind her. Ellie sat down in the straight-back chair that had been her command post for the past three days.

"Ellie, I am going to go out to take a walk," Lee said.

She said what she knew was obvious, "Lee you really like to walk, don't you?"

"Yes, I like to walk. I think I am pretty good at walking and I have gotten Christie to walk more. She said she noticed having more energy after our walking. Things are clearer in my head when I walk and sometimes I am very surprised I have not even noticed how far I have walked."

"Maybe you should get a pedometer; it will tell you how far you've walked."

"But, I do not want to know how far I have walked. I know if I have walked enough by feeling the backs of my legs. I know how big those muscles should feel and if at the end of the week, if I need to, I will walk up and down hills."

Ellie turned her head to look at her brother, never seeing the slight smile Lee's words brought to her father's face. "You take your time," she said." That sounds like a good system." She knew that if anything happened to her, her brother would never be able to sit in the command post.

Lee knew he had to get outside and as he opened the door, he let out the gasp of a long-submerged snorkeler breaking the surface. He had to have the oxygen of his walking to think about everything Reid had said. He would have to walk over to Mrs. Plennington's spa right now. Christie would be at work. Christie would have to tell him about the state university and tell him everything Reid said wasn't true. Once Christie cleared everything up, then Lee could go back to worrying about his father. First things first, he thought as he began the three-mile walk to the spa. He looked back at the one building of the hospital still visible through the trees. There was another mall opening up, maybe six stores not much different than the -- he counted -- the eight strip malls on either side of the highway now snarled by a web of wires from which traffic lights dangled. As he walked through the unfinished parking lot he thought about all that grass gone forever, grass that would never gently lift each of his steps. He was now on the edge of the road, uncomfortably close to groaning trucks and impatient minivans. He knew the lights were changing when he heard the engines leave their idle and he tried to move back as far as he could from the road without breaking stride. It was easy to twist your ankle on the gravel and debris on the side of the road. This was not one of the places he would walk if he had a choice. He wondered if Ellie thought he just went out for a walk around the hospital grounds. He caught himself when he stepped on a piece of broken plastic. Just over the rusted, green metal bridge, with the big rivets, began a stretch of fields where struggling grass lay under the threat of lot-for-sale signs. Lee knew it wouldn't be long.

Beyond the new mobile homes standing under a galaxy of different colored aluminum pennants tossing in the breeze, the full, green branches came into view. Lee smiled, almost thought of waving. His feet pushed forward in a more determined gait. The warm sun had brought the beginning of a sweat to his workout. The trees seemed to draw a boundary in front of houses that had been in town long before the invention of the traffic light. He was soon in the park that hosted the Dan Calvert for Council Rally. The knoll looked the same as the morning they arrived to begin preparations for what Lee had been led to believe would be the defining moment in the campaign of a real man of the people. He looked at the spot where his father threw the football at him. That was another man, not his father.

Lee wondered if Dan Calvert would be going to jail. Christie had told him about Dan Calvert. Terri Herman had told him also. Lee hoped Terri wouldn't be sent to jail. She just did what her brother told her. She wouldn't do well in a jail cell. Maybe she and her brother had left and were now somewhere managing the campaign of another man of the people. He remembered Sanford Black's battle plan for the rally. One good thing about Sanford, he stuck to his guns; he didn't care if some people wanted other flavors of ice cream. He told Lee at the end of the rally that if he had to do it again, he would go solo with vanilla. Why give people something they want just because they want it? You give them one thing and there will be no stopping them. Sanford said if the people knew what was good for them, they wouldn't need the good people who aspire to political office. Lee agreed when Sanford asked him never to forget that basic principle of politics.

Lee lifted his foot on to the sidewalk. The broad shoulders of the trees above switched off in a flick the sun's heat. Mrs. Plennington's spa was maybe ten blocks away, but it was ten blocks of green lawns with fine edges, mulched shrub beds, stone walkways, trees with an armor of strong bark and towering branches that gave even more authority to well-sculpted houses. Houses, Lee thought, that might have been around when President Theodore Roosevelt visited the town which according to the historical sign was 1902. The first street was Augusta and following the alphabet, he would turn left on Harrison, and then it was another three blocks to the Spa. He loved to walk on these streets. Sometimes, people out in their yards or walking their dogs would recognize Lee from all of his walks and wave. Some people just stared. But he loved this area of town; loved it even though he knew he would never be able to afford one of these houses.

He pulled from his pocket, the slip of paper his mother had given him. Maybe he would call her. She had asked him to call her. He put the piece of paper back into his pocket. Thoughts of his father in his hospital bed, thoughts of his mother whom he should call because he hadn't seen her in over ten years were washed away with the force of a fire hose by his thoughts of Christie and everything that Reid said might happen. He tried to turn the water off; his mother and father were more important at this point. But the forceful spray continued and kept his mind on only one thing.

When he got to Harrison Street he turned in the opposite direction of the Fitness Fling Spa, went two streets over, headed in the direction of the hospital and when he got back to Augusta, turned and headed back to Harrison. He did this twice. He had to kill time. Christie worked till five; she had told him she would be at the hospital at six-thirty. He walked and walked. He got to the spa at four o'clock. Mrs. Plennington's office was dark. He had never seen it dark before. He looked around, but he didn't see her. This made things even more disturbing. Did it mean that Mrs, Plennington wasn't at her spa or would she jump out from some door and ask him some tricky questions, put her hand on him, and make him smile that frozen smile? He kept an eye out for her as he walked toward Christie. Her back was towards him as she discussed some exercise with a group of four elderly women. The women turned their attention from Christie to the advancing Lee. Christie turned. "Lee, what are you doing here? Did something happen to your father?" She rushed to him while her class waited for his answer.

"No, my father is still at the hospital and I think he is getting better. He was sleeping when I left."

"Then why are you here now? Remember I said I would meet you at the hospital and I would tell you about my visit? You know," she whispered so the elderly ladies wouldn't hear, "to the state university."

"This is about your visit to the state university," he whispered back. "I need to talk with you now."

"Now? I'm in the middle of a class."

"But it has to be now. I have tried to wait till later, I have walked for five hours around and around trying to wait till later, but I have to talk to you now."

Christie's impatience evaporated as she saw a particularly troubled look on Lee's face. "Ladies, I'm terribly sorry, but you'll have to excuse me for a minute. Maybe you could brush up on that exercise we started with."

Christie led Lee to a partition behind the check-in desk. As she patted her neck and face, the towel became an atomizer spritzing a citrus orchard scent his way. "Lee, what's this all about? I thought something had happened to your dad. You're sure he's okay?"

"Yes, my father is doing better. I will have to go back to the hospital soon. My mother will be there tonight. I was very glad to see my mother and so was my father, I did not think that would ever happen, that my father would be glad to see my mother. But my father has changed."

"Lee, I need to get back to my class. Come back in an hour, I'll go home and change and then we can go to the hospital."

"I need to speak to you now, Christie, about the state university. After your trip to the state university, do you think you will go there in the fall?"

"Well, I liked the school and they were very encouraging about financial aid."

"So, you are going to go?"

"Lee, I said we can talk about this later." She looked at her class. One woman, running in place, was clearly annoyed at this break in her training regimen.

"I need to know now."

"Yes, I think I would like to go."

"Do you remember you said you loved me and I said I loved you? I will always love you. No matter what, even if you are away at the state university. But I need to know if you will always love me no matter what, even after you meet all those other people going to college. I will love you forever. Will you love me forever?" The other exercisers stopped their chatter and while not as annoyed as the woman running in place, nevertheless began to stare at Christie and Lee. Christie gave a nervous I'll be right there wave.

"Lee, what's gotten into you? You're just going to have to wait. I told you to come back in an hour."

"So, you are not going to tell me that when you go away to the state university, that no matter what you will love me forever?"

"I am not telling you anything right now. I want you to come back at five o'clock. I have got to get back to my class."

"I will not be back here at five o'clock," said Lee as he strode away.

"Lee!" But it was too late, he was in the doorway, then gone.

"Mrs. Plennington, Christie left us just standing here. She just left us and went chasing out the door after some boy she had been having an argument with." That's exactly what the woman who had stood with folded arms would say. Christie walked back to the exercisers. She'd have to stay a few minutes after five.

Lee walked for the next hour. It was over. Reid had been right. Christie didn't have to say anything. Lee knew if he showed up at the state university in a disguise, he'd see Christie walking with a new boyfriend and talking with all her college friends about things that he'd never be able to understand. He thought about his father. It was getting dark. He slurped the last of a large chocolate shake that had been drained with none of the enjoyment that comes with savoring a chocolate shake. He tossed the cup into the trash and then walked back four blocks to stand in line behind a man ordering a dinner of a double cheeseburger, large order of French fries, apple pie, cookie and Diet Coke. The same girl who had waited on Lee earlier handed him another large chocolate shake. "Like these things, hey?" she said. She wasn't pretty and she wasn't funny. He looked behind the counter, at the customers in the seats, at the people in line behind him. None of these fast-food makers or fast-food eaters people cared about him. He wasn't angry at them, even as he felt himself freefalling into the big barrel where all these people lived. He'd have to get to know them; there would be no way now of ever getting out of the barrel. He wondered if they would ever talk about anything but the food and drinks they were making and ordering. Ellie and his mother could take care of his father. They would have to understand that they could only wave to him from the rim of the barrel. He wondered if his sister would plead with Christie; please help my brother get out of the barrel. Lee saw Christie angrily refusing. Your brother embarrassed me so at the spa, Christie told Ellie. Christie was probably already thinking about having a new boyfriend at state university.

The second shake was gone as Lee came to the end of the street which like an off ramp of an airport led to the J street and then to the main runway toward the hospital. Regular visiting hours were over in an hour. He looked at the pay phone in front of the convenience store. He should call, but what would he say? Everyone would be angry. He reached for the card he had gotten from the nurse and deposited several coins into the phone. His stomach hung unfamiliarly over his belt, just slightly, and the two shakes began to harden like poured concrete. Sugar streamed through his head and his muscles tingled. His body hung heavily on the phone post. Five rings. Maybe he should call a cab.

"CCU?" came a voice that drilled each letter into the other.

"This is Lee Fitts. My father is in the CCU and I wanted to see if my sister or mother . . . "

"I know they are both looking for you, please wait one second."

Lee knew they would be mad. He hadn't bothered to call his mother the whole day. She would probably leave again. Ellie wouldn't be happy. Even though she had put herself in charge of their father's care, Lee had no right not to be there. And Lee's father was sure to have asked for his son.

"Lee, where are you?"

"Ellie, I'm very sorry. I know I shouldn't . . ."

"Lee, don't speak and listen to me. How long will it take you to get here?"

"Maybe forty-five minutes if I walk fast."

"Try to get a ride or take a cab. Dad, is not doing very well. The doctors are not sure what caused it. Get here soon. You need to get here soon." Lee heard a click and then hung up his phone.

He looked at a faded sticker for a cab company on the phone. He could barely make out the numbers, but found there was no more change in his pocket. Panic pulled at him. His body hadn't expected that anything, even panic, would have thought Lee was in any shape to run. But his legs like a team of resting horses awakened by the snap of desperate reins, propelled him. Past Jefferson, Independence, Hanover, as he thought about the G, F, E, D, C, B, A streets in front of him, he felt a stitch in his side. Listing to one side, he rubbed at the area just above his belt. Running turned to a fast walk, at least until Edwards Avenue. He ran faster now, trying to make up for lost time. The two shakes were toying with him and he thought he would have to stop to puke. By the time he got to Boyce, the feeling passed, but he was still holding his side. He was starting to cry, and pulled his hand from his side to wipe his eyes. He wondered how many times his father had asked for him? Should he have tried to get a cab; maybe he would have been at the hospital by now. Why hadn't Ellie or his mother offered to pick him up? They must be really mad at him. Or maybe they did not want to leave his father. Lee repeated to himself that even if his father weren't doing very well, the doctors would do something. It wasn't as if his father were going to die while they drove to where Lee was. At Augusta Avenue, a thought draped in black veils landed hard; maybe his father was dying.

The last light from Augusta faded as Lee hit the fields. His shoes pounded over a frayed mat of litter and twisted arms of weeds. Rumbling trucks and SUVs laughed at the speed limit signs and were not reluctant to grab the shoulder on which Lee was running. Lee moved away from the road. The stitch had eased up some and he didn't have to bend any more. He found himself picking up the pace as he looked ahead at the quilt of ever-changing reds, yellows and greens that hung above the streets between the strip malls. Beyond those stores was the driveway leading to the hospital.

The dim lights masked how close the tramp hauler was coming toward him. Realizing at last, Lee stepped quickly in almost a leap. His foot landed on a baseball-size chunk of asphalt hiding in a sinister green canopy. He rolled, the truck was even with him now, but as the macadam shot out from under his heel, the spin took him away from the road. In that split second, he waited for the landing and one of two things: a thanks to God *or* a cry to the heavens for help. There was no thanks; his ankle had twisted badly, his palms stung from the debris that had bitten into them, and his head had hit something hard. As he got up he saw the truck's lone rear light flicker in the distance. He could walk, but the pain spiked up his leg. He patted at the cut on his head, some blood, but the flame from the abrasion soon died. He was on his way again, like the soldier he had read about in the front lines of a Civil War battle who had been wounded, but knew his duty demanded that he continue until he reached his objective. He was almost to the last of the strip malls before the turn into the hospital. The pain from his ankle buckled his knee and he began to hop through that last parking lot. An elderly couple bringing groceries to their card stopped and apprehensively watched the hopping boy with the gash in his head. They unloaded their groceries and quickly got into the car not knowing if the hopping boy would turn and start after them.

Lee began up the hospital drive and was now supporting his leg by bending it back and holding on to the cuff of his pants leg. When his arm couldn't hold any longer, his foot lowered to the ground and the ankle burst with pain upon each step. He slowed as he got to the entrance and leaned on the rails as he walked into the hospital. Walking across the hall to the elevator, his leg, surrendering to the pain, buckled and he leaped for the railing. He clung to the inside of the elevator. The door opened and he saw his father's doctor at the end of the hall. Lee walked past his father's room. The view from the hall allowed him to see his father's legs under the covers just as they had been that morning.

He'd go in and apologize to his father for not being there after he spoke with the doctor. Dr. Centers, the young doctor who Lee had come to believe could fix anything, shook Lee's hand. He noted Lee's limp, but said nothing. He motioned Lee into a small conference room, where the nurse on duty when his father was admitted, sat at a white table with used coffee cups and someone's crumpled lunch bag pushed to one side. She placed the coffee pot back on the heating pad and handed a cup to the doctor who suggested that Lee sit down.

"I'm sorry. We did everything we could, but it happened very quickly. His pre-existing condition, the vascular mass, it ruptured across from the earlier repairs we had made. I'm sorry. I know your sister and mother tried to get in touch with you. I believe your mother left a while ago to see if she could find you. Your sister and her husband were in your father's room; they may have gone downstairs."

"Is my father . . .?" Lee knew he didn't need to finish his question. The look on the faces of the doctor and the nurse had given him his answer.

"We're very sorry," the nurse said. "Do you want to go to your father's room?"

Lee arose from his seat. He felt no protest from his injured ankle. Is this, he wondered, what someone says to you when your father dies –we're sorry? He looked at the doctor who had brought the cup to his lips and took a swallow of coffee. He wondered how many times over the years the doctor had to say he was sorry and then, not able to do anything else, sipped his cup of coffee. There was probably nothing more final that someone could say other than very sorry.

He approached his father's room as if the older Fitts were in a clearing in some fairy tale's enchanted forest. There were his father's legs. He stopped. He had misunderstood the doctor and the nurse. They were very sorry for something else. He believed in the magic of their medicine, a magic that had kept his father alive. He knew when he turned the corner and walked into the room, his father would be resting much as he had been that morning. But the magic had ended. The tubes were gone from his father's body and his face had been washed and his hair combed according to how some nurse's assistant thought it should be. The monitors were dark, the electrical frenzy wiped from their screens and their stand pushed away from the bed.

There were no tears in Lee's eyes. He was still taking it in. His father looked no different than at any other time he was sleeping, but medicine, everything the hospital had to offer was through with Jim Fitts. No one needed to check his charts, no one would have to bring him anything to eat or drink ever again. The warmth of his father's body was leaving. Lee pulled up the blanket to try to save that warmth for as long as possible. Maybe it was only a temporary chill. After all, who wouldn't have such a chill after going through what Jim Fitts had been through? Lee tried, but he knew it was over.

He looked at Ellie's Bible; the one she had gotten at her confirmation. He began to think in slow motion as he stared at the book. When she was small, it always went right back into the box after she finished reading it. He had never seen his sister as mad at him as the time he got cookie crumbs down deep into the pages of her Bible. She complained for months that she hadn't been able to get all the crumbs out. Amidst the worn colored ribbon markers was a torn piece of white paper. Lee opened to the page; it was Psalm 91, the psalm Ellie asked Rev. Taylor to read to her father. Lee didn't know why his sister had requested that particular passage, but Ellie and Lee both saw their father's jaw muscles clench as the biblical music made its way to his ears. He looked at the open book then looked at his father. Lee began reading Psalm 91 – his voice seizing at some points – one last time to his father. There were words Lee didn't understand. He didn't know what "pinions" were and he didn't know what a "buckler" was and he didn't understand why if God wouldn't let any evil come to someone who believed in Him and if he kept away "the plague that stalks in the darkness" and "the sickness that lays waste at mid-day" then why would his father not have gotten better? Maybe God didn't think Jim Fitts believed hard enough, that he should have loved God more. "With long life will I satisfy him, and show him my salvation." That must be the case, Lee thought as he slowly closed the book, because his father was only forty-five years old. Lee wished that God could have been more understanding, yet as he thought more about it, maybe his father was just beginning the second part of his long life.

"Lee," his sister said as she put her arms around him. The two stood huddled in the twilight of the psalm's pronouncements. "He called for you. Your name was the last thing we heard him say. I thought you would be back before we lost him. Mother left an hour ago to look for you; she has Christie looking for you too."

Lee and Ellie looked at the man lying in front of them. It was coming to them; he would never open his eyes and climb out of that bed.

CHAPTER 36

The days after Jim Fitts' funeral wobbled like mercury over the lines of the calendar. Lee sat most of the day at the table and stared into Jim Fitts' empty chair. He slept on the couch at night. His mother realized she would have to stay longer; her son was slipping further away. He answered "yes, Mother" or "no, Mother." Rev. Taylor had been little help, even though she found bits of sunshine in his homey sermonettes. Something about him was different to her. She noticed it first when he spoke at the funeral. It was as if he were holding back some of his compassion and keeping it for himself. Ellie would spend short periods in the morning with them and the bridge between mother and daughter that had been damaged in the maelstrom was now open to light traffic. Reid stopped by several times. If ever anyone could hold up both ends of a conversation it was Reid. He really cared about Lee. "Best friends, man. You know we'll always be best friends," she heard him tell her son. He brought cookies the first two visits, "Got to eat, man, you're losing too much weight." Both bags lay unopened on the table. "Ankle's getting better, Mrs. Fitts, yeah, swelling's gone down a lot."

Christie came over after work. She had stood beside Lee, often hand in hand, at every part of the grieving process. Lee asked her nothing about the fall, about state university. His mother had heard from someone about it, but Christie painted her answers in such broad strokes of washed-out colors that no one could tell where she would be in the fall. Lee knew, and when she visited and held his hand as they sat at the table, he felt that something inside him should care. Christie's hand, her presence, her watching television was the comfort that most soothed him, but it wouldn't bring back his father. He had taken the big hit that makes ones that follow automatically easier to absorb. If she left for the state university, that would have to be that. He thought that would just have to be that. Christie's hand slipped from his as she kissed him and rose from the couch to go. He feared that one time when she did that and left it would be for good.

Marian Fitts would be away for three days. There would be a lot to do. She'd call Goodwill to come for the few pieces of furniture in her apartment and assorted small appliances. She thought the paperbacks that had sheltered her in their worlds the past ten years would fill two, maybe three boxes. Some she would bring home to Lee; she would read to him. Most of her clothes would go as well. There would be no room in that small house where she and Lee would be living. She had enough in savings till Lee received his share of Jim Fitts' life insurance which would be about ten–thousand dollars. She had been reading the classifieds. Maybe, she could get something part-time until Lee got better. She had been wrong to leave those years ago. It was her turn now. In her mind was the fierce determination of a lioness returning to cubs she had lost. Ellie could be turned. It would take some time; patience was key.

At the airport, shortly before boarding, Marian tried to reach her supervisor in the garden department; no answer again. Her boss, Reggie, short for Regina, Wilcox, hadn't been happy about Marian's leaving during the crucial days of setting up the spring stock of flowers, shrubs, tools, fertilizer; everything the guild of amateur gardeners emerging from their cocoons demanded. Her supervisor's only world was the garden stock which she commanded with a well-cultivated determination that shone strongest as she raised with her fork lift to the highest level a pallet of landscaping stones. She had agreed grudgingly to let Marian leave; it was only supposed to be for a few days, but it was now seven. Her employee had taken advantage of her; Marian knew that's what Reggie was thinking. She was probably angry and when she got that way, she drove her forklift a little more carelessly. Marian saw little hope of getting a reference which she knew she would need when she got back and looked for a job.

Lee went back to the table after opening the door. Reid followed and sat across from him. "Don't got long, got a load of lawns to get to. Damn, the start of lawn season is one big merry-go-round. I mean the smell of that spring grass gets you pumped. We have a summer like last year though and that grass will be brown in another month. We get paid to cut it regardless, that's the good thing about the landscape business," Reid said as he reached down to tie the frayed laces on his work boots. "You're looking better man, looking better. But I tell you, you got to eat. Did you have breakfast?"

"I did not have breakfast, but I did have a glass of orange juice."

"Glass of orange juice? You need more than that." He got a bowl, milk and a spoon. "Lee, I'm not leaving till you finish the Raisin Bran, all of it, and I told you I ain't got much time, so I'd appreciate you cleaning up that bowl pretty quick."

Lee began to eat, chewing as hard and fast as he could, mouthful after mouthful.

"What's that?" Reid asked as he pointed to a small metal box, one of the boxes that gift cookies come in, on the table next to Lee's arm."

"CRUNCH, GARBLE," Lee said.

"Wait a minute, finish what's in your mouth, I can't understand what you're saying."

Lee swallowed. "I found this in my father's closet. It was under some old sweaters."

"Well, what is that stuff in the box?"

Lee pulled at the edges of the top which he handed to Reid. "These are some of my father's mementoes. These are things I know are, I mean were, very important to my father."

"What do you mean mementoes?"

Lee pulled out a sheet of paper folded into thirds, now ivory-tinged, and limp as a dollar bill due to be retired from circulation. He removed a small pin. "I got this for perfect Sunday School attendance one year. I felt bad because Ellie was going to get one too, but got really sick. I remember she was crying and my mother and father were crying, and I was crying, but she was the sickest I ever saw her, and my dad said she would have to stay home."

"What the hell is that, some kind of model car?"

Lee lifted out a red, wooden car, with black plastic wheels. "This is the Pinewood Derby car my dad and I made when I was in the Cub Scouts. They had this big long track going downhill, and our car won the first race, but only came in second in the finals."

"What's that paper say?"

Lee unfolded a small piece of note paper and handed it to Reid.

"Says here, 'Dear Mr. Fitts, I usually don't write a note like this, but wanted you to know that I've been watching Lee in PE class; the boys have been playing flag football. Lee and several of the boys were kicking the football. I couldn't believe my eyes when I watched Lee kick the ball. He had five of five over the crossbars, the last one from thirty-five yards out. He has poise, timing, and what an old kicking coach told me only the best have: quick muscle twitch that just snaps that leg around. I never saw anything like this in middle school. You may want to contact Coach Richards on the football team. Sincerely, Ed Cannon.' So, I guess this is what started the whole thing with your father. Damn, Ed Cannon, I hated that jerk. He always had me running laps because I didn't clean my gym uniform. Pretty clear what was the big-time thing in your father's life. You know I found something in my father's closet once, that was before he left, under some comforter that stunk like hell. Know what it was, a bag of skin magazines. 'Member I brought one into school one day?"

"Yes, I do remember, but I did not think it was very nice for you to show it to those girls."

"Whadya mean, they all seen stuff like that before. Anyway, your father was all over that kicking stuff like nothing I ever seen. Remember all the books he got you, and the kicking stand he made out of an old hacksaw, and the kicking coach, and the kicking camp. He had you in the NFL, man. Ever think about doing that anymore?"

"I do not think I am in very good shape and my ankle still hurts me."

"You're in great shape, you walk all over the damn place all the time and that ankle will be fine. It's gotten better already, hasn't it?"

"I guess so."

"See. You know dear old dad probably would be pretty happy looking down from that cloud up there and seeing his boy slamming them right between the uprights. I guess, he's up on a cloud, he was really sorry there toward the end about the way he treated you. He probably just couldn't help himself. I told you, he got dreams just like anyone else. Damn, look at the time, I got to get going, I'll call you."

Lee put everything back into the box, walked it to his bed and shoved the container underneath. He opened the closet and looked at the last of the half-dozen footballs his father had bought him. It had the LF monogram his father had written in permanent marker between the tip and white band on each of the balls.

Langford High wasn't far from Lee's house. He looked at the football field, still, as if resting for the fall season ahead. He saw himself at all the spots on that grass from where he had fired upon the goal post. He got home before five and Ellie was there with his dinner. She was pleased that he was getting out of the house and noted the reduced limp in her brother's stride. She gave him a hug and left to meet D.H. Christie arrived at seven, just as she said she would. He had never known Christie to be late. As he got into the car, Christie's perfume hit him like a body-sized powder puff.

"Your ankle seems to be getting much better," she said, moving several magazines from the floor in front of the passenger's seat. "But do you think you should be kicking footballs all over the place?"

"I will not be kicking footballs all over the place. I will not be kicking footballs for a while, but I wanted to go to Hank's Sport Shop to get the footballs. You cannot get this type of football just anywhere and I hope Hank's still has them. I want to have my footballs when I am ready to start kicking. My father always had six footballs in the mesh bag when I would go to kick."

"Did you call to see if they have the footballs in stock?"

"I did not call because while most of the people working at Hank's are very friendly, they sometimes do not know where everything is or sometimes things get misplaced. I could call and ask if they have the footballs I want and they would put me on hold and when they come back they could say they do not have my footballs. But it has happened before that if I went to the store and looked real hard, even in those places where the footballs are not supposed to be, I find my footballs."

"Just got a new shipment in," said the salesman at Hank's. "Second aisle over, third shelf from the bottom."

Lee gazed at four, five, six, seven; Hank's had seven of the footballs Lee wanted. There couldn't have been any more satisfaction on the face of a soldier of the Lord who happened upon the Holy Grail. Lee placed each one of the seven cardboard containers into his Hank's shopping cart. Christie, like a scientist taking notes in the field, struggled to understand the mystical communion between Lee and his precious cargo. He turned the shopping cart into the main aisle and headed towards the checkout counter.

"I have to write down my plan; I have to have a plan for when I go into training. I will write my plan down when I go home," Lee said as he reached his hand behind him to touch the two large plastic bags. He almost forgot what he planned to ask her. "I need to ask you a favor, Christie. Can you stop at Mrs. Aggarwal's house?"

"Who?" she asked as they started out of the parking lot.

Lee explained who Mrs. Aggarwal was. He told her about Raymond. About how he would be helping him with some exercises. And how happy he thought Raymond would be to have the football.

Christie looked at Lee; her quivering smile accompanying her caress of Lee's hair. "Lee, you are such a good, kind person helping that little boy like that. It's no wonder that I love you."

He smiled at her.

Christie slowed the car as she approached Lee's house. "Lee, what exactly are you training for?"

"I am going to be in training so that I can kick the football farther and farther every time. I have to see if I can be as good as my father thought." He thanked Christie for bringing him to Hank's but didn't ask her in. He didn't even think that he was losing time he could be with her before she left for state university. August twenty-fifth was what she had told him the day before; she'd be gone in three months if she decided to go.

"I will start my training tomorrow; I will walk to your house Christie. I will bring a pizza that we can have for dinner. Will you be back from work at six o'clock?"

"Yes, I will be back at six, but Lee that is too far for you to walk on your ankle. You're going to make it worse if you're not careful; that's just too far to walk. I can pick you up and then we'll get our pizza."

"No, Christie I have to walk to your house. That is the first part of my training program that I figured out in the car. I have to start my program tomorrow. My ankle will not let me down."

"All right, Lee," she turned the ignition key. "I'll see you tomorrow at six."

Lee spent the next morning with a spiral notebook with stubs from carelessly torn pages clinging to the wire spine. He pinched the remnants away and wrote out his training plan: what exercises he would begin, estimates of the amount of time he'd have to walk each day, and when he would read the books and magazine articles on kicking he found in a shelf in his father's closet. He made it to Christie's house fifteen minutes earlier than he had anticipated. His ankle felt like it was ready for the deep plant of the pivot step upon which his body would rest as his leg followed across like a gun's hammer. After pizza and a salad with the special health dressing Christie made, she drove him home so he could begin reading the books his father had bought. He walked to her house for the next five nights even after his mother came home. Marian Fitts had cut from her waist the heavy chains that for the last ten years of her life were anchored in the concrete of guilt and confusion. She was home now, more energetic than ever; she would piece it together. A large part of that energy she drew from her son. There was a new purpose in his manner that was not there when she first returned. She watched as he read and made notes, and sometimes she heard him talking to himself: "I can do that, I know I can do that. I remember Dad saying that I had done that well. I can do it again."

Lee decided his ankle could have Saturday off. He called Christie to have dinner with him and his mother. The three gathered around the small table that once hosted only Hungry Man dinners. It was meat loaf now, with baked potatoes, green beans, and crescent dinner rolls. As he concluded his six-word blessing, Lee's head remained bowed.

"Is everything all right, Lee?" his mother asked.

Lee couldn't know yet if everything was all right, but he nodded anyway as he took his first bite.

CHAPTER 37

Mrs. Aggarwal phoned asking Lee if he could be at their house at 9 the next morning. He left home early so he would not be late for Raymond's exercises.

"Good morning, Lee," Mrs. Aggarwal said as she motioned him to come in. "This is my father, Mr. Gupta."

"Good morning, Mr. Gupta," Lee offered his hand and the older gentleman extended his.

"Good morning, Lee," Mr. Gupta said formally as he withdrew his hand. Raymond was sitting in a small chair with a tray and was staring at the window.

"I must be going now to work. As I said, Raymond's caretaker will be late this morning, so your being here now means we can do Raymond's early morning exercises. Father will show you what to do. You're being here means so much to us."

"I am glad that I can help and I will listen very carefully to Mr. Gupta's instructions about Raymond's exercises."

Mr. Gupta returned from the kitchen with a jar of peanut butter and what looked like a wooden tongue depressor. Lee thought Mr. Gupta was going to have a morning snack and maybe there weren't any clean spoons.

"This will help Raymond develop muscles in his mouth and strengthen his tongue." Mr. Gupta said. Raymond turned toward his grandfather. The boy's head was tilted and his arms bent and stiff. What might have been a smile at Lee vanished as Raymond opened his mouth and his grandfather smoothed a large portion of peanut butter on to the boy's tongue. "You stay on this side of Raymond and I'll stay on the other, because he will start moving his head and his arms as he gets the peanut butter off his tongue. Mr. Gupta gave Raymond one more large serving of peanut butter.

Lee had never seen anything like this. "Raymond seems to like peanut butter," was all he could say.

"Yes, he does, and we think that this exercise is helping him make stronger sounds with his tongue. We will wait a while until we do the next exercise and we will wait with the others until his therapist comes. Would you like something to drink or eat?

"No thank you," Lee said. Raymond stared at Lee and smiled. Lee wondered what other exercises were to come.

Mr. Gupta went into the other room as Lee stood by Raymond. The grandfather returned with a wooden frame, maybe 4'x5' with two openings at the larger ends. He laid it on the floor; it was about 12" high and across the top were ropes woven into small squares.

"I will need your help with this my friend. We need to get Raymond out of his chair and down by the frame."

Lee was very happy that Mr. Gupta was his friend and he believed they together could do a good job for Raymond. As Mr. Gupta lifted Raymond's tray and undid the belt holding him in the chair, he motioned to Lee to lift the boy and carry him to the frame. Raymond's arms were tight as Lee placed him down in one of the open ends of the frame.

Mr. Gupta got down on his knees and bent down so that he could see Raymond at the other end of the frame. "Raymond, come to grandfather. Come to grandfather."

Lee watched as Raymond started to crawl under the rope. He wasn't sure how he was to help the boy who with legs pushing and arms pulling along the floor suddenly stopped.

"Lee, reach in between the ropes and give Raymond a little push, tell him he is doing a good job," Mr. Gupta said. And Lee did and did again until Raymond had dragged himself to the other end of the box. "Now we let him rest for a while, then I will send him to you under the ropes. This builds his muscles and shows him how to use his arms and legs."

Lee would be back five more times when the therapist couldn't show. He would remember the look of love Mr. Gupta had in his eyes as he helped his grandson. He would remember the glimmer in Raymond's eyes as he made it through the rope box. And finally, he would remember how appreciative Mrs. Aggarwal and her husband were to have Lee help them. We will have you back for a nice dinner they told him. This was one good thing that came from working for Dan Calvert, Lee thought.

CHAPTER 38

For the third Sunday in a row, Ellie had come up with some reason she wouldn't be able to go to church. Lee had offered to go to the service Ellie said she would attend only to have his sister say she wasn't sure if she felt well enough to go to church at all. Marian Fitts said that when the time was right, they'd all go to church together. Lee, Christie and his mother slid further down the pew to make room for the broad-shouldered man who had arrived late. He smiled a thank you to Lee then bowed his head of stubbled gray hair on to bold hands defined by the prominent veins and sinew of a workman, or possibly of a seasoned athlete.

Lee looked at Rev. Taylor as he walked to the front of the altar. The pastor's smile seemed forced; as forced as it was last week, and the week before. Lee had always taken comfort in what he thought was fact: God gave to Rev. Taylor, just as he most likely did to other pastors, the ability to glide effortlessly into that big reassuring smile that had arms that could wrap you in a big, loving hug. Lee was concerned this week. It was clear there was something the matter with Rev. Taylor's smile. Lee thought of the dying flicker of Tinkerbell, and he prayed for Rev. Taylor just as if Peter Pan had been there exhorting him.

There were instances when certain words, a plaintive chord from the organ, or the smile of a father toward his fidgeting son, would make Lee's eyes mist up as visions of a loving Jim Fitts passed in front of him. At such times, Lee heard a blur of sounds as Rev. Taylor spoke. Jim Fitts, however, knew the words soon to come were meant for Lee.

". . . a bright cloud . . ." Lee saw it immediately. ". . . overshadowed them. And from the cloud a voice said, 'This is my Son, the Beloved; with Him I am well pleased . . ." Lee's grip on top of the pew in front of him tightened, drawing the glances of Christie, Marian Fitts and the lanky man next to him. Lee wiped his tears away.

In the fellowship hall, Lee gravitated toward the piano where in earlier days he had conversations with Mrs. Plennington. She hadn't been at church for some time, although she had sent the family a very nice card and fruit basket, and came to the funeral home to pay her respects. She spent most of the time speaking with Lee's mother. The only thing Lee heard her tell his mother was what a nice son she had and how he had grown into such a fine young man. His mother thanked Mrs. Plennington who then gave his mother a hug. She next hugged Ellie, then D.H., then Lee. Lee placed his arms limply around Audrey Plennington's shoulders. The older lady's hug was more powerful, more clinging in an unobtrusive way of which she was master; no one other than Lee caught it. Her eyes turned from comforting to inviting to comforting so quickly that Lee wasn't sure he had seen what he thought he had seen.

Christie and Lee's mother now stood next to the piano where Audrey Plennnington would stand after church with her cup of coffee issuing to Lee invitations, some subtle, some formally engraved. Christie and Marian Fitts radiated a peace that washed from that place in a soft, warm light the uncomfortable memories that had lingered by the piano.

Lee stretched one leg, then the other; his training regimen knew no limits. His ankle stood firm and he reached for his toes. He would be ready for tomorrow; even if it were only from a short distance; he could hear the ignition as his instep made contact with brown leather.

"Lee," Christie said softly as she watched him. "You're not out on the football field and people are starting to stare."

"I am sorry. I did not even realize that. I am just getting excited because of tomorrow."

"I know tomorrow means a lot to you, but you have to learn to pace yourself."

"I was not even thinking about tomorrow, but then Rev. Taylor started talking about the son that the father was well-pleased with, and then I started thinking about my dad and the ball . . ."

"Lee, you haven't done this in so long; it might not come at first. Please don't think it's going to come back right away. You can't get upset; you have to accept what happens. Promise me you will accept what happens."

Lee stopped stretching and looked up at Christie; he had never looked at her defiantly before. "You think I am not going to be able to do it?"

"Promise me!"

Before Lee could answer, he saw Rev. Taylor making his way through the flock. The smile would come on and off as if it had a photoelectric cell making contact with one parishioner after another with whom the clergy-man would stop to talk.

"Someone just told me something about Rev. Taylor's brother; doesn't sound good" Marian Fitts whispered to Christie. The smile on Warren Taylor's face clicked on as he walked toward the piano. He had his arms on the shoulder of the man who had been sitting next to Lee in the pew. Christie knew now where she had seen him before.

"Good morning everyone. Marian, it's so nice to have you back with us. And Christie; my lifesaver, came along just when I needed that ride, good that you were able to join us this morning. Lee, everyone, I want you to meet Clement Ezzer. Clement will be joining us here and I wanted all our good folks to get to know Clement," Rev. Taylor said. Marian and Lee reached for the new parishioner's hand.

"I'm Christie Veit, we've never been introduced but I go to St. Lukes's and I remember seeing you there."

"Well, very nice to finally meet you. This is a great place, great people, great pastor, I think I'm going to be very happy here, yes very happy here," Clement said with energy in his voice that might well have next exhorted the group to join him right then in a ten-mile run. "Don't get me wrong, Christie, I like St. Luke's, the people, what they're doing, but I don't know, hard to put my finger on it. I heard about this church and was mighty impressed with what's going on here. I guess I just need fresh challenges sometimes, fresh challenges."

"I certainly understand. There's that time when people have something inside that says, time to try something new; see if you can do it," Christie nodded.

"Yes, yes, all true, I guess," said Rev. Taylor. "Lee, here's something I'm sure you'll find of interest. Clement was a kicker for the state university football team, and not just any kicker; he was an All-American and drafted by the NFL. What year did you graduate, Clement?"

"I was afraid you were going to ask that," Clement chuckled. He playfully squeezed Rev. Taylor's arm and smiled. "Let's just say it was after Joe Willie Namath led the New York Jets to their first Super Bowl title."

"Super Bowl III, 1969," Lee blurted out.

"So, you're the young fellow Warren's been talking about; got a pretty good kick do you?"

"I used to have a pretty good kick; at least that is what my dad always told me. He told me I was going to go somewhere with my kick, to the NFL. But I have not kicked a football in a very long time and my dad died several weeks ago so I do not think I am going to the NFL."

"I'm sorry to hear about your father. Maybe you and I can talk about a few things I learned along the way. Why don't you give me your phone number," Clement Ezzer said as he got a small notepad and a pen from his blazer pocket.

"I would like to get together to hear what you have learned along the way," Lee said before reciting his phone number.

"Okay, got it, got it. We're going to get together."

"Mr. Ezzer, Christie is going to state university in the fall."

"Please call me Clement or Coach if you'd like. And that's great Christie, you'll really love it there. It's a big place though, don't want to get lost. Only kidding, you'll love it; it's a pretty exciting place. Some of the courses were rough; they were tough ones, but I have to admit I wasn't the best student in the world. Did graduate though, and I tell you even with all that All-American hoopla, the fact that I graduated, got my degree, that meant more to me, and I know it meant more to my mom and dad. Say, Christie if you'd like, you, Lee, and I can grab lunch one day and I'll tell you all about state."

"I'd like that," Christie said.

"Well, I'll look for you folks next week after the service. Thank you, Rev. Taylor."

"Coach, we are at the piano right here in the fellowship hall after the service," Lee said, wanting to make sure Clement Ezzer knew where to go next Sunday.

"Pleasure to meet you, Clement," Marian Fitts added, as the sunlight of this man's presence awoke in her a hope that God was somehow reaching out to help her son. "He's such a nice man, seems very sincere, don't you think so Christie?"

"Yes, I agree."

"Warren, how's your brother?" Marian asked.

Warren Taylor was always uncomfortable when one of his sheep asked him about his personal life. But it didn't take long for word to travel through the flock. He only hoped they didn't know how bad things had gotten. "My brother will be fine. The Good Lord knows the burden we can shoulder and the relief we enjoy when He's strengthened us. Your concern means a lot as well; that too is a blessing from God."

Rev. Taylor turned and began his trek to the counter outside the kitchen window where a few donuts remained next to the large urn of coffee.

"Clement Ezzer is a very nice man. An All-American, he must really be able to kick the ball. Maybe I will understand state university better by listening to Clement, but I will still miss you Christie."

Marian Fitts also did not look forward to that day. "He's a very nice man. What a pleasant surprise this Sunday morning had in store for us," Lee's mother said.

Lee slept during the last hours of the afternoon. The stand of white PVC piping that he had made earlier lay by his bed. It was a simple device, saw lengths of the white plastic pipe, attach with some elbow joints and there you had it. You could place the football at almost any angle.

Lee's dinners at Christie's had developed a pattern. She would have a large glass of ice water waiting for him and he would brush a kiss on her cheek which would be leaning his way. Their dinner was simple: lettuce, but with a special vinaigrette dressing made ahead of time, carrots or freshly-cut green beans, and either grilled chicken breast, canned tuna, or center cut pork chops split in half, so that one chop fed two. They took to the dinner table naturally; they could have been married for several years. Christie spoke about the spa and new fitness programs. She spoke about the two new tires she had to buy for her car, but she was okay, because she put part of her salary away for just such an expenditure. She was also saving more for expenses when she was at state. Some of her financial aid would be in the form of loans and she wondered if she would have to get a part-time job between classes. Her parents had pledged some money, but she knew they didn't have much. She was careful not to speak about going away. Lee handled it poorly. She would stare at the painting on the wall behind Lee: a small boat moored by a casually-tied knot to a failing dock. Looming in the background was a fog of spun cotton wedged between a threatening sea and a sky stirring sharp shards of cloud. It had happened several days ago for the first time: first she saw herself in that boat then she and Lee, then Lee, poor Lee, being dragged far from the dock from which the boat had slipped its bond. Maybe he was right to be concerned about her going away, maybe she should stay.

Lee reached for her dish and placed it on his. He looked at her; her thin fingers, the one with the tiny green sparkle on the gold band, her arms with a light glossy tan that disappeared under the edge of her thin top that stretched tightly around her shoulders and breasts. Her thin neck rose to meet the fall of fine light brown hair.

Lee made a funny face. The young school girl that had long ago made him feel the first tingle of love, smiled. Christie was prettiest when she smiled, when the firm round mounds below her eyes pulled to almost bursting and her eyebrows arched as if wings in ascent. The days till state university loomed. Maybe as the prediction of a weatherman for a bad storm that never materialized, state university would have life only as a faulty computer model.

They sat together after dinner on a love seat that really could only claim to be a large chair. They listened to music. Lee would sit stiffly with his arm around Christie. She would occasionally nudge his chin with hers and he would kiss her ear and sometimes it would lead to more.

They had spoken about Clement Ezzer at dinner and he knew he had more that he had to tell her.

"Coach Ezzer called me this afternoon. He said for me to call him coach and told me all about a kicking camp he has in the summer for high school and college students. He told me to think about it and he also said that if I wanted he would meet me at the high school so he could see how I am doing. I told the coach that I would like to meet him at the high school, but as I was walking over here, I started to feel that I had made a very bad mistake. I do not think he will think much of what I can do, because I have not even started to practice my kicking. I will begin tomorrow and Reid will meet me at the field after he is done with work. But Christie, I am not sure I can do it, I think I better call the coach and tell him I cannot make it Saturday afternoon. I could be very embarrassed."

"Lee, please don't worry so much. I'm sure that the coach is just trying to be helpful. I was very impressed with him. See how you do the next couple of days, if you still feel uncomfortable call him, but be honest with him."

"I have to make sure I stretch; I will never make it if I do not stretch enough. There is nothing more important to being a good kicker than stretching. I have found that I have been able to stretch better a little each day. My father always told me about stretching, and I read it in all my books and magazines."

Christie pulled away slowly. She turned, her eyes like a referee calling time out during an important game. "Lee, I know this is important, but try to keep this whole thing in perspective."

"This is not just kicking, Christie. This is about more than kicking."

CHAPTER 39

"Beautiful day for kicking the old pigskin. Damn, look at that field," Reid Fletcher said as he turned his pick-up into the Langford High parking lot. "I got to see if I can talk with someone at the school about getting that grass patched up, needs some quick-grow seed and needs sod in spots. They just haven't been taking care of this field the way they used to."

"I think they will work hard over the summer to get this field into good condition. I have seen them do that; they always make the field look nice when the season starts." Lee said.

"Damn, I hope you're right, man. I didn't think I'd find these things, a little scroungy, but they fit pretty good and they'll get worked in once I'm out there shagging those kicks of yours coming in from fifty yards." Reid finished tying the frayed, dirty laces of a pair of stiff, faded red leather sneakers and tossed his muddy work boots into the back of his truck.

"I am nervous, Reid. I am very glad you are here with me."

"No reason to be nervous man. Look, I told you I'll be with you all week. We'll get you ready for this Coach Ezzer on Saturday. Say, you sure this guy is on the up and up? I mean you sure he was an All-American and is this big kicking expert?"

"I like the coach; he has been very nice to me and it was Rev. Taylor who told me the coach had been an All-American. I do not think the coach would lie to Rev. Taylor."

"Yeah, if he knew what was good for him, he probably wouldn't go around lying to the Rev. Here, you carry the bag with the stand and I'll get the balls. Man, those are beauties, four, five, six. Those babies aren't cheap."

Lee finished getting on the new pair of soccer cleats he had begun breaking in the week before. The shoes, the crisp tang of new football leather from his quiver, the pinch of breeze toward him carrying the grass and hard dirt smell of the field beyond the waist-high chain link fence, the goal post just waiting; it was like Lee had never left.

"Did you bring a magazine?" Lee asked.

"Yeah, my boss let me borrow this magazine; it's got all these garden lay-outs and tells you how to build these retaining walls with old railroad ties."

"That is good, because I have to warm up and stretch for at least twenty minutes. I hope it is not too boring for you."

"Don't worry about me, just do what you have to do and tell me when you want me out there."

Lee jogged back and forth across the field several times. He walked slowly toward the upright until stopping, he looked at it as a fighter would stare into the eyes of an opponent in the center of the ring before the match. He began the regimen of stretching that his father once directed with a harsh voice always telling his son he could do more, that the young legs could be lifted higher and held for longer. Though his muscles trembled and threatened to snap, Lee found that his father had been right. At the command to bring his leg down, Lee would feel a jolt of energy rushing to his toes. There was pulling to stretch the thighs, then the calves, then twists to loosen the ankles. The ankles, there was no trace of the injury that had hobbled him the night his father died. Lee worked on the hamstring, then the back. He pranced sideways, alternating steps. He shook his arms and the current flowed to his hands. He jogged past Reid, who by now had finished reading about retaining walls and shrub placement.

"I think I am ready. My legs feel like they are ready." He kicked his leg above his waist several times.

"That's good man; that's good. Let's go do it," Reid said as he reached for the mesh bag containing the six judges that would soon tell by their flight and trajectory if a flicker of Lee's magic had survived that morning of horror.

As Lee walked toward the middle of the field, he saw for a moment Sam and Christie Veit near the sideline, talking then turning to look in Lee's direction just as they had that afternoon. Sam would probably be playing football at state university. Lee might have gone there too. The morning that had snatched away Sam Veit had sent Lee and Christie on to a much longer path toward each other. Lee wondered if he and Christie would be together now if not for that morning. "Keep your mind on what you're here for son," came a forceful voice with little tolerance for anything that distracted from making the football rotate perfectly turn after turn as it sailed over the crossbar. "You are right Dad, you are right," Lee said.

Lee stood at the fifteen-yard line. Counting the ten yards from the goal line to the back of the end zone where the goal post was anchored, meant his first kick would be from twenty-five yards out. He took a ball from the mesh bag, squeezed it as if he were a discerning melon buyer and put the ball back into the bag. The fourth piece of fruit was the one on which Lee would initially pin his hopes.

"What are you doing?" Reid asked from behind the goal post.

"I have to find the ball that will do the job."

"C'mon, they're all the same. I just looked at them."

"No, they are not all the same; not now. When I get the first over the crossbar, then they will all be the same."

"Jeez," Reid muttered into his cupped hands. "All right, all right, find the right one."

Lee set the top pipe of his PVC stand at just the *right* angle on the *right* one. The new ball, it's white, unblemished lettering glowing in the late afternoon sun, looked fully the NFL caliber it was. The afternoon would tell if the ball were wasted on Lee.

Lee took three steps back then paced his shorter steps to the side. He looked at the ball, he looked at his foot, he rocked on his left leg, he looked at the goal post, he moved toward the ball, his right leg beginning to whip, his instep making contact: "PHUMF," "TOINK." PHUMF was the bad sound coming from his foot and the ball meeting in the wrong place. TOINK was the second bad sound as the ball hit the upright. The ball landed way to the side of Reid.

"Okay, okay, that's the first one in how many years? Don't worry about it man, just get another ball. It's gonna come, it's gonna come. Just put it right into my arms, right down the middle."

Lee stared at the bar, then at Reid. "PHUMF," "TOINK."

"Okay, okay, that's good consistency. You hit the other upright, just got to aim that gun a little more in the middle. The middle; look for the middle. All right, get another ball. C'mon."

Lee looked up to the cloud. He heard nothing. He reached in for another ball and closed his eyes as he shook his head. Reid looked now like an impossible target. Lee rubbed his palm on his instep, seeing from the touch the sweet spot he would have to hit. One leg planted, the other whipped. "PHANK," came the sound of his foot smacking the leather wall around the bladder of air. He waited as he was supposed to and didn't lift his head, but he knew that sound. Reid held his two arms straight up as the ball gunned over the middle of the crossbar by six-feet.

"That's what I'm talking about, that's what I'm talking about. You woke up that kicking genie on that one. Hurry up and get another ball, before you start to do too much thinking. Better yet, don't do any thinking."

The next ball flew the same path, but at least three feet higher. The next was back five yards and landed in the same spot.

"Damn, Mister Kicking Man be back in town. Try the left hash mark." Lee moved from the center of the field and took several practice follow-throughs at the clipped angle.

"PHANK." Another "PHANK," as he connected from the right side of the field. Reid started gathering the balls and tossing them back to Lee.

The next half-hour was full of "PHANKS" from all over the field and Reid scampered after balls and continued his profane cheers which became more and more punctuated by a shortness of breath. "Son-of-a bitch, you got it down now. Time for a little break, that leg has got to ease in, got to ease it in."

Lee turned his back to the goal post and broke into a smile. He didn't want anyone else to see. He looked up at the cloud which was now behind him. Small wreaths of white formed a smile as bubbly as Lee's. Lee knew that Jim Fitts had counted each one of the balls that breached the crossbar in a perfect arc of end–over-ends.

"Okay," Reid said after he joined Lee in the middle of the field. "That's good man, that's real good. You really nailed them. Come on give me a little smile. You were knocking the crap out of those balls and you know it."

Lee smiled as he began to put the balls back into the bag.

"That's the spirit, man. I ain't see you smile like that in, in a real long time. That's good man, nice to have something to smile about. I think you got something to show Coach."

"Yes, I think I did better than I expected this afternoon. I hope the coach will be happy with what he sees on Saturday."

"Oh, he'll be happy. If he ain't happy with the way you've been kicking, know what? He ain't a real coach 'cause he don't know nothing about kicking."

"But I know he's a real coach."

"Why are you putting those balls away? You got to try a couple of those long boys. We got to see what you can do on the kick-offs, see if you got what it takes on the long ball."

"I thought we could wait on those."

"Wait? You've only got four more days after today till Saturday and I heard them calling for some rain maybe later this week. Suppose you're hurting in the long ball department? We better find out sooner rather than later. Tell you what, just do one so we can see what we're working with. I'm going to stand about twenty yards in front of the end zone, you know, to give you a way to measure if you can get the ball at least to the twenty- yard line, then we'll know how much more oomph you need to get into the kick to get it back further."

"Okay, maybe one kick, my leg is a little sore, I don't want to . . ."

"Lee, this is the big time, you want to be in those NFL films where they have that music playing in the background and then the kicker lines up in slow motion to get that ball sailing through to win the big game or what? You think that guy's leg might not be sore? I know how to handle these things; we're just talking about one kick."

Lee lined up at the thirty-five-yard line. He took a black, hard plastic block from his bag and placed a ball, its lettering now slightly scuffed, on to the holder. He stretched his legs then rolled his shoulders as he waited for Reid to get to the twenty-yard line, some forty-five yards away.

Reid turned and raised his arm. "Look, you don't have to get it as far as me. We just need to see what kind of height you're getting, get an approximate hang-time, and see what kind of spin you can get on the ball."

Lee walked back from the ball, looked at Reid, rolled his shoulders then took strong strides to the ball: "PHANK" and a follow through that almost landed him on his back.

Reid's eyes locked on to the field in front of him where he expected the ball to land. Like a radar dish struggling to track the unexpected, his eyes lifted sharply. The perfect end-over-end hadn't been consulted about landing short of the twenty-yard line and soared above Reid's turning body until it zeroed in on the ten, landed, then rolled out of bounds at the five.

"Son-of–a bitch, did you see that? I can't believe it. I got lost on the hang time watching that, but has to be at least four seconds. You got the package man, it's a gift, man, just no other explanation. Almost took my head off trying to watch that baby go right by me."

Lee watched as his friend went to retrieve the ball. He brushed off the kicking tee and put it into the bag.

Marian Fitts and Christie showed up at the field the next day. There was no way Lee could keep them away after Reid's Emmy-award winning narrative of what had taken place as Lee began "his quest for stardom."

"This is not a good idea, Reid," Lee said as he saw his mother and Christie wave from the top of the stands.

"This introduces that element of having to perform before a crowd. What do you think those stands are going to be empty when you get called into the big game?"

"But, I still am not ready for the big game. I need to do my stretching."

"Okay, okay, start your stretching, I'll be checking the wind and looking for some good spots for you to kick from."

Lee brought to his stretching the conviction of a shaven-headed, saf-fron-robed ascetic. Lee neither saw nor heard his mother, Christie or Reid. The kicker's legs worked a loosening routine on muscles that had proven themselves the day before. The back, the arms too were prepared as well for their role during that snap second when the restive solitude seven yards behind the line of scrimmage explodes.

It was much as it had been the day before. Lee did miss on two kicks, the first from twenty yards out, and the last from a tricky angle on the left. But the form was there; the quick muscle twitch that snapped Lee's leg like a medieval catapult and made him a genuine competitor.

"You got it man, I'm telling you, I think you did better than yester-day. You got some good early lift then those babies sailed home to their mommas," Reid yelled out to Lee as he looked up to see nothing but a blue sky. "Did you see him kick those babies? Perfect end-over-end, and this is only his second day!" Reid called out as he walked up the stairs to where Marian Fitts and Christie were sitting. The two nodded at Reid with satis-fied smiles.

It was the same the next day and Thursday would have been the same except for the call early in the afternoon from Reid.

"Look, this is kind of bizarre, so just stay with me on this as I explain," Reid told Lee. "I got a call last night from Audrey Plennington. Remember I told you that before I picked you up, I was putting up those little cards about me doing landscaping jobs? She saw the one I put up in the grocery store and well, I guess my new little business has its first customer. But here's the rub, Mrs. Plennington said she's having a party this weekend and wants all her beds mulched. She wanted to know if I could do it today. I told her it was too big a job for me, even if I could get the mulch delivered – and it is going to get delivered early this afternoon -- and that I didn't know if I could find someone to help me on such short notice. She told me to ask you, no, she insisted I ask you, that you could use the money. And then on top of everything, when I told her how much it would cost, she said there's another fifty dollars in it for us if we definitely get the job done today. But man, it was kind of weird how she was pretty firm about me getting you to help. So, there you have it, I mean I know you got this big kicking thing with your coach and everything on Saturday, but you've been kicking the crap out of the ball and you'll be fine. Then on Friday afternoon we'll get back down to the field and pick up where we left off. Whadda ya say, Lee? This means a lot to me, I mean this is my first job in my new business and I'm sure if I do a good job, well, Mrs. Plennington must have a lot of well-off friends she can recommend me to."

It was easier for Lee to hold the phone as if he were waiting for Reid to say something further then to focus on the answer his friend was waiting for. Mrs. Plennington's house? Missing a day of practice two days before he was going to meet his coach? Now he knew, it was easy as he thought about it. He would say "What?" and Reid would say "Just kidding man, I'll pick you up usual time and we'll head over to the field."

"What?" Lee asked.

"C'mon," came the response from Reid. "I need you on this one man, this is big to me."

Reid wasn't kidding. Lee had heard everything perfectly. What his best friend was asking could derail everything. His big chance with Coach Ezzer could go down the drain. "Is there some way we could do this job for Mrs. Plennington next week?"

"Man, I told you, she's having this big party on Saturday and when she saw my sign thought she'd get this work done before the party. I told you that, man."

"Yes, now I remember, you told me that. Reid, I am afraid that if I miss a day of practice, it will make me not good enough for when I see the coach on Saturday." He knew he could never say he was afraid of what Mrs. Plennington might do.

"Lee, listen to me. Is there anyone who wants you to do good on Saturday more than me? Is there anyone else who has been spending more time and working as hard as your best friend –me- so that you can get to be the best damn kicker your coach has ever seen? Do you think I would ask you to miss practice today if I thought it would hurt you? Do you?"

"No. I will help you with your landscape job at Mrs. Plennington's house this afternoon."

"All right now you're talking; now I hear my best buddy talking. I will call you back in a half-hour."

The phone rang five minutes after Lee put it down. "This is getting to be like a damn soap opera. Look, my boss just gave me holy hell for being on the phone so much today. He's got me driving over to work this piece of hill I didn't think I'd have to work on till tomorrow. Bottom line, I'm going to be here an hour longer this afternoon than I thought, so this is what I arranged. My guy who's dropping off the mulch should be there by now. I told him to leave a rake, pitchfork, and wheel barrow. I need you to go over there and get started laying that mulch. Call a cab, I'll pay you back when I see you, and get over to Mrs. Plennington's house right away. We got to get this job done before dark. Try to get as much done as you can till I get there."

Lee knew Mrs. Plennington would be there. Maybe he could call her and tell her about Saturday. He could tell her he needed to practice. But as he rehearsed his appeal, his mind heard the sound of Reid's friend's truck as it came up Mrs. Plennington's driveway and backed up into the turn-around. The truck's container lifted, dumping a huge pile of mulch right where Lee knew the guests coming to Mrs. Plennington's party would park.

He opened the drawer, pulled out the small yellow-pages and looked up the number of a cab company.

CHAPTER 40

The sun shone through the dogwood trees surrounding Audrey Plennington's house. The mulch was piled on the blacktop of the large turnaround that slanted towards the open lawn in the backyard. A wheel barrow, pitch fork and rake were next to the mulch. Lee paid the cab driver and walked toward the pile. Maybe Mrs. Plennington hadn't heard the taxi; maybe she didn't know Lee was there. He started to load the mulch and kept his head down. He took the first load towards one of the large shrub beds and worked it in around the bushes. He was soon back with another load and then another. Pin pricks of sweat started to mix with bits of mulch on his arms and hands. He was about to dump the fourth load.

"Lee," came the voice he had hoped not to hear. The storm door slammed shut. "Oh, I've got to get that thing fixed. But Lee, it's so good to see you. That bed looks so nice. I told your friend Reid I knew you would do a good job. Tell me, how you've been?"

"Oh, I have been fine, Mrs. Plennington, but I do not think I have time to stop and talk right now, because we have to get all this mulch spread before dark. Reid should be here any minute."

"Reid actually called before you got here and said he got held up on the job for a while and thought he'd be later than he planned."

"Well, if that is so, I better work even faster so we can get this job done in time." Audrey Plennington's light green sun dress fluttered at her knees as the tepid breeze drafted through the dogwoods. "Lee, you need to take a break, you've already done quite a bit." She was almost next to him. Her hair had been recently combed, combed well, and tied back in a black ribbon that made the fine brown strands seem lighter than they were. He wondered if she would talk about Christie and he looked down the driveway hoping that Reid might arrive sooner than expected. Lee looked at his watch; he'd been working for almost thirty minutes.

"Maybe I can take a break when Reid gets here, but just a short break."

Audrey Plennington looked at her watch. She still had enough time. "Now Lee, I don't want you working yourself to death. You know something happens here on my property, you hurt yourself or something, and I'm responsible. Now you've got to take a short break, I insist. I made a pitcher of sweet tea, a special recipe of mine, with a slew of fresh mint from the garden. And, I've never seen anyone able to resist my double-fudge brownies; they're fresh out of the oven. There will be plenty left for your friend when he comes."

"But . . ."

"Lee, I think I know what's best."

He lay down the rake. "Mrs. Plennington, I am all dirty. I have mulch all over my feet and my hands, and my pants, and my shirt. I will get mulch all over your house."

Her pincers pulled the silken strands tighter; he was not going to get away. "Nonsense," she said as she bent over in front of him to brush off the bottom of his pants. "There, that's fine. I've got the girls coming tomorrow to clean for the party. So, there's no problem; there is no problem at all. Now come, come," she said as she pulled him toward the house.

The open, spacious house was as he remembered. The pitcher of tea sat next to a basket of brownies. Bright flowers and greens stood tall and full in an ornately-cut vase that twinkled in the sun.

He had forgotten for a second why he had been hesitant to take a break; to come inside the house. The hand pulled him toward her and off balance he found himself against her as she locked her arms around him. Her low pleading voice shot a paralyzing sting into his body: "Lee, I am so lonely, I need someone to be with me. I need you to be with me."

He started to struggle but thought that to break her tightening grip, he might hurt her. He stood motionless as she dug her head into his chest. Her perfume launched on another front, its heavy essence washing over Lee. "Mrs. Plennington, I have to get back to my mulch. I know Reid is going to expect me to have done more than I have done already. I know he wants to get that bonus money he told me about if we get the job done by dark."

Her grip, if anything tightened. "Lee, please do not think about the bonus. I'm going to double it, regardless of what you get done." He felt her arms slide quickly down his back. Her hands dug into his backside. "Lee, I am a very wealthy woman and I'm told a very attractive one as well. You can have anything you want. I can buy you anything and you can have me." One of her hands grabbed one of his and placed it on her backside. He felt his heart beats throbbing in his ears. Her venom was jetting through his body.

"Mrs. Plennington, I . . ."

Her hand dug harder into him and she dug his harder into her. "Lee, we have to go upstairs, or do you want to do it right here?" Her passion drained some of the strength from her hands and he broke free.

"Mrs. Plennington, I have to go back outside."

"Lee, you're not . . ." The half-burps echoing from the muffler were like the notes of a bugle above the pounding hooves of horses carrying cavalry to the rescue. Reid's truck came to a stop in front of the mulch. "Lee, stay here." But Audrey Plennington felt the power draining from the wiles that had permitted her to overpower the younger man.

The door caught and slammed behind Lee.

"What have you been doing man, is this all you got done?" Reid asked as he pulled another wheel barrow and rake from his truck. "We got to get this done by dark, this whole thing by dark, or we don't get the damn bonus, you know that."

"I was working pretty hard, but then, then I had to use the bathroom."

"Had to use the bathroom? Man, that must have been a major dump. Now come on, we got to get busy."

The door slammed again.

"Hello, Mrs. Plennington. Reid Fletcher, thanks again for giving me this business. You're gonna like the work we do. Let us know if you want us to do anything else while we're here. Lee and I can do whatever you want done."

"Nice to see you Reid. Don't work too hard; it's getting hot out here. And don't worry about finishing, get as much done as you can, you'll still get your bonus. There's sweet tea and double-fudge brownies on the table when you want some. I'm going up to lie down for a while."

"Seems to be a nice lady; guess you can never believe all you hear. Not bad looking either for someone her age. Heh, what do you think Lee?"

CHAPTER 41

"**Y**our kicks looked good yesterday. Doesn't seem that missing Thursday affected you. I know you were concerned it might," Christie Veit said as she signaled to turn into the school parking lot where they would meet Coach Clement Ezzer.

"Yes, I was concerned. I did not want to miss my kicking practice on Thursday but I knew I had to help Reid with a job he got for his new landscaping company. There is Reid's truck. I am glad he is right on time," Lee said as he turned to make sure for the third time that his bag was in the back seat.

"Yesterday was such a great day. The first day I've had off in months. I stayed in bed till late morning then just rested. I read some and watched a little TV. It was so nice to be out of that spa even if it was for only one day. Where did you say you and Reid were working?"

Lee saw the coach. Clement Ezzer waved to him. There was a man in a blue T-shirt and red shorts standing next to the coach. "We, it was someone who had read one of Reid's cards about his new business," Lee mumbled. "There's the coach." Lee noticed that the man next to coach was wearing soccer shoes.

"Okay, don't you treat this day any differently than all the days you kicked like a monster," Reid said as he put his arm on his friend's shoulder and took the mesh bag of now friendly footballs. "You hear what I'm saying?"

"I hear what you are saying, but I am still nervous."

"Don't be nervous, man. Christie, tell Lee not to be nervous."

"He'll be fine after he finishes his stretching."

"Yeah, that's right. Hear that? You'll be fine when you get done stretching."

Clement Ezzer was wearing a light blue nylon pullover jersey and tan soccer shorts. A clipboard and folder rested on a mesh bag of footballs nearby. The man standing next to the coach also had a mesh bag at his feet and his hand was around his ankle as he pulled on and began to stretch his leg.

"Morning everyone." The coach inhaled deeply. "Mornings don't get much better than this."

"Good morning coach," Christie said.

"You are right; mornings like this do not come often," Lee said before turning to Reid. "Coach, this is my friend Reid Fletcher who has been helping me practice my kicking this week."

"Good morning coach," Reid said, his voice trailing in a nervous falsetto.

"Morning Reid. You a kicker too?"

"No, no sir, just helping out."

"Well, that's very nice of you. Heard your friend Lee was pretty good aways back."

"Coach, you're going to like what you see. No doubt in my mind, Lee's got to be the best darn kicker in the state."

"Sounds mighty impressive, I'm looking forward to seeing what Lee can do. Oh, let me introduce you to someone I've been working with over the years, Bobby DeFlore. Bobby's been kicking at state for the past three years, first team all-league and on his way to breaking the all-time school scoring record. Bobby's been going to my kicking camp, it's a three-day deal I run locally. In any event, Bobby's been going to my camp for what is it, the past five years?"

"Actually, coach, it's been six years," Bobby Deflore added matter-of-factly even as he fought to suppress the laugh he knew could pop through as he thought about the stupidity of the stupid man's claim about Lee's kicking prowess.

"That's right, that's right six years. Say, Lee I brought you some information about my camp. Might be something you'd be interested in, but you know, thought it would be a good idea to see today where you are, you know to see if you and my camp would be a good fit. Bobby here called, just happened to be home this weekend, and I told him to come over this morning if he had time, to join us."

Reid and Lee looked at Bobby. The kicker had to be over six feet, maybe 190 pounds, with calves the size of small pot roasts and the thighs of an Olympic sprinter. The rest of his body was trim and his black hair was short, but neatly parted.

"Good morning," Bobby said, his broad smile bringing a round-ed-boyish charm to his face as he sought authenticity in his greeting. "You're Christie?"

"Yes, that's Christie," Coach said. "She and Lee . . ."

"Coach told me you're going to state in the fall," Bobby cut in. "If you have any questions about school or the area, let me know. We have some good people at school, and we usually know how to have a good time."

"Well, I'm not one hundred percent sure I'm going. I've visited and, well, it is a very nice campus, and the people I met were very nice to me."

"I'll give you my number, and we can get together sometime; I'll answer whatever questions you have."

"That's kind of you," Christie said. Coach called over to Bobby and handed him a new kicking tee. Christie looked at Lee, then at Reid. Lee fidgeted almost as if he shouldn't be there. She snapped out of it and put her mouth to his ear. "I'm going to go sit in the bleachers. Remember how good you are. Don't let this guy shake you. I love you."

Ezzer Clement worked Lee and Bobby through a half hour of vigorous stretching. "Okay, Bobby can answer this one," Coach said as he watched the two kickers finish a slow jog. "What's the most important part of a kicker's regimen?"

"Stretching, Coach."

"You're darn right. "STUR-ETCH-ING!!! Need to spend a little more time on your stretching Lee. More stretching means more yardage, can't forget that. Bobby, come over here to hold, we got to see what Lee's got here."

Reid went down field in his awkward run; he'd never be on any athletic team. He stopped about thirty yards away and waited for Lee's kick. Bobby brought the mesh bags over to the coach.

"Okay, Lee show me your set up, and then do a half-speed follow through," Coach Ezzer said.

Lee paced off his steps and with head down approached the spot where the ball would be. He pivoted and his kicking leg followed through.

"Lee, you got to keep your head down after the kick. It's an important part of the process. You lift your head too soon and you don't know what that ball is going to do. Do it again." Lee did. "That's better, much better. That's keepin the old noggin where it's supposed to be. Okay, regular speed this time." Bobby made the motion to the invisible center, grabbed the invisible ball and placed it down as Lee's foot soared by.

"That's a three," Bobby said encouragingly.

"Doggone right that's a three-pointer. Quick, got that quick muscle twitch. I was almost a hundred percent sure when I saw you turning on that jog," Coach Ezzer added.

Bobby got a real ball from the invisible center and placed it in a blink before Lee's instep launched the ball about five yards over Reid's head. Another and then another landed within ten yards of each other. Coach walked over to the goal post and marked out a rough thirty yards. Each kick sailed through the uprights as they did at forty. At forty-five, one went through, the other sailed two yards to the left.

"How long you been kicking?" Bobby asked.

"I did kicking when I was younger. I started again last week after I bought my new footballs."

All right, time for point-afters, let's see your PATs." Coach motioned them to a point he figured was seventeen yards from the end zone. The ball sailed through.

"Lee, what did you let up for? That motion has got to be just as fast, just as powerful whether you're doing PATs or you're fifty yards out. Your body has got to fine tune just one set of all-purpose mechanics. Now try it again. That's it, that's it. All right now hold one for Bobby, you try one Bobby."

Bobby pulled at his legs and then grabbed at the grass in front of him. His foot was a blur as it passed Lee and shot the ball end over end some fifteen feet over the crossbar.

"That's the way it's done, Lee," Coach said. "Okay, okay let's take a few from the thirty-five; you guys alternate on a couple of kick-offs. Reid, see if you can find a goal line down there somewhere so these guys have some-thing to aim for."

Lee sent a perfect end-over-end to the fifteen. Bobby's was a little higher and landed just short of the ten. Reid like a man on ice with no skates, followed the unpredictable bounces. Lee's next soared to the five, just after Reid had set himself up at the ten.

"Nice hang time, darn nice hang time; 4.4 seconds," Coach shouted out.

Bobby set the ball on the holder, twisting the ball and squeezing it in what was surely some ritual he had developed over the years. His mind thought about Reid's stupid statement about Lee being the best kicker in the state. Couldn't be, but what about what he had seen today? This guy had never played anything beyond junior high ball? Bobby's leg snapped around and his body lifted off the ground. It was every bit as high as Lee's, but into the end zone; not what he wanted on a kick off.

"That was a very good kick, Bobby. You are some kicker," Lee said.

"Yeah, thanks."

"Okay, okay, guys come over here a second. Thanks for getting those balls Reid.

Bobby, last night I got a call from a friend of mine, we played college ball together, now he's a big-time assistant coach in the NFL up in New York. We've spoken a couple of times over the past few years about prospects and I told him about the good things you've been up to Bobby. He asked me about you last night and I said you were home for a few weeks. He said he was free next weekend and if I could find a field somewhere maybe half way, he'd like to see what you can do. He also said, it'd be a good excuse for him and me to get together again after all these years. So, we got two old war horses getting together who'll be shooting the breeze. Then we get this morning, and I tell you, Lee, both Bobby and I agree, you showed us something out there. You've got some rough edges no question, but I'll tell you this from what I've seen, the mechanics, the concentration, the power, well you don't see that package too often. I'd like both you and Bobby to come up and see my friend, Ed Turley. I'm not promising anything, but I'll tell you this, if one of you has it, Ed's the man that will see it.

I've marveled over these years at Ed's talent to see that special something that means somebody's going to make waves big time. I think it'd be great if you both could let Ed take a look at what you've got."

Bobby DeFlore nodded. "I'll be there coach." His ears told him at first that the invitation to Lee was preposterous, but his eyes had seen in Lee what the coach had just described. Through years of drinking in everything about kicking, Bobby's mind had developed an at-the-ready clipboard listing every attribute needed. Lee Fitts had a superior rating in every category.

"Good, good, Bobby, I'll call you once I get all the particulars. Lee, how 'bout you?"

"Well . . ."

"Coach," Reid said. "You know, Lee is a little shy sometimes. I can drive you up in my truck. I mean this is a great opportunity. I mean you heard Coach say how famous Ed Turley is; I mean this is Ed Turley, NFL."

"Reid, I appreciate your enthusiasm, but this is something Lee has to want and he's got to want it pretty good." Reid looked at Lee about to say something then stopping.

Lee took a deep breath and looked at Christie over in the stands. "Yes Coach, I would like very much to see Ed Turley. Reid can drive me up in his truck."

"Yeah, that's right, we'll go up together, the two of us."

"That's good," Coach said. I'll call you this week also. And boys, one thing, if you plan to get some practice in this week, be careful, go light. No way you'll heal in time for next Saturday and Ed Turley is not going to bother with you."

Reid sat up and leaned between the two front seats. He told Christie everything Coach Ezzer Clement was preparing for the following week and how he and Lee would be driving up to meet Ed Turley. Damn, Lee had shown that Bobby D. More like Booby D. If Lee were at state, Booby would find himself with a permanent spot on the bench. Christie looked in the rear view as Reid continued on about what he called the "Strange World of the Kicker" which few people really understood. Lee sat looking ahead and saying nothing. After lunch, they returned to the school parking lot so Reid could get his truck.

"You should be proud of your boy there, Christie," Reid said as he got out of the car. "Wait till old Ed Turley gets a look at Lee. Just think of the seats we'll have on opening day."

"Good bye Reid," Christie said in a low voice as if not to wake someone crying out hallucinations as they slept.

"What? Oh yeah, thanks for the lift. Lee, you take it easy this weekend, don't be getting injured or anything. I'll call you and we'll get back into training on Monday."

"Good bye, Reid. I will be careful this weekend."

"Seems as if Reid has this whole thing all planned out for the two of you," Christie said in voice as far away as Lee ever heard it.

"I think Reid is very excited. Reid gets very excited; at least he does not get excited about cable television any more. That was really getting him into trouble. Would you like to come with us next weekend? I would like it very much if you would come with us, because I am very nervous when I think about what the Coach was saying. I mean, I would not want to disappoint him in front of his old football teammate."

"Lee, I think the coach probably knows what he's doing; he's been at this a long time. Thank you for inviting me. I would really love to go, but maybe it's better that it's just you and Reid. I think it's better that maybe you have as few distractions as possible. Plus, I doubt Audrey would give me the time off, especially since I took off Friday."

"Christie, I saw the way Bobby DeFlore was looking at you, and he is this big important guy at state university and I am not, I mean I just barely finished high school. I wish you did not have to go to school there. And you were smiling at him. Are there any more courses you can take at the community college?"

"Lee, we have been through this so many times. I have told you how I feel about you and I don't care how you think Bobby DeFlore was looking at me, and if I were smiling then that's because it was the polite thing to do. I smile at a lot of people. If I do go to state, I wish you'd see that it was because it would make me happy and that I could get a better job in the end and if we want to think anything about us and the future, then we better make sure I get the best job possible."

"Does that mean you think I can never get a good job too?"

"Lee, I didn't say that."

"My sister's car is in front of our house," he said and then paused.

"Lee, look at me. Why don't you just rest this weekend, spend some time with your mom; maybe you two could go to a movie or go out to eat. I seem to be upsetting you."

"I do not know what I will be doing with the rest of my weekend if you want to be by yourself."

"Lee, that's not what I meant. Lee look at me. I told you I love you and I know you love me. I know how much this week coming up means to you. I told you I haven't even decided if I'm going away to school. Let's not talk about it anymore. I'll call you on Monday. You can come over for supper if you want, okay?"

"Okay Christie. You are right, all of a sudden I am very nervous about this week."

"You'll be fine, I wouldn't say that if I didn't mean it," she said as she leaned over, turned his head and kissed him.

Marian Fitts and her daughter sat at the table, a half-eaten coffee ring and two mugs in front of them. They were smiling; they were talking as mother and daughter; two women realizing how much a part of each other they were, the intervening years notwithstanding. They had Lee tell them several times what was happening the following weekend just so they were sure they understood fully what he was describing. Ellie got up first and hugged him. Marian Fitts motioned for her son to come closer as her eyes welled with tears. He heard them talk about blessings, about mysterious ways, about how happy Jim Fitts would have been.

"Lee, that is such good news. You should be so proud of yourself for getting such an opportunity. I know your sister and I are so proud of you. At least we get a little good news today. Ellie was at church this afternoon, helping with the flowers for tomorrow and well she heard about Rev. Taylor's brother. He died yesterday, seemed he was severely overweight, someone said over four-hundred pounds. Well, anyway, Rev. Taylor will be gone for most of the next week. Ellie said people who had seen him said they had never seen Rev. Taylor so upset. He kept saying he should have done more, that it wasn't his brother's fault that he was so overweight, that he should have been more patient with his brother. You know Rev. Taylor; he always seems to come up with a smile, even if it's at the last minute. I've never seen him seem troubled by anything. Ellie said that people that saw him yesterday, they were trying to comfort him, said they have never seen anyone so upset, just completely broken, sobbing, and everything. We must be sure to remember Rev. Taylor in our prayers."

CHAPTER 42

Christie Veit looked at herself in the full length, bevel-edged mirror. Encased in a frame of darkened carved wood, it hung between two matching posts. It had been an expensive purchase that day at the auction house, maybe her single most extravagant act of treating herself ever. The mirror was the only piece of furniture she owned for which she had plans to place in her dream house. The mirror would tell her on those occasions when she needed to hear it, that she was a very attractive woman, her hair, her face, her figure, other than the color of her blue eyes which she would have preferred to be green, she wouldn't change anything. She was quick and resourceful with the "no thank you's" she dispensed over the years to men she didn't care for. Lee was different; it became unmistakable to her after spending so much time with him since the previous fall. He was good and hers to protect. Her brother Sam "had been snuffed out by a savage, twisted fate slipping past the vigilance of a loving God," said scribbled words punctuated with red marker on a postcard with no return address among the many pieces of mail she received after her brother died. Her early, ephemeral infatuation with Lee became linked to a vengeance borne from that one anonymous note she could never forget. She would cheat the dark power from claiming another victim. She didn't blame God; she was just confused.

Yes, she would protect Lee at all costs. She might have to forgo college; she knew Lee was coping badly with the prospect of her going away. But how would they support themselves? Maybe she had done all she could for Lee. After all, his mother was back now; she could take care of him. And what about Bobby DeFlore? She saw that look in his eyes as the star kicker from state university spoke with her. If she became Bobby's girl she knew she would be popular, well-known as she walked with him on campus and went to parties, and watched in the stands as he played football and broke the school scoring record.

Bobby was a silly thought. Her life would be with Lee; somehow, she would make it work. But when Christie returned from her three-day weekend, Audrey Plennington was ready. It had never crossed Christie's mind. She thought the odds greater that she would win the Mega Jackpot Lottery on one of those occasions when the top prize got over two-hundred million dollars. Audrey brought a surgeon's skill to making a story sleazy. In her pert, condescending manner, she described an afternoon in a prose full of suggestive blanks that Christie's reluctant mind could not refrain from filling in. She examined the mirror, looking carefully for any defect the reflection might define.

When she heard the knock at the door she looked at the clock and rushed over to turn off the burners on the stove. She took one last look in the mirror before opening the door.

"Hi Christie. That smells very good. I know that is roast chicken and I can smell Stove Top stuffing. That is another favorite dinner of mine. I brought an apple pie for dessert. My mother said I should bring something over to celebrate about seeing Ed Turley this weekend, so she bought me an apple pie. I told her apple pie was your favorite," Lee said as he leaned forward to kiss her on the cheek. She took the pie and pulled away.

"Christie, is there something wrong?"

"Maybe you should tell me if there is something wrong."

"I do not know what you mean, Christie."

"I find it hard to believe her sometimes, but at other times she can be very convincing and if you must know, I was sick in my stomach when she told me."

"Who told you what that you got sick in your stomach?"

"Well let's try someone we both know; someone it seems you might know better than I thought: Audrey Plennington."

"I do not know what you are talking about Christie."

"Last Thursday, you were at Audrey's house?"

Lee's head dropped.

"I was at Mrs. Plennington's house because I was helping Reid with his new landscaping business. She saw one of his cards about his new business and she needed to have the mulch put down before her big party last weekend. Reid said she recommended me for the job. But then Reid got in trouble with his boss and so he had to stay at that job longer. Then he told me to take a cab and start working on the mulch because he said Mrs. Plennington would give us a bonus if we got the job done before dark."

"Remember I asked whose house you were working at, and you never answered me? Why didn't you tell me you were at Audrey's?"

"I was scared, I get very confused sometimes when I am around Mrs. Plennington.."

"Were you in the house alone with her?"

"She asked me into her house, she said I needed to take a break and that she had fixed me a snack."

"Did you hold her?"

"Did I hold her?"

"Did you? I'll tell you what she told me and two of the other instructors at the spa. Just picture her saying this. 'It was nice seeing Lee at the house on Thursday. He wanted to come in, he was so thirsty and had been working up such a sweat. I gave him some sweet tea and brownies. He gave me such a big hug almost wouldn't let me go, guess it was his way of saying thanks. He said he really liked being at the house. I'm glad I made him happy; he's had such a rough life, and now with his father gone, well, I hope he'll be all right. He's such a nice boy, guess not really a boy anymore.' That's what Audrey Plennington told us at the spa this morning."

"She hugged me first. It did not happen the way she said. I did not want to hug her, but we were alone in the house and I did not know what to do. I was very happy when I heard Reid's truck coming up the driveway. I was able to get out of the house then."

"Is that all that happened?"

"Lee hesitated. He would beg to be forgiven if she knew otherwise. "Yes, that is all that happened." He held his breath, hoping he saw no signs in her expression that Audrey Plennington had said anything about where her hands were.

"Lee, do you remember being upset about how you thought Bobby DeFlore was looking at me. How do you think I feel when Audrey Plennington tells me all this?"

"It will never happen again. I will not go back to her house again even if Reid needs help. I will not come to the spa anymore, and if Mrs. Plennington walks over to me when I am at the piano in the parish hall after church, I will walk away in a hurry."

"Lee, you can't give her a chance to make something out of even the tiniest thing."

"There will not be even the tiniest thing, Christie."

"There are so many things we have to work out Lee," she said as she put her arms around him. Lee's arms wrapped around her and he watched in the mirror as she placed her head against his chest. There was nothing more beautiful than looking at his hands firm around her waist. Lee rested his head on hers. She pulled back, smiled and kissed him. "Let's get your chicken and stuffing. We'll have a nice dinner. You've got an important week ahead of you."

CHAPTER 43

Wednesday afternoon, minutes before Reid was due to pick up Lee, Coach Clement Ezzer called. "Okay Lee, just spoke with Ed Turley. Got a pencil and paper?"

"Yes, I do Coach, I have them right here."

"Okay, okay. We're going to meet Coach Turley at the football field at St. Leo's College."

Lee listened carefully and wrote down the interstate and exit numbers and the street names to St. Leo's College. He read them to the Coach.

"Good, good, I figure it will take us about four hours and Ed wants to meet us at ten o'clock sharp and he wants you and Bobby all warmed up before he gets there. You still planning to drive up with Reid?"

"Yes, we plan to drive up together and get there the night before so I can get a good night's sleep."

"Good, good, that's good. I'm going to tell Bobby to do the same thing. You sure that truck of Reid's will make it okay?"

"I asked Reid that same question and he said no sweat. He said that his truck could make it clear across the United States if it had to."

"Okay, I guess I'm glad we're not going across the United States. Coach Turley is looking forward to seeing you boys but he's not going to have a lot of time. He really doesn't need it you know; he's had a lot of years that tell him pretty quick if he likes what he sees. Do your best Lee, do just what you were doing the other day. Just don't bring that head up too fast. Remember what I told you and you'll do fine and then we'll see. What's to be is to be, life is as simple as that."

"Yes, coach I will do my best and I will remember everything you told me. I have been working hard so I can do a good job on Saturday. I will be stretched and ready at 10 o'clock."

"Good, good. I will see you then."

Marian Fitts took Lee, Reid, Christie, Ellie, and D.H. out for pizza on Thursday night. They laughed as they hadn't in many years, sometimes at things Reid said even though he wasn't trying to be funny. Christie wiped pizza sauce from Lee's face and Marian said she had never known Lee from the time he was very young to eat pizza without getting sauce on his face. Ellie's Coke slipped and most of it landed in D.H.'s lap. D.H. tried not to laugh at first, but burst out so that a tiny bit of mucus hung from his nose which made Ellie laugh even harder as she reached to wipe his nose. "Mrs. Fitts, you better get a hold of this unruly group," Reid deadpanned.

"It's so good seeing everyone having a good time," Marian Fitts said, her wide eyes focusing on a picture she wanted to hold on to forever.

Three pizzas were gone and the pitchers of soda were almost empty. D.H. poured what remained so that everyone had enough for a toast. "Here's to Lee; here's to his doing the best he can do and letting him know we're with him no matter what."

There were a lot of smiles, and a tear in Marian's eye as she watched Lee and Christie embrace and say their goodbyes before he and Reid left to get ready for the next day's travel.

"I can take you home, Mrs. Fitts," Christie said as she returned to the table.

"Are you sure? Ellie and D.H. had planned to take me."

"It's not a problem at all."

"Very well. Ellie I'll talk to you later and thank you and you too, D.H. for making this such a pleasant evening."

"That it was, Mom," she said as D.H. nodded.

"Lee tells me you work for Audrey Plennington. I understand she has a nice exercise facility."

"Yes, I do, it's just part-time, but the pay is decent and it helps me stay in shape."

"I haven't seen Audrey since I returned. We spoke a bit when I came home. She was my very good friend when I left, but we didn't keep in touch as we probably should have. She was a very good friend and helped me tremendously after the crash – she was a very good listener. I tried to think I helped her also when she had her problem." Marian realized she might have gone on more than needed.

"Is she all right?" Christie asked as she thought this might shed light on why Audrey was the way she was.

Marian looked at her. "Maybe I've said too much, but, well, you and Lee have gotten so close and I see for myself how kind you are. I'm sure we'll be sharing a lot in the future. Please don't think me a gossip. Audrey is a very good person; it's just that she went through so much."

"Went through?"

"About a year before the event that changed all our lives, Audrey went through a very nasty divorce. Her husband had been abusive, physically and emotionally. It was amazing the job she did to hide that. However, she was crushed beyond belief by her husband's carrying on. Not just one woman either. He was going out with several; all from town. And he did nothing to hide it. It seemed the more brazen it was, the better he liked it because he knew it humiliated Audrey. He spent money with little regard. It was all Audrey's money that she got from her family when she turned twenty-one. Audrey was beautiful and I imagine she still is, but she was destroyed and spent her time at home in the fetal position. Her parents stepped in, hired a big-time divorce attorney and it all ended pretty quickly. I often thought about her as Lee was recovering and thought at times that what she went through had the same destructive force as that train hitting the school bus. I spent a lot of time with her, trying to help, and it often seemed that she'd never snap out of it. Yet, an amazing transformation took place when Lee was hurt. It seemed she poured her emotional energy into helping me and my family. And it seems too that now she has become a successful business woman."

"That is an amazing story. I'm so glad it seems to have a happy ending," Christie said, although not sure why she said happy ending. Christie had begun putting the pieces together: Did Audrey think Lee was safe, wouldn't harm her, someone she could control? And would she be as conniving as necessary to get him?

"Oh, one thing, Audrey did mention, she has started seeing someone." Christie's body tightened. "Yes, actually someone I knew; John Cantoli from church. He was always such a nice man. He doesn't go to our church anymore and Audrey has visited his new church a few times. I'm happy for her. John is a very nice man; I'm sure she'll fill me in when we get together."

The car stopped and Marian opened the door. "Thank you, Christie. I'm so blessed that my son has found someone as nice and caring as you."

"Lee is someone special; I am very fortunate." As she drove off, there was a huge sigh of relief. She gave thanks that Lee appeared to be free from further entrapment and she prayed also that Audrey would find happiness with John Cantoli.

CHAPTER 44

Lee thought how lucky he was to have Christie as he watched the summer landscape that hugged the interstate. He then thought about a goal post that seemed to be moving further and further away.

"Damn, I'm glad we left when we did," Reid said as he finished the water in his Thermos. "This traffic is getting worse; vacationers, got to be vacationers. We should have about another hour. I didn't sleep too good last night, must be all this excitement. I keep thinking this guy who's going to be watching you is an NFL coach. Do you believe that? Ever think you'd be kicking in front of an NFL coach? How did you sleep last night?"

"I did not sleep as well as I would have liked. I spoke on the phone with Christie for a long time. We spoke about a lot of things. She kept telling me to hang up so I could get some sleep. She said I was going to need my sleep."

"You and Christie are pretty damn close, man. Oh damn, let's not even get into what could happen if she goes to state. I'm sure things will work out okay. Just got to keep Booby away from her. Yeah, it will work out fine. She's got to know that guy's a jerk. I knew it first time I saw him. Damn good kicker though. I don't know about you, but I just want to get a quick hamburger or something and get to the motel. I want to hit that old sack early and you should too. Matter of fact, as your unofficial trainer, I'm going to order you to get to bed early."

"I just have to call Christie when we get to the motel. I told her I would call her."

"I'll call her and tell her we got here safely. Geez, you'd be on the phone half the damn night."

The clock said 3:07 when Lee awoke. He closed his eyes, but that was as close to sleeping as he would come for at least another hour. He tried to detect a pattern in Reid's snoring. Maybe there would be a large enough pause in the bursts of rattling air coming from Reid's pillow that would give Lee just enough time to fall asleep. But Lee couldn't break the code. Somehow his body finally blocked it out, one of those miracles that somehow the body pulls off. The next time Lee awoke it was to the sound of the alarm which went off precisely at the six am time to which Reid had set it the night before.

"Turn that son-of-a-bitch off. Can you turn that thing off?" Reid implored.

"But you said we should get an early start this morning."

"I was wrong. Even I can be wrong you know. Now turn that damn thing off."

Lee reached over and fished for the lever and the shrill noise came to an end. He visited the bathroom then put on his shorts and flip flops and opened the door. The morning was cool and the bright rectangular light shining down on the parking lot caught lazy drops which when apprehended in the glare, exploded into mist. He walked the length of the terrace and looked at the pancake house that was well into the business of the day. He wondered if Bobby DeFlore was up. He thought about the field at St. Leo's; there were puddles in the parking lot. He wished he had brought another towel to wipe the footballs. It would be over by noon and he and Reid would be on their way home. He turned towards the room looking still at the pancake house. They should eat soon. His flip flop hit a spot by the railing, green fuzz had turned into a wet sponge by the leaking gutter above. It was the ankle he had twisted as he ran to the hospital that night. The flip flop went flying as he bent in the direction of the turning ankle. He held his leg up; no pain. He placed his foot down. "No," Lee grunted. He lifted his foot up then stood on it. He walked back to the room, each step sending the same spike. This wasn't something he would shake off.

He closed the door, sat on the bed, and carefully massaged his ankle. He stood on his foot. "Owww," he said, falling back on to the bed.

"What the hell is going on, didn't I ask you to go back to bed?"

"Reid, I think I sprained my ankle."

"You did what?" the unofficial trainer said as he whipped away his covers. He looked at the ankle which was starting to bulge. "Holy shit, how the hell did you do that?"

"Outside, it's raining, I slipped."

"Okay, stay right there, stay off of that ankle," Reid said as he reached for the ice container. He returned with a full bucket and wrapped a towel full of ice around the ankle. They both looked at the ankle as if searching for a magical chant that upon completing would produce an ankle as good as new.

"It is my plant ankle, at least it is better that it is my plant ankle. If it were my kicking ankle, it would be all over right now."

"All right, all right, let's stay calm, let's think this through. Aw damn, this isn't going to work, there's no such thing as a one-legged kicker."

"Reid, I think . . ."

"All right, listen, I told you to remain calm. Damn! All right, this is what we're going to do. You stay right there, I'm going to run over to that pancake house and get us some breakfast. You got to eat now, get that energy into your system. Keep that ice on, if we keep that swelling down and wrap that baby tight with an Ace bandage I think we got a fighting chance. Aw shit. I'll be right back with breakfast. You know there is no turning back, don't you? You ain't gonna get another chance like this. You look at me, don't let your mind start playing tricks on you. Even if your ankle is messed up a little, you're still a better kicker than Booby. You got that? No turning back!"

"No turning back."

Lee and Reid arrived at St. Leo's at 8:45. Bobby DeFlore was lying on the field, someone about his size in shorts, cleats, and cut-off football jersey was pushing Bobby's outstretched leg back.

"Bobby is here already," Lee said as if looking at an invincible adversary.

"Now I'm telling you be calm, that's the best Booby is going to look all day. C'mon let's get our stuff and get on the field before the coaches get here."

Bobby DeFlore and his friend watched every hobble that Lee took as he walked toward the sideline. "What happened to you?" Bobby asked still trying to reconcile the limp with what looked like Lee's determination to get ready to kick.

"What do you mean what happened to him?" Reid answered.

"I was talking to Fitts, he can speak for himself, even though it takes a while."

"Look," Reid said. "I'm surprised at you, big-time kicker and all. You never heard of 'Kicker's Limp?' That's a training aid older than time. I guess to you that big Ace means something is a matter with Lee's ankle. Wrong! We wrap that bad boy tight, makes the blood pump harder to the muscles and give you more power and snap. Some people think it's not Kosher, but there's still no rule against it."

"You idiot, what the hell are you talking about?" Lee was hoping for further explanation as well.

"Bobby," the friend said as he motioned towards the parking lot. Coach Ezzer waved as he spoke with a man in a yellow baseball hat, wind breaker, and long shorts that splashed on muscles not common for a man who like Coach Clement must be in his early sixties.

"Reid, Coach wants us all stretched out by the time he and Coach Turley got here," Lee said.

"We'll start stretching, get in as much as you can. Damn, the ankle any better?"

"It hurts like heck."

"That's okay, don't worry about it. That's normal."

"Bobby, Lee, this is Coach Turley. An old friend of mine, two old war-horses from when they didn't have those fancy Gatorade squeeze bottles. When we got a break during a game, some kid would run out on to the field with a bucket and ladle. If you didn't get to that water early on, well, when it got to you you'd be getting a good helping of grass and snot with your water."

"I don't remember back that far," Coach Turley said. "Damn, Clement you must be much older than me." Both coaches laughed. That was the last time anyone on the field saw anything faintly resembling a smile on Coach Turley. This is one serious son-of-a bitch, Reid thought to himself.

"What happened to your ankle Lee?" Coach Ezzer asked.

Lee explained. "That is why we got to the field a little later than we wanted. I am still not done with my stretches."

"You going to be able to kick?" Ezzer Clement asked in much the same manner the target of the firing squad is asked if he would like a last cigarette.

"Yes, I will be able to kick," Lee said, suppressing a grimace as he placed his weight on his bad ankle."

"All right, seeing as we're a little early, finish your stretching."

Reid worked Lee through his routine as Bobby and his friend talked on the sideline with the coaches. "How does it feel Lee?"

"It does not feel the way I would like it to feel." On his back, Lee looked into a sky where the sun peeked through a traffic jam of clouds. The clouds were the paint of his imagination. He pulled himself from the grip of tears; no magnitude of throbbing would let slip from his hand this day so important to his father. He didn't care if his father in the end had talked about being wrong. Jim Fitts's son knew what mattered to his father and it mattered more now to Lee.

"Okay guys, ready?" Coach Ezzer called out, even though he was telling them more than asking them. "This is going to be simple, I've told you already a bit about coach Turley. He's one of the best football minds in the country and for one thing, you guys are getting a shot not many other guys get. Coach has a limited amount of time, so we're going to get started right away. Five kicks each from different spots on the field, then two kick offs. Bobby, you go first, from the twenty-five." The two coaches walked to the sideline.

"Hey Lee," Bobby said as he and his friend turned toward the twenty-five. "Sorry Christie wasn't able to make it today. Hey be a buddy, here's my phone number; I told her I'd give it to her so she can call me about state."

"Give me that," Reid said as he stuffed the paper into his pocket. "What a frickin booby."

"PHANK," went the ball as it left Bobby's foot and cleared the crossbar by a mile.

Reid reached for the ball from the imaginary center and placed the pigskin down. Lee started through his motion and felt the bite and burn that consumed his plant foot and shot up his leg. "PHUMF," One of the loudest "PHUMFS" Lee had ever heard came from the ball before it slammed into the upright and bounced away from the crossbar. Room charge, gas, tolls, breakfast at the Pancake House, damn, we just wasted a lot of money, Reid said to himself.

Lee bent over and clenched his fists. With an iron concentration powering into his body, he walked on the ankle and continued in his mind to stare down -- much as one would seal watertight hatches -- the barbs of pain ready to shoot up his leg.

Bobby and Lee got "PHANKS" on kicks from thirty-five and forty. On the left hash mark, Bobby's was more centered than Lee's. The two kickers walked to the fifty.

Bobby PHANKED right down the middle.

"Easy Lee, you can take this guy. I mean with your ankle and all, I haven't seen anything like this," Reid called out to his struggling friend.

Lee took his steps back and to the side. Reid's hands went down, the ball planted a little to the left, but Lee's foot snapped past Reid with ferocity and purpose. It was a PHANK that Reid thought could have launched one of those space shuttles at Cape Canaveral. The ball lacked only a fiery trail as it sailed a perfect end-over-end some ten feet higher and a little to the right of Bobby's kick.

"Let's get it to the thirty-five. Reid, see if you can find that goal line down there so these guys have something to aim for," Coach Ezzer said.

"You go first, Bobby said. "Your ankle must be getting pretty sore by now."

Lee was holding his shin. He knew the familiar rush of adrenalin; he wished it to all parts of his body. The ball slipped on the tee and Lee walked up to reset the ball. His plant was the most painful yet, but he felt pain in a different way now. "PHANK." The ball was high, a good hang time, a real good hang time he said to himself. It fell about a yard in front of Reid who was standing on the ten. Bobby DeFlore PHANKED the ball into a lower trajectory landing it several yards between Reid and the goal line.

The pain was unlike anything Lee had ever felt. He fell over as he lifted the ball into yet another seconds-gobbling hang time which plopped on the two-yard line and rolled laterally several yards before stopping.

Bobby DeFlore, holder of all kinds of records and awards, NFL prospect, looked at the spot where Lee's ball landed. "Luckiest damn bounce I ever saw," he said. He placed the ball on the tee and walked back in steps more carefully paced than ever. "PHANK." The ball went too far, sailing over Reid's head and bouncing out of the end zone. Bobby kicked the grass in disgust. A receiving team would have the ball on the twenty-yard line.

CHAPTER 45

"All right, if I remember, this exit puts us about four hours from home," Reid said as his fingers searched for any remaining fries in the bag on the middle console.

Lee shifted the bag of melting ice on an ankle now bluish, stiff, and puffy. "Yes, it will be good to get home."

"Did one helluva job out there today. Damn, had old Booby on the run. You're gonna hear from Turley, I know you're gonna hear." Reid looked up at the envelope and remembered Lee's mother's instructions to give it to her son on the ride back home. "Oh yeah, almost forgot, your mom wanted me to give you this on the way back."

Lee opened the envelope and removed the single sheet of paper. It was written in his mother's hand but the uneven signature was his father's:

Lee,

I've asked your mother to give you this when she thought best. I want you to know that I have always been proud of you. I am very, very sorry for the way I acted at times. You are the best son and have had to be very brave. I will always love you no matter what you do.

DAD

"Well, what's it say?" Reid asked.

"Something really feels like it's changing today. Damn, something feels so different. Can't put my finger on it. It's pretty funny though." Lee said.

Reid's neck snapped sideway. He looked at his friend then locked his gaze straight ahead. Maybe he was imagining things; maybe he hadn't heard Lee correctly.

Ed Turley chomped into his cheeseburger. Both coaches had ordered the special, large house salads, and iced tea.

"Well, what's the final verdict?" Clement Ezzer asked.

Coach Turley swallowed and then took a sip of iced tea. "Clem, it's been great seeing you again. And I'm glad you arranged for me see to your guys. I can see why you were so high on the boy."

"Yeah, I thought you might like what you saw. Bobby's going to have a monster senior year."

Ed Turley took another sip of iced tea to help his tongue dislodge bits of cheeseburger from his teeth. "I'm not talking about Bobby; I'm talking about the Fitts boy. Sure, I know Bobby's more polished, but Bobby's gone as far as he can go. Lee is still rough, but he's got potential like I haven't seen in a long time. Kids like this don't come along often, and remember he was doing all this with a bum ankle. I'm going to want to work with him, bring him up to the complex. Maybe even Europe would be good for him for starters. I've got some friends over there with the pro team in Barcelona. I'm going to have to think this whole thing out."